aug i7 l

STOLEN IDENTITY

By Lucia Van Der Gulik

Do Suzanne

Enjoy my first novel

Lucia

STOLEN IDENTITY

by Lucia Van Der Gulik

Published by Lucia Van Der Gulik, Ontario, Canada.

Stolen Identity: a suspense novel / Lucia Van Der Gulik

Second Edition

ISBN 978-1-456-49030-0

Transcribed by: Ann Wallace

Edited by: Eleanor Colwell, Janine Black, Allison Itterly, Melissa Yellowlees, Amanda van der Gulik

Book cover artwork by Octavia Cheetham

Dedication

In loving memory of my dear friend Ann Wallace,
this book is dedicated to you.

Acknowledgements

First and most of all I would like to give a huge thank you to my daughter Amanda who has helped me with this book from beginning to end.

I also would like to give my husband an enormous thank you, for all the things he did for me because of my book, and for his patience with me. I know you had many lonely evenings while I sat in our computer room writing my novel.

And thank you to my daughter Melissa. Who helped me with some editing.

Thank you to my son-in-law, Rob, who built my StolenIdentityBook.com website for me and helped me with all the formatting of my book.

A special thank you to Ann Wallace, who, just before she passed away, transcribed my story for me. I'm so sorry that you never saw the end result, however I believe you can see my finished novel now, and you are smiling as you are looking down on it.

Thank you to Eleanor Colwell for editing my first draft, and encouraging me to keep going.

Thank you to Janine Black for doing the second editing and helping me make my story come to life.

Thank you to Allison Itterly for the final editing.

Thank you to Octavia Cheetham for the beautiful artwork on the cover.

Thank you to all my family and friends who have listened to me go on and on about my book.

I am so happy and grateful that I could and did write this book.

Table of Contents

CHAPTER 1

"Anna-Marie! Hurry! Put on your apron," motioned Helen as she wiped the bar with a soggy washcloth. "Peter's not here yet. He rang that he'd be a bit late this morning. He doesn't need to know that you're late."

Peter's Diner was a quaint, cozy, corner restaurant with red and white-checkered tablecloths and a long sit-down bar. A jukebox stood in the corner. It was the type of place where people could feel at home, and it was located in the friendly little town of Greenville.

Helen had been working at the diner for over twenty years. Peter knew that a large part of his business was because of her friendliness. Customers adored her. She was a real motherly type—with her graying hair tied back in a bun, her snugly body and her warm comforting smile.

Five months ago, when Anna-Marie stumbled in, Peter was nice enough to give her a job waiting tables. Helen had taken Anna-Marie under her wings from the very first day they'd met.

Anna-Marie Winters was a beautiful 17-year-old with long straight, blonde hair and light blue eyes. She didn't know how beautiful she was as her poor self-esteem caused her to be very shy. Her mother had died when she was nine years old, leaving her father to raise her on his own. She didn't know what her mother had died from, but she knew she was very sick. She remembered how scared she felt seeing her mother hooked up to all those tubes and machines. She had run out of the hospital room as soon as she saw her mother lying there like that. She'd been so frightened. Now, she regretted not staying longer and saying good-bye to her mother. She just couldn't erase from her memory, weeping uncontrollably in that cold hospital hallway, and feeling all alone.

Her father did the best that he could for her, or so he thought. His work took him away from home most of the time—he was a traveling salesman, selling inventory to big department stores—leaving Anna-Marie to be raised, for the most part, by a host of housekeepers.

Her father, a tall, muscular man with salt-and-peppered hair, was difficult and demanding, notorious for being hard on his staff and his daughter. Because of his attitude, he had a high turnover of household help. Therefore, Anna-Marie pretty much raised herself. She was never praised for anything she was good at or did right, but her father was quick to tell her whenever she did something wrong.

Anna-Marie slipped the polka-dot apron over her head and tied the string tightly around her waist. She paused. Her palms gently rubbed her belly—her growing belly. Five months ago, she found out that she was pregnant.

"If you stand around all day, you're not going to make any money. Look at all those tables that need waiting," Helen said as she hastily pointed across the room.

"I think I feel it moving," Anna-Marie softly replied. Tears welled in her eyes. When she first found out she was pregnant, she wanted nothing more than to disappear into thin air. She was only a child. How could a child possibly raise a child? But there were moments like these—as she stood in the bustle of Pete's Diner—when she wanted nothing more than to be a mother.

Five months ago, Emily, a girl in Anna-Marie's history class, invited her to her older brother's party. Anna-Marie was hesitant if she should go or not, mainly because her father would never approve. But, something inside of Anna-Marie stirred. Sure, she had friends whom she did homework with, friends whom she gossiped about boys and teachers, but Emily was different. Emily—a "popular" girl—signified a different world that Anna-Marie was not a part of. Not that Anna-Marie wanted to be popular—she was too shy for such things—but maybe, just maybe, she could ignore her fears, anxiety, shyness, her father's looming voice in her head, and just let go.

As Anna-Marie got ready in her room, she couldn't stop shaking. Was it the anticipation of her father catching her or the fact that she was about to embark into unknown territory? Her shaky hand applied mascara. "Calm down, it's not a big deal," she told herself.

A picture of her mother sat on her dresser. In the black-and-white photo, her mother wore a long, flowing dress—her long, straight blonde hair parted down the centre. Her mother wasn't smiling, but there was kindness in her eyes.

Anna-Marie didn't remember much about her mother—she had been too young—but there were certain things she couldn't forget. Her mother's smile and how she always smelled like eau de cologne. She still remembered the clear glass bottle with swirls of blue and the silver top, and handkerchief that her mother used. Sometimes, she swore that she could smell it, as if her mother was close by watching over her. Anna-Marie picked up the photo and softly kissed her mother's face. It gave her strength.

As Anna-Marie descended the stairs, she heard her father coughing in the living room. *Just act normal*, she thought.

"Where are you going?" her father asked sternly while looking at his watch.

"I'm supposed to meet Julia. We have this dumb group presentation that's due on Monday. I won't be home late." Her voice shook.

Her father arched an eyebrow then went back to reading his paper. She had almost wished he asked more questions, inquired more, just to show that he cared. He didn't look up once as she headed out the door.

As Anna-Marie approached the party, music blared, and scattered all over the front lawn were people she had never seen before holding plastic cups. She hesitantly walked up the driveway and made her way through a crowd inside.

Beer bottles littered the living room. Jugs of wine were perched on the fireplace mantle. A keg of beer sat in a metal tub full of ice. People all around her laughed and chugged beer.

"Have a drink!" a boy shouted and shoved a plastic cup in her hands. Anna-Marie smiled, and then placed her lips to the cup's brim. It smelled like rubbing alcohol. As the boy watched her take a sip, she couldn't help but notice how red his eyes were. She took a big gulp, felt a burning sensation slowly make its way down her throat, into her chest, and into her stomach. She coughed. Her eyes immediately watered.

The boy laughed and gently patted her shoulder. "Did I make the drink too strong?"

"No," she stammered, "It's just how I like it," she lied. "Thank you." Whatever was in that drink started to make her feel light-headed, yet happy, without a care in the world. She took another sip. Then another. She didn't feel shy at all, in fact, quite the opposite. The boy called over two of his friends and made Anna-Marie another drink. She smiled, and then leaned her back against the wall for fear of falling down. But, for once in her life, she was having fun. And, that was the last thing she remembered clearly.

Everything else was hazy in her memory; a mixture of booze, loud music, and someone pulling her down a hallway toward a bedroom. She stumbled. She remembered the way the bed felt soft against her skin, how her head was so heavy she could barely lift it. And the boys. The three of them. Their faces were a blur, and she could smell the alcohol on their breaths as they inched closer. She started to panic, to yell and plead, but the music was too loud and nobody heard her.

Anna-Marie awoke on a bench in the park near her home. It was 2:00 a.m., cold, dark, and she was scared. How she got there, she had no idea. On getting up from the bench, her body ached and she felt very drowsy. Her dress was torn. What had happened? It felt like she'd wet her pants. Her head pounded. She shivered in the cold air. The party. The alcohol. The boys. The bedroom. She started walking home, crying the whole way.

When Anna-Marie approached her doorstep she hesitated. She waited for a moment. Inhaled, then exhaled. She shakily placed her hand on the knob and turned. As she stepped inside, everything was still except for the sound of her father's snoring. Anna-Marie crept to her room, lay down on her bed, and, with her mother's photo clenched tightly between her arms, cried the rest of the night.

When Anna-Marie discovered a month later that she was pregnant, she panicked. She went over every possible scenario—should she keep the baby, or get rid of the baby? She couldn't get rid of the baby, she just couldn't. What would her father say? She'd wished her mother was still alive, especially now when she really needed her.

Anna-Marie knew she had to tell her father.

She sat at the table, wringing her hands on her lap. "Dad?" she whispered. The sound of her voice sounded foreign. "Dad," she said again.

Her father stood at the stove flipping eggs into a pan. The oil crackled in the air. He didn't acknowledge her.

Anna-Marie took a deep breath. She had gone over this conversation a million times in her head, but saying the words aloud seemed impossible. She bit her lip. Her whole body was shaking. The time was now.

"Dad, I'm pregnant," she said with a trembling voice, but loud enough to be heard.

Her father paused, and didn't turn around for what seemed like forever. And then it happened. He spun around, spatula gripped in hand, and burned holes through her body with his piercing blue eyes.

"What did you say?" He inched closer, not taking his eyes off her. She saw the vein in his forehead pulsating.

Anna-Marie shifted uncomfortably in her seat. Her eyes scanned the table. "I'm pregnant," she whimpered. "I went to this party and these guys..." her voice trailed off.

"You're a slut!" her father screamed. He slammed his fists on the table causing Anna-Marie to jump. Her heart pounded.

"Please let me explain," she croaked. "I was taken advantage of. These guys left me in the park..." She was trying to explain, but her father's presence scared her. How could she explain what happened? Her father would never understand.

"No daughter of mine would let this happen." He paused. "I don't want to see your face again." Turning his back to her, he whispered. "Get out of my house."

In that moment, Anna-Marie couldn't focus on anything but the slump of her father's shoulders and how she had disappointed him. She felt numb, and alone.

Anna-Marie had no other family to turn to—no aunts or uncles. Her only grandparent was living in a nursing home with Alzheimer's. There was no one except Isabelle, her closest friend, and the only person she felt totally comfortable with.

Isabelle was two years older and had finished high school. She had found a job upon graduating and moved into her own apartment. She had grown up in the same condo as Anna-Marie and was somewhat like a big sister. Anna-Marie was most drawn to Isabelle's positive attitude and sense of humour. She invited Anna-Marie to move in with her for a little while, and managed to get her the job at the diner.

"You look very upset, Anna-Marie. What happened?" Helen asked, snapping Anna-Marie out of her thoughts.

On the brink of tears, Anna-Marie's body trembled. And then the waterworks poured. Tears ran down her face. She blurted, "Oh, Helen, I don't know what to do." She kept repeating herself. "I don't know what to do. I just don't know what to do."

"Come on, Anna-Marie, sit down," Helen gently said as she told Kathy, another waitress, to take care of Anna-Marie's tables. "Tell me what's wrong. What's the matter?"

Anna-Marie sat down and blew her nose before she continued. "Oh Helen, I don't know what to do. I went to the doctor this morning and found out that there's another heartbeat. I'm going to have twins. What am I going to do? I don't know what to do." Her voice squeaked and her hands shook. She tried to compose herself.

Helen sighed and looked at Anna-Marie with love in her eyes. She felt so sorry for the girl. Anna-Marie was such a good worker, a good friend. Why did this have to happen to her? "Anna-Marie, I don't know what to say. I'm so sorry, but we'll figure something out. Are the babies healthy, and what about you? Is everything okay with your pregnancy?"

Her health wasn't the issue. She was fine, maybe a bit overworked in trying to save up some money, but two babies? She could barely think about taking care of one.

"Have some breakfast sweetie," Helen urged. Anna-Marie shook her head. "Just sit here, Peter's not here yet. Don't worry about it. You need to eat to keep up your strength. I'm so sorry. We'll figure something out, don't worry."

"I cannot take care of twins. I can hardly take care of myself; I don't know what to do," Anna-Marie sobbed. It was as if she was in a trance.

Two women sat at the table nearby and waved for Helen. Helen quickly poured Anna-Marie a cup of coffee and then approached the table.

"Pardon me," one of the women said, "but I couldn't help overhear what you two were talking about. I'm sorry for that girl, and I know what she's going through. I've helped many girls in her situation, and I might be able to help her, too. I'm with an adoption agency. Here's my card."

Helen thanked her customer but she knew Anna-Marie was very much against adoption. "She says she wants to take care of the baby herself. Which, of course, is difficult now because it's not just one baby anymore," Helen explained.

"She might consider putting one of them up for adoption," the woman said.

Helen was shocked at the suggestion of separating the twins. But, in reality, Anna-Marie couldn't possibly look after two babies. Even though Helen didn't like the idea, she had to ponder the possibility. "Thank you very much," Helen said as she left.

After Helen handed Anna-Marie the card, Anna-Marie sat staring, twirling the card over and over for what seemed like eternity. With tear-filled eyes, Anna-Marie said, "I won't do that! I won't give up my baby!" The thought made her nauseous. From the moment she had decided to keep her baby and raise it by herself, something switched in her body, her mind, and her soul. It was fate. She was going to take care of her baby no matter what the circumstances. But now, there were two. Two tiny hearts. Two heads. Two pairs of legs. Two sets of arms. All growing inside of her. How would she manage?

"You might not have a choice. At least think about it for a while. You still have time to make a decision either way. So, why don't you hang on to the card until you decide what's best. Okay?"

Anna-Marie, still crying and almost choking on her own tears, hesitatingly agreed.

"I'll think about it. Thank you, Helen."

"You're welcome dear," Helen said as she took Anna-Marie in her arms. "And you know that I'm always here for you if you need to talk."

"Thanks Helen. I'm so grateful for you and Isabelle."

Helen squeezed Anna-Marie. "Okay, I can see that you're not really eating anything. Wipe away those tears. Let's get you ready to work before Peter walks in. Otherwise, we're both in trouble." Helen smiled, trying to lighten the situation.

Anna-Marie stood up, and with a forced smile dabbed the tears from her face with the corner of her apron. She placed her hand over her belly. Two heartbeats. Then picked up her dishes, still more than half full of her breakfast, and walked toward the kitchen.

CHAPTER 2

The phone rang. Anna-Marie wanted to pick it up but her twins were crying and bothering the customers. She had her hands full at the moment. She had been trying to serve the customers and feed the babies at the same time. Frustrated, Anna-Marie ran to the phone with one crying baby in her arms while the other sat hysterical in the carriage.

She hastily picked up the phone. "Pete's Diner, this is Anna-Marie speaking, how may I help you?" But the phone kept ringing and ringing. She hung up the phone, but it continued to ring. She unplugged it from the wall and threw it across the room. The phone ringing, the cries of her children, she placed her hands over her ears and screamed.

"Wake up, you're having a bad dream," Isabelle said as she stood over Anna-Marie's bed.

Anna-Marie peeled opened her eyes and tried to catch her breath. "I can't do it," she murmured. "I can't take care of two babies and work at the diner."

"Sshh." Isabelle tried to calm Anna-Marie down. "You know Betty has already volunteered. Please try to be at peace with that."

Betty, Isabelle's older sister, already had three children of her own. And yes, Betty had insisted that it was no problem, saying that one more would not make a difference. Anna-Marie knew that Betty had quite willingly volunteered to take care of her baby but that was before she knew she was having twins. Two more would be a handful, especially babies.

Isabelle sat on the edge of Anna-Marie's bed. She pushed her brown hair from her shoulder and rested her hand on top of Anna-Marie's arm. "You know that Betty and I are here for you. We'll help you, and I know that Helen will help you, too. Just remember that you're not alone."

Still visibly upset about the nightmare, Isabelle threw her arms around Anna-Marie and they held each other for a long time. Anna-Marie just needed to be held and loved.

"Okay, get up, get dressed, and we'll have some breakfast," Isabelle said kindly.

Anna-Marie got out of bed, took a shower and got dressed, then went to her dresser to comb her hair and put on her make-up. There, staring at her among the various knick-knacks was the adoption card that Helen had given her from the woman in the diner.

It had almost been two weeks since Anna-Marie found out that she was having twins. How could she feed two mouths and still maintain a job? At the moment, Anna-Marie was not in a position to find a better job, and the diner didn't pay her very well. She was relying on Betty to look after the baby, but two babies made things more complicated. She could not expect Betty to take care of twins without paying her a decent wage.

Overwhelmed, Anna-Marie finally decided to give the woman a call about giving her babies up for adoption. At the thought, she trembled. She couldn't stop thinking about the two heartbeats.

Isabelle interrupted her thoughts. "Breakfast is ready. It's getting cold!"

"In a minute," Anna-Marie said. She stared at herself in the mirror. She looked a lot like her mother, the same heart-shaped face, the same big, blue eyes. Would her mother be proud of her? Would her mother agree with her decisions?

As Anna-Marie entered the kitchen, Isabelle was already seated stuffing eggs into her mouth. She had made scrambled eggs with toast, some fruit with yogurt, and juice and coffee. Anna-Marie sat down and placed her hand on Isabelle's shoulder. "You're a good friend, Isabelle." She forked eggs onto her plate.

"No worries," Isabelle said.

As Anna-Marie poured a cup of coffee she blurted, "I'm thinking of giving the babies up for adoption."

Isabelle stopped eating and listened with wide eyes.

"I can't take care of two babies. I really wanted to take care of my baby, but two of them are just too much. My doctor has been suggesting adoption, but I didn't want to hear it. But now, I think that she's right." Anna-Marie paused to catch her breath then continued rambling. "I mean, who am I kidding? I can't take care of two babies by myself, even with the help of you and Betty. Sooner or later I'll be on my own with two babies to look after and I'll have to go to work. I just can't do it. It's too irresponsible."

Anna-Marie felt like a weight had been lifted. For two weeks, all that consumed her was the thought of adoption, but to actually say it aloud, and to someone who would understand, felt liberating.

Isabelle squinted her eyes, finished swallowing the food in her mouth, and placed her fork slowly on the table. She knew that once Anna-Marie accepted the fact that she was pregnant, she was excited about having the baby. This was just her fear talking.

"Anna-Marie!" Isabelle said. "You could give one baby away and keep one. That's what the woman from the adoption agency told you."

Whenever someone mentioned separating the twins, Anna-Marie's heart cracked. "I don't think it's fair to the babies if I separate them. I know what it's like to be raised alone. I mean...I had no brothers or sisters. No siblings to play with. What if something happens to me? At least if they both go to the same place they'll have each other." Anna-Marie started to cry again. Her emotions were definitely getting the better of her lately.

"Come on Anna-Marie, give that woman a call, but don't tell her that you want to give both babies away. Just talk to her and see what options you have. It can't hurt." Isabelle looked concerned.

Anna-Marie exhaled. "Okay, I will give her a call." She wiped her eyes, took a couple of deep breaths, got herself back together again and picked up the phone. With trembling fingers she dialed the number on the card. It took a few rings before anyone answered, but then a woman said, "Good morning, *Live and Let Live Adoption Agency*. Sylvia speaking, may I help you?"

"Oh...um...I'm Anna-Marie Winters. You were at Pete's Diner a couple of weeks ago and you gave my friend your card. I'm the pregnant girl who's expecting twins." Her voice sounded loud and scratchy. Isabelle rubbed her back.

"Yes, I remember," Sylvia said with a comforting voice. "I overheard the conversation you were having with your friend that you are pregnant with twins. I would love to talk to you. Have you decided what you plan to do?"

"No, not yet," Anna-Marie answered. She shifted in her seat. "That's why I thought I'd talk to you. Maybe you can help me make up my mind. I really don't know what to do."

"Well," Sylvia said, "it's difficult talking about this over the phone, so why don't we meet somewhere? How about the diner where you work? Would that be okay?"

"That would be good." Anna-Marie answered. "Maybe tomorrow morning, around 9am? We could talk before I start work."

"Sounds like a plan, Anna-Marie. Don't stress about anything; it's not good for the babies. We'll find a solution you'll be happy with. I'll see you in the morning."

Anna-Marie hung up.

"Now see, that wasn't so bad," Isabelle said. "I can see relief on your face. What did she say?"

"She said that we'll find a solution and I'm going to meet her tomorrow before work."

"I'm glad you phoned her," Isabelle said and gave Anna-Marie a hug. "Everything will be fine, but we need to hurry up and get to work. Let's put the dishes away and get out of here."

Anna-Marie felt as if a weight had been lifted. Maybe there was some sort of sunshine on the horizon.

*****

The following morning, Anna-Marie arrived early at Pete's Diner in anticipation. Every time the door opened, a bell sounded and Anna-Marie jumped. And, just as she expected, a few minutes before 9:00, Sylvia sauntered in carrying a leather brown briefcase and a smile.

Anna-Marie led Sylvia to a tiny table by the corner window. She offered Sylvia some coffee, her hand shaking as she poured. Sylvia's wild red hair seemed tame in the morning light. "It's okay, dear," she said. "Have a seat."

Anna-Marie composed herself and sat down.

Sylvia smiled. She had a kind face, and soft brown eyes. "Let me start out by saying that my agency has helped many girls, a few who have been in similar situations, also expecting twins. You have a few choices: you could give up both babies, or give up one and raise the other. But before we go into any details, I need more information. Tell me everything you can think of so I know what our next step will be."

Anna-Marie swallowed the lump in her throat and proceeded to tell Sylvia the whole story—how she got pregnant and how her father kicked her out. Initially, she felt very embarrassed, but Sylvia was very understanding. She understood exactly what Anna-Marie was going through.

Sylvia sipped her coffee, stared out the window for a second, and returned her gaze. "I was raped," she bluntly said. "Just like you. Although, my parents didn't desert me. They were with me all the way."

Over the next twenty minutes, Sylvia told Anna-Marie her story. She was 14-years-old when it had happened. Her parents had wanted her to give up the baby for adoption. She remembered how difficult it had been, but she felt she had made the right decision.

"About four years ago," Sylvia continued, "I found out that my son, who I gave up for adoption, was a happy young man living with very nice parents. He was also doing very well in school. I had finally realized that I had made the right decision. It's like I had closure on the biggest decision of my life. Of course, it doesn't always turn out like that, but it can, and that's when I decided to become an agent for the *Live and Let Live Adoption Agency*. I have helped many girls and I have made many couples very happy." Sylvia paused, as if reflecting on her own history. "I'm sorry, Anna-Marie, that I interrupted you but I just wanted you to know that I know what you're going through. So, please continue."

Anna-Marie told Sylvia the rest of her story. How worried she had been. How Isabelle had taken her in and found her the job at the diner. Isabelle, Helen, and Isabelle's sister Betty had been there for her when she'd needed them most. Anna-Marie started to cry. She couldn't help it. She had so much on her plate lately, but Sylvia encouraged Anna-Marie to just let it all out.

"Go on, Anna-Marie, just cry for a while."

Suddenly, Helen came walking out of the kitchen. She saw Anna-Marie crying and put her arms around her. "What is it, honey?" she asked concerned.

"Oh, nothing, Helen," Anna-Marie replied as she blew her nose into a handkerchief. "Everything's fine. Sylvia is here to help me."

Then Helen looked at Sylvia and gave her a hand. "I'm Helen," she said.

"Yes, I thought so," Sylvia said. "You're the woman I gave my card to."

"Yes, I am," Helen nodded. "And I'm very happy you did. I'm happy that Anna-Marie finally decided to give you a call. Thank you."

"But please, Anna-Marie, go on with your story," Sylvia asked while Helen refilled their coffee mugs.

Anna-Marie continued with her story, telling Sylvia that in the beginning she was very upset about being pregnant and didn't know what to do. She explained that after awhile, with the help of Isabelle and Betty volunteering to help out, she started liking the idea of having the baby. Excitement was growing within her.

"That was until two weeks ago," Anna-Marie explained. "When I found out that I was having twins." She choked back her tears and continued. "Since I've had your card, all I've been thinking about is what I should do. Yesterday morning I had an awful nightmare. I was busy serving customers and I was taking care of my babies at the same time. I can't do both, I just can't. So, I decided to give both of the babies up for adoption, but Isabelle talked me out of it."

Anna-Marie grabbed Helen's hand. "Helen," she said, "I think I'm going to take your advice and give up one of the babies and keep the other." Anna-Marie started to cry. "I hope it's the right thing to do."

Helen took Anna-Marie in her arms and held her for a moment. "Believe me, honey, it's the right thing to do."

"But what about the baby I'm going to give away? How do I know that it will be placed in a good and loving home?"

Sylvia cleared her throat. "We have a lot of nice prospects – married couples who are unable to have children of their own. Professional couples who are financially stable. I have a couple in mind, and I would like for you to meet them."

Waves of panic consumed Anna-Marie. She looked to Helen for advice. "I don't know. Helen, should I do that?"

Helen looked slightly nervous and bit her lip. "You should at least meet them. I'll come with you," she said.

Anna-Marie couldn't express enough gratitude for having Helen by her side. It was as if Helen had taken the place of her mother, a woman who cared and loved her as her own.

"Okay," Anna-Marie whimpered. "I'll meet them."

Sylvia reached into her briefcase and pulled out a stack of paperwork that Anna-Marie would need to fill out. "Take as much time as you need, sweetie," Sylvia said. "And, if you don't like the couple, we can find someone else that you do like, okay? And always remember, you can change your mind."

Anna-Marie held the paperwork in her hands – so heavy for her weak fingers – but felt at ease.

CHAPTER 3

Mary's day at work was hard and long. The kids were rowdy and she just wanted to go home and relax. When she pulled into her driveway, she parked her car and got out. As she walked to the front door, she stopped to get her mail, then unlocked the front door and stepped inside.

The first thing she did was kick off her shoes and put on the kettle for a nice cup of tea. While she waited for the water to boil she surfed through her mail. Junk mail, a phone bill, and then her heart stopped. An envelope from the *Live and Let Live Adoption Agency*. Could it be? She ran her fingertips along the edge of the envelope but decided to wait for her husband John to come home. It only seemed fair.

John and Mary Wells had been trying to adopt a baby for the past two years, ever since they found out that they could not have children of their own. They had been married for ten years, and five years into their marriage they wanted to get pregnant. After three years of trying and with the encouragement of doctors, friends, and family, there was still no result. After numerous tests and consults, it was determined that Mary would never bear children, a fact that still didn't seem real.

The envelope shook in Mary's hands. John had suggested that they adopt a child, and at first, Mary was against it. She wanted to experience the joys of motherhood, the feeling of life growing inside her belly, the pangs of childbirth, holding the wailing baby in her arms knowing that she and John had created life. But that wasn't reality. Finally, she had agreed and it had taken two years for any positive news, if this letter contained positive news at all.

Mary was a 2nd grade teacher who loved kids and her job. While she got a chance to be around the little rug rats day-in and day-out, a piece of her heart yearned for a child of her own. With John, a lawyer for a real estate firm, they made up the typical middle-class couple—a nice house, financially stable, but something was always missing.

The teakettle started to whistle, snapping her back to reality. She was so nervous that she shook while pouring the hot water into the mug. "Ouch! That hurts." She murmured as she accidentally spilled hot water over her hand. "Be careful!" she told herself. "Sit down, relax, have some tea." She kept talking to herself, but it wasn't helping. She got up again and paced back and forth through the living room.

Then she heard the rattle of keys to the front door. The knob turned. Mary bolted to the front door to greet John.

John stood in the doorway, put down his briefcase, and hung his coat on the wall hook. After ten years, he still thought his wife was beautiful. The way her green eyes sparkled, how her sandy-blonde hair bounced up and down. "What is it Mary?"

She waved the envelope. "It's from the adoption agency," Mary squealed.

John felt his heart pound. He took the envelope out of Mary's hand and ripped it open. They stood side by side and read the letter.

To Mr. and Mrs. Wells

Dear John and Mary:

Finally the news that you have been waiting for, I know how anxious you were when we met at the Live and Let Live Adoption Agency for you to adopt a baby. I have looked through your credentials and I am pleased to announce that you have been considered for the adoption of a baby in three months time. The natural Mother, Anna-Marie Winters, is 17 years old and 6 months pregnant; the father is unknown. However, before we finalize anything, you will have to meet with Anna-Marie. She will have questions for you and you will have questions for her. This will be a meeting between the two of you, Anna-Marie, and me. It will be a very informal meeting. This meeting is to help Anna-Marie feel comfortable about who she is giving her baby to. I hope you can understand that. She is very concerned that the baby will be placed in a good and loving home.

I recommend that the both of you and me meet prior to this meeting to discuss any questions you will have of Anna-Marie and she may have of you.

I'll be waiting your response.

Yours truly,

Sylvia Green

Before John placed the letter on the table, Mary already had the phone in hand, ready to dial.

*****

They had all agreed to meet the next Saturday. Greenville was about a four-hour trip from Eastwood City where John and Mary lived. Arranging it on the weekend meant that they could be assured plenty of time with Anna-Marie. They decided to leave around 5:00 P.M. on Friday so they could be at their destination around 9:30 P.M. depending on traffic. The bed and breakfast they booked was close to where they were going to meet Anna-Marie and Sylvia.

The trip went well; they only stopped once for a little break and arrived well before their estimated time. Their accommodation was lovely, but neither of them could sleep that night. They were both very nervous and anxious. After all, this meeting could change the rest of their lives. They desperately wanted to make a good impression. They held onto each other until they finally fell asleep.

*****

There was a knock on the door. John woke up from the noise. He sat up, and answered, "Thank you, I'm awake." They had asked for a wake-up call. He shook Mary. "Wake up, honey."

Mary slowly turned, then moaned. Suddenly, she sat up. "Oh, John," she said. "What time is it?"

"It's time to get up sweetie," he said, brushing the hair from her face. "But don't worry we have plenty of time to shower and eat breakfast." He kissed her on the cheek, then rolled out of bed and jumped into the shower.

Mary wiped the sleep from her eyes and yawned. Nerves

jumped through her veins. She arose from the warm bed and sifted through her suitcase, laying out the outfit she was going to wear. She walked over to the vanity mirror. "I'm going to be a mother," she said with a smile.

After shoving breakfast down their throats and getting lost twice, they finally arrived at Sylvia's office with high hopes.

Sylvia sat behind a large oak desk, and offered John and Mary coffee, water, tea, anything they needed. Mary fidgeted in her seat, "We're fine," she said as she grabbed her husband's hand. "We just ate."

"Well then, sit down." Sylvia said. "Anna-Marie will be here soon. I just wanted this little time for us." Sylvia asked them a few more questions, but the important questions were already asked long before this meeting.

"I'm so nervous about meeting Anna-Marie," Mary exclaimed.

Sylvia smiled. She had seen these nerves before in other couples. "You're going to like her, and I'm certain that Anna-Marie is going to like the two of you as well."

What seemed like forever finally arrived. A knock on the door. And there they were, a young girl and an older woman cautiously walked into the office. All of their eyes met.

Sylvia broke the silence. "Here, let me introduce you, John, Mary, Anna-Marie and Helen." They all shook hands and sat down.

As Anna-Marie sat down, Mary couldn't stop staring. She was beautiful. Long blonde hair, big blue eyes, and a face of innocence. Her belly protruded outward, but she sat upright, perfect posture, and held her hands in her lap. Nervously, she fiddled with a ring on her thumb. This was the girl who would make Mary's dreams come true. Funny, how it came in the form of a 17-year-old. She knew the story of how Anna-Marie had become pregnant and was expecting twins. She couldn't imagine how difficult it would be to give up one of the babies for adoption. Mary wanted nothing more at that moment than to reach across the table and grab her hand.

John cleared his throat and addressed Helen, "Are you family?"

"No," Helen said, "I'm a friend of Anna-Marie. I'm here to give Anna-Marie support."

And then Anna-Marie spoke. Her voice sounded mousy and high-pitched. "I didn't have any family to come here with me, so that's why Helen is here. She's my family." Anna-Marie watched the reactions of John and Mary, how their eyes squinted and mouths drooped. She could tell that they genuinely felt sorry for her and she liked them immediately. The way that they held hands and stroked each other's fingers told her that they truly loved each other.

"Of course," John said, "I'm sorry." He felt sorry for her. Despite all that she had been through, he was quite impressed with her presence. He knew she had suffered a lot but managed to overcome it. There was peacefulness in her eyes.

John continued, "Do you have any hobbies?"

And that broke the ice.

Maybe it was the nerves, but Anna-Marie did not hold back. She told them that she liked to play the piano and sing. She liked acting as well. She was once in a school play and she was good at it, at least that was what the teacher had told her. She went on to say that she had lots of fun acting and she wanted to take acting lessons, but her father refused. He believed that "All actors are the same. They smoke, use drugs, drink too much, and they get divorced after only being married for a little while." But, he let her take piano lessons. Her father had an old piano that she used to practice on. He was never home to hear her play, so he never knew how good she had become.

When Anna-Marie finished, she felt dizzy. She couldn't believe she said all those things, especially about her father to strangers. But there was something about these people that she trusted.

Mary said, "I'm happy that you have a hobby like that and I hope you can continue. Do you still play the piano at school?"

Anna-Marie answered, "Well, at the moment I can't, because I had to quit school to get a job and support myself, so I don't have a piano right now, but maybe one day I will again."

Then Helen asked, "What about the two of you? What do you do? Sylvia has told us that you are a professional couple but she has not told us what you actually do for a living."

One at a time, John and Mary explained what they did for a living. Anna-Marie was happy with the fact that Mary was a teacher, so she was used to being around children. Mary was going to take a leave of absence as soon as they adopted the baby so she could be home with the baby. Anna-Marie liked that idea.

After all the nerves and stress, Anna-Marie was happy that she decided to meet John and Mary. She could see that this couple was very excited about having the baby, and she had a good feeling about them. The biggest decision she had to make didn't seem so difficult anymore.

*****

A couple days later, Sylvia called Anna-Marie. "You sound good, Anna-Marie, what's up?"

Anna-Marie's voice beamed through the phone. "I really liked them. I have a good feeling, and I'm happy I got to meet the couple that's going to adopt one of my babies."

Sylvia said, "So, you're okay with that? You're going to give up one of your babies for adoption to the Wells?"

"Yes," Anna-Marie said. She paused. It was not an easy decision, by any means, to give up one of the babies, but she really had no choice in the matter. She was not ready to take care of two babies and all she could do was hope that she was making the best decision, for everyone.

Anna-Marie was close to tears again, but she knew she had to be strong. She wished she could keep both babies; she felt so much sadness. She felt guilty about separating them, of not being able to take care of both of them, but at the same time, she knew that she could not keep both.

Sylvia said, "I'll let Mr. and Mrs. Wells know that you have made your decision. I'm sure they'll be very happy." Sylvia then told Anna-Marie that she would make all the arrangements and she would put in motion all the paperwork.

Anna-Marie felt somewhat lighter, relieved of the heavy burden she had been carrying. Even though she felt very distressed, there was still a part of her that felt at peace. She knew in her gut that she had made the right decision. Everything would be all right.

CHAPTER 4

"Push, Anna-Marie. Come on, you can do it. Come on. Push!"

For the past 14 hours, Anna-Marie had been in labour. The stark-white hospital room made her uncomfortable. Helen squeezed Anna-Marie's hand, cheering her on. But the pain. Never in her life had Anna-Maria experience so much pain. Waves of nausea overwhelmed her as her body gave in to exhaustion.

"Please, can you do something for the pain?" Helen pleaded.

The doctor replied, "I'm sorry, I can't. It's too late for that now. She's already going through transition. But don't worry, she's doing a great job."

At that moment, Anna-Marie decided it was now or never. She gritted her teeth, clenched her fists and pushed with all her might. She screamed at the top of her lungs.

A few seconds later, the tiny wail of a baby filled the room. Sweat beaded on Anna-Marie's forehead, and though her face was ghostly pale, she smiled. The nurse quickly cut the umbilical cord, tenderly wrapped the baby in a soft blanket and was about to bring this precious bundle to Anna-Marie when she could see the next contraction was already coming. So she laid the baby into the bassinette and went to tend to Anna-Marie instead. All Anna-Marie wanted was to hold her child, but more contractions came in quick succession. She gripped Helen's hand so hard she thought she would break her fingers.

"Just breathe deep," Helen soothed.

"Oh Helen, I can't do this anymore," Anna-Marie cried. "I can't do it." A bolt of pain jabbed through her back then into her stomach and groin. Would it ever end? Would she make it out alive?

"Push real hard," the doctor said. "You're almost there. Come on, Anna-Marie, you can do it!"

And there it was. Anna-Marie let out another ear-piercing scream and five seconds later they heard the second baby cry. A beautiful sound after almost 14-and-a-half hours of labour.

Completely exhausted, Anna-Marie knew that she was still not out of the woods. The cramps started again, the after birth was coming, but the worst was over. And she didn't care. All she cared about was seeing her two sweet little babies.

There were moments in one person's life that seemed surreal, almost magical. When the nurse placed both babies into Anna-Marie's arms, she was so overcome with love that she started to cry and smile at the same time.

"Helen, I did it, I really did it."

She stared at their faces, all purple and wrinkly, their gaping mouths with naked gums. How their tiny fingers tried to hold on to her fingers. Their tiny nails, so microscopic. Their beautiful soft, thin hair. How they looked like dolls. Two perfectly-formed little girls.

The nurse had confirmed that they were identical twin girls.

The only difference between the girls was that one of them had a distinct small birthmark in the shape of an "S" under her big toe, on the bottom of her foot.

One by one, more nurses bustled in and out to help clean up Anna-Marie and the babies. Anna-Marie didn't want them to take the babies away, but she was safe, they were safe, and she needed rest.

She fell asleep almost immediately with visions of her tiny princesses.

*****

Sylvia has been waiting in the waiting room for almost an hour with John and Mary. They were all so excited. Helen notified Sylvia as soon as the babies were born. Sylvia called John and Mary right after that. They came as soon as they could.

John and Mary had been very busy the past three months since they had met Anna-Marie. They had made one of their bedrooms into a beautiful nursery, and a child-seat already sat fastened in their car.

Sylvia said, "Anna-Marie is doing really well, at least that's what I heard from the nurse. The nurse said that she'd call me when Anna-Marie wakes up, and she thinks that should be soon. Apparently, she's been sleeping almost eight hours."

The nurse finally told Sylvia that she could visit Anna-Marie. John and Mary waited anxiously in the waiting room.

When Anna-Marie woke up, all she saw was a nurse. "Where's Helen?" she asked groggily?

"She went home to get some rest but she'll be back soon."

"Can I see my babies?"

The nurse nodded, left, then returned and placed the babies into Anna-Marie's arms. What an incredible feeling! She looked at the babies with tears in her eyes. Sylvia said that she could name the babies, but it was up to the adoptive parents whether or not they kept the name or chose one of their own. Anna-Marie had already chosen names for them, Sonia and Celia. She decided that the baby with the S-shaped birthmark would be named Sonia and the other Celia.

With the twins held lovingly, one in each arm, Anna-Marie knew that she had to make the second most difficult decision in her life: which baby would she give up for adoption? Tears rolled down her cheeks. How did someone make such a decision?

Just then Sylvia walked into the room. "Oh, Anna-Marie," she said. "They're beautiful." She sat on the side of the bed and stroked one of the girl's arms. "I know what you're going through, and in your case it's even more difficult than it was for me. I never even got to see my baby. All I knew was that it was a boy. They just took him away as soon as he was born." Sylvia paused and looked at the floor.

"Sylvia…" Anna-Marie said.

"I wanted you to have the opportunity to make the decision yourself," Sylvia interrupted.

"I can't do this. I don't know which one to give up. They're both so beautiful and they're both mine."

Sylvia gently caressed her arm. "You have to make up your mind, Anna-Marie. Why don't you do a coin toss?"

Anna-Marie looked at Sylvia in disbelief. She could not believe that Sylvia said that. Was this some kind of joke?

"I know it sounds crazy, but it's one way of doing it," Sylvia said, and then she went on to say, "A coin toss: heads for Sonia and tails for Celia. That way it's left up to fate to decide."

Anna-Marie swallowed hard. She wasn't thinking clearly, but she needed to make a decision and she couldn't do it alone. She apprehensively went along with Sylvia's idea. She didn't want to give up either one of them, but she had to. A coin toss would take away the raw emotion of the feeling of having to choose one over the other.

"Ready," Sylvia asked holding out a quarter.

"You do it," Anna-Marie whispered.

As Sylvia tossed the coined, Anna-Marie clenched her eyes shut and prayed that it would all turn out all right. After a moment, Anna-Marie asked for the verdict.

"Heads," Sylvia said.

Anna-Marie choked back her tears. She stared at Sonia's little face. "I'm sorry, I'm so sorry I have to let you go, but you're going to have a good life, I promise. And I will always love you. Please remember that." Sonia wiggled in her arms; Anna-Marie kissed her sweet little nose.

Reluctantly, she handed Sonia to Sylvia as tears ran down her face. As soon as Sylvia had Sonia in her arms, Anna-Marie couldn't contain herself. She felt like she was going to die. "Oh, no," she cried. "Please give me back my baby one more time. I need to hold her one more time."

Anna-Marie placed Celia down on the bed in between her legs so that her arms were free to hold Sonia. Anna-Marie held her tight against her.

"Anna-Marie, I'm sorry but Mr. and Mrs. Wells are here waiting for Sonia. Sonia will be very happy with them."

"My little angel," Anna-Marie cried and handed Sonia back to Sylvia. Then she picked up Celia again and held onto her, vowing to never let her go. She cried for a long time after Sylvia had left the room, but the nurse gave her something to calm her down. Soon after, the nurse took Celia from Anna-Marie and took her to the nursery. Anna-Marie dozed off from emotional and physical exhaustion.

As soon as Mary and John saw Sylvia walking in carrying Sonia, they stood. And then they saw the beautiful little bundle that she was cradling. Sylvia presented them with their new daughter. Mary had tears in her eyes as she gently cradled her new baby in her arms. Mary thought her heart would burst; she would never forget that moment as she stared lovingly into her daughter's eyes.

"Anna-Marie named the babies Sonia and Celia. This baby is Sonia, but you don't have to keep the name. You can change it if you wish," Sylvia said.

Mary looked at her baby. "Oh no, Sonia is a beautiful name. We'll keep it."

John couldn't hold back his tears. He gently rubbed the top of Sonia's head. After ten years of marriage, they were no longer just a couple. They were a family.

"Can we see Anna-Marie?" Mary pleaded even though it was already agreed that it wasn't the best thing for Anna-Marie. Mary just wanted to make Anna-Marie feel better and let her know that Sonia was in good hands.

"No," Sylvia said, "Anna-Marie is a young girl who had to make a very difficult and emotional decision. As you know we recommend that you have no further contact with her at all. It will be easier for her to heal and get on with her life. She will need all the strength she can get to concentrate on raising her daughter Celia."

"Yes, of course. Thank you so much, Sylvia," Mary said with teary eyes. "We're so happy and we'll take good care of Sonia. You can tell Anna-Marie that for us."

Sylvia replied, "I'm sure you will and I'll be sure to tell her."

*****

After the four-hour car ride, John and Mary arrived home. They fed Sonia, changed her, and they looked her over from head to toe. And she was totally perfect. Sonia was a beautiful baby.

"Oh, look at this John," Mary said as she noticed the birthmark on the bottom of her foot.

"Oh that's kind of cute," John said as he grabbed her little toes.

"Yes it is. It looks like an "S," don't you think? An S for 'special', because Sonia is our special baby. This baby is our special little girl," Mary said, as she picked up Sonia and cuddled her.

Mary handed Sonia to John, but John was afraid he would break her, so he quickly kissed her and gave her back to Mary. Mary then put a nice cozy sleeper on Sonia and placed her in her new crib.

With a big smile on her face and a tear of warm emotions in her eyes, she adoringly whispered, "Oh little baby Sonia, the S-shaped birthmark underneath your little foot means that you're our special little girl."

CHAPTER 5

After a few days in the hospital, Anna-Marie went home with Celia cuddled in her arms. Even though Anna-Marie was only seventeen years old, she started growing up really fast. She had to. She was a mother now with a huge responsibility.

Just two weeks after coming home, Anna-Marie went back to work. She couldn't afford to stay off any longer. She took Betty, Isabelle's sister, up on her offer to baby-sit. Anna-Marie was very grateful to Betty for helping her out. Betty knew how much Anna-Marie needed the help, and she knew that Anna-Marie had no extra money to pay her. Betty told her that when the time came and she was able to pay, then she could do so. Until then, it was not a problem. Anna-Marie knew that Betty would let her know if Celia became too much, but she still felt guilty for not being there for her own child. However, she knew Celia was in good hands.

She left Celia with Betty before she went to work, and then picked her up after her shift at seven-thirty. This arrangement worked out well. It allowed Anna-Marie to work every day without having to worry about her baby, make some money, until the day would come where Anna-Marie could support them both.

Anna-Marie dragged herself through many of her shifts at

work. Celia's nightly cries left Anna-Marie with a lack of sleep, feeling like she was almost running on empty. Although it was very difficult, she was strong and determined that she would make it work, and she did.

After about a year, Anna-Marie found a better job at a well-known bar. She was a cocktail waitress and the tips were a lot better than at the diner. She couldn't believe that she made double the amount of money in tips in her first shift alone. And the work was actually easier because she only had to serve drinks. She was so happy with the money she was making.

Betty no longer babysat Celia. She found that it was getting to be too much. So Anna-Marie found a new babysitter for her. Isabelle and Betty remained good friends to Anna-Marie, as did Helen. Celia was crazy about Helen, and when she was old enough to talk, she called her "Grandma."

When Celia was about five-and-a-half years old, Anna-Marie had saved up enough money to take a trip. From the day she gave Sonia up for adoption, she had planned to find her. Over the past five years, Anna-Marie took a quarter of each pay cheque and put it in her savings account. All she knew was that Sonia had gone to live in Eastwood City, which was about two hundred miles from Greenville where Anna-Marie and Celia lived.

"Celia, hurry up, honey, we have to get going," Anna-Marie said. "You haven't got your coat on yet, and where is your teddy bear?"

"It's in my backpack," Celia said proudly as she put on her coat. Celia was just as beautiful as her mother. Straight blonde hair and eyes as blue as the sky.

"Is that bag too heavy for you sweetie?" Anna-Marie asked Celia.

"No, Mommy, I can do it. See!" she said as she put her arms through the backpack loops.

"But isn't that's too heavy for you."

"No, Mommy I can do it! I can even put my boots on with the backpack on me, see!" Celia had become quite an independent little girl having been taken care of by different babysitters, with many children to compete with for attention.

"Okay then," Anna-Marie said with a sigh, "just hurry up. It's cold today, so make sure your coat is done up and your hood is on." Anna-Marie checked to make sure that Celia was warmly dressed. She then took Celia's hand and picked up her suitcase. As they left, she noticed that it was really getting cold outside and the early morning sky had a dark overcast. Anna-Marie was disappointed in the weather. "Well, you can't do much about that," she thought.

Anna-Marie decided to make the best of it because today was the day she had been waiting for.

At the bus central, she purchased two tickets for Celia and herself. Anna-Marie had not told anyone about her trip. Only her boss knew that she was going on a week's vacation. He didn't ask where she was going, and of course, she didn't tell him. She did not want her friends to know because she knew they would try to talk her out of it. Nobody was going to stop her. Celia may also have inherited a bit of her independent streak from her mother.

Anna-Marie knew that she was not supposed to do this, but she wanted so desperately to know how Sonia was. Every time she looked at Celia she saw the ghost of Sonia standing next to her. All these years she had been thinking of her and hoping she was doing well.

The cold air stung their faces. Anna-Marie and Celia sat on the bench waiting for the bus. *Sonia. How wonderful it would be to see her face again. Would she look exactly like Celia, missing front tooth and all?* Her heart leapt.

Suddenly, Anna-Marie snapped out of her trance. She panicked. Celia was not next to her anymore. She quickly looked around, and then with a sigh of relief, saw her not too far away playing with a little boy. "Celia," she called. "Stay close to me."

"But Mommy," Celia said, "I'm playing."

Anna-Marie got up from the bench and walked toward Celia and the little boy. "What's your name, little boy?" she asked.

"Kevin, and I'm a big boy," the little boy said.

Then a man came walking up and grabbed Kevin's arm. "Here you are. I told you to stay with me and to never talk to strangers."

Anna-Marie could see that the man was very upset. Celia then stood up and said, "I'm not a stranger. I'm Celia. And we're not talking, we're just playing."

Anna-Marie had a hard time holding back a chuckle. "I'm sorry," she apologized and then extended her hand. "Hi, I'm Anna-Marie Winters and I'm really sorry. I was just daydreaming for one second and then my daughter was gone and I saw her here playing with Kevin. At least that's what he told me his name is, and he also told me that he's a big boy, not a little boy."

The man smiled. "I'm Sebastian Haines, and I have to confess that I too had just taken my eyes off my son for just a second. I'm sorry if I sounded angry, but I was really scared when I didn't see him."

"It's okay," Anna-Marie said. "Don't apologize. I know what it feels like, but we're all okay. We're just waiting for our bus to arrive."

"Oh, so are we," Sebastian said. "We're going to Eastwood City."

Anna-Marie started to smile. "That's where we're going as well."

Anna-Marie didn't trust men because of her past, but she had a good feeling about this one. She was comfortable talking to him, and he was very easy to look at as well. Sebastian was tall with dark blond hair and blue eyes. He had a warm caring smile, and she could see that he was very protective of Kevin.

"Oh! Look there's the bus," Anna-Marie said.

Sebastian suggested sitting close together so that the kids could talk to each other. Anna-Marie liked that idea hoping for Sebastian's company. They boarded the bus and set out on their journey.

Sebastian and Anna-Marie each had a window seat in the same row with the kids beside them on the aisle seats. Celia and Kevin were talking and playing with a little toy Kevin had. All they had between them was the aisle, so they had lots of room to play.

"Why are you going to Eastwood City?" Sebastian asked. "You got family there?"

At first she thought about making something up, but for some reason she couldn't stop the words from spilling out of her mouth. "Family, you could say that," and then she explained her story, making sure to keep her voice down just in case Celia overheard. It actually felt good to tell someone what she had been keeping inside for so long.

"I'm going to try to find my daughter, she's five year's old. I gave her up for adoption," Anna-Marie explained.

Sebastian raised his eyebrows. "Now you're getting me all confused," Sebastian said. "Who's this little girl here with you now? I assumed that she's your daughter and she looks about five years old to me."

Anna-Marie's emotions were getting the better of her. A lump rose up in her throat as she held back tears. She uttered, "Yes, she's my daughter, but she was one of a set of twins. I had two—Celia has a sister and I couldn't take care of both of them, so I had to give one up for adoption. Not one day has gone by that I haven't thought about her."

"Oh, I'm so sorry," Sebastian said.

"It's okay," Anna-Marie said. "It was a long time ago. I just want to make sure that she's happy. I named her Sonia, but they might've changed her name."

Celia and Kevin were playing during the entire conversation, or at least, that was what Anna-Marie thought.

Suddenly, Celia asked, "Mommy, who's Sonia?"

Anna-Marie froze. "Oh, nobody, honey, you just play."

Then Sebastian said, "Why don't you come and sit here with

me, and Kevin can sit next to Celia. That way we can talk more freely and the kids can play more easily."

Anna-Marie stood up and so did Sebastian, both instructing their children to change seats. Sebastian offered Anna-Marie the window seat so she could have a nice view.

Anne-Marie took the window seat mouthing the words "thank you" to Sebastian. Kevin thought this was great, as he went to sit next to Celia. Kevin had a little car that they were playing with.

Once they were all seated, Sebastian whispered to Anna-Marie, "How are you going to find Sonia?"

Anna-Marie said, "I really don't know. It's probably a crazy idea. All I know is that she's living in Eastwood City. That is, if they still live there. What about you Sebastian, why are you going to Eastwood City?"

"I'm going there to help my brother. My brother's business is growing very fast and he needs some help, so he asked me to come and work for him," Sebastian said.

"And you can just go, that must be nice," Anna-Marie quipped. Soon after her comment she felt her heart begin to ache as Sebastian told her his story.

A year ago he had lost his wife to a rare disease. His parents took him and Kevin in after his wife died because he had a nervous breakdown and couldn't work. Before his wife died, he had a decent job—he had been the accountant for his father's woodworking company.

His brother, Simon, didn't want to work for his father. He had wanted to start his own company, and he did, with his father's blessing and encouragement. He went to Eastwood City, to set up his own shop, and he was doing very well.

"But now he needs some help, so he asked me. I think it's his way of helping me out," Sebastian said as he winked. "Anyway, I'm better now, so I decided to go and give it a try. I couldn't go back to work for my father; he sold his business. He was ready to retire."

"I'm sorry that you lost your wife, and I'm happy that you're able to move on now," Anna-Marie said sympathetically. "Do you have a place to live there?"

"Yes, I do," said Sebastian.

"I hope everything works out for you," Anna-Marie said and she really meant it. She liked Sebastian; he was a nice man. Kevin seemed like a well-behaved little boy and Celia had lots of fun with him. Anna-Marie was happy that they met Sebastian and Kevin. And it really did feel good to open up to someone.

The kids were still playing with Kevin's little car, but after a while, they got tired and fell asleep. It was very cute to see them lying against each other. They slept for a long time. Anna-Marie and Sebastian talked a lot and realized that they had a lot in common. They even talked about meeting somewhere once they were in Eastwood City.

When the kids awoke from their nap, Anna-Marie offered some snacks and shared them with the kids. Once the kids were fed, they continued to play with Kevin's little toy car.

After about three and a half hours into the trip it began to rain heavily. The rain quickly turned to sleet. The bus driver had slowed down considerably; the kids were still happily playing with Kevin's car. The car had dropped on the floor in front of their seats, so the both of them hopped down onto the floor.

As Sebastian was about to tell the children to get back to their seats, the little car rolled into the aisle. He bent down to grab the little car before it rolled away. Right at that moment, the bus started to skid on an icy patch as they went through a curve on the road. The bus began to fishtail when the driver lost control. It smashed through a guardrail and careened down an embankment.

Thunderous screams were heard throughout the bus as unsecured passengers were tossed around like rag dolls. It seemed as if the bus rolled over and over.

It was almost as if it were in slow motion. Anna-Marie smashed her head against the seat in front of her and then against the window beside her. Searing pain surged through her head as the screams became more piercing. The bus finally came to a halting stop. All that could be heard were moans amongst the eerie silence. There was broken glass, people, things, and blood everywhere.

Sebastian had been thrown to the other side of the aisle where the kids were seated. The impact caused the seats in front to buckle. Sebastian ended up pinned between the seats in a bent over position. He could not move his body except one arm and his hand.

Kevin softy whimpered, "Daddy, Daddy. I'm stuck."

Then he heard both kids crying. Kevin was pinned under the seat by one of his legs. Sebastian told the kids, "Be as still as you can and someone will be here soon to help us." Sebastian's speech was starting to waver. He wanted to comfort the kids, but felt himself slowly slipping away into unconsciousness.

Anna-Marie tried to keep her eyes open. She tried to speak but no words came out. She went back in time. She was in the hospital, holding both Celia and Sonia, and gave one of them away. With all the strength she had left, she called out, "Celia, Celia where are you? Are you all right?"

During the crash, Celia had slid under the seat in front of her. Celia had been sitting on the window side and Kevin on the aisle. In a shaky voice she answered. "Mommy, Mommy, I'm okay." As she crawled out from under the seat, she knew that Sebastian had told them to stay still, but she was frightened and wanted her Mommy. She managed to get around Kevin to the other side of the bus where her mother was. She crawled up beside her and immediately knew something was wrong.

Anna-Marie blinked slowly and stared into her daughter's big blue eyes. How beautiful she was. She tried to lift her head but couldn't move. Her body felt numb. *I'll always love you*, she thought, but couldn't speak the words. Her eyelids felt heavy. Her daughter. Her beautiful daughters. Her angels.

Celia began to cry. "Mommy, Mommy, please wake up!"

CHAPTER 6

"Hi, honey. How was your day?" John said as he walked into the kitchen.

Mary had just pulled the chicken out of the oven and placed the hot pan on top of the stove. She pushed her hair from her face with the back of her hand and smiled as John leaned over and gently kissed her on the cheek. After fifteen years of marriage, they were still so in love.

"Where's the little one?" John asked.

"In the backyard. You can call her in. Dinner's ready," Mary said.

John opened the back door and called for Sonia. "Sweetie get inside, dinner's ready."

Sonia, who was tall for her five years of age, pleaded, "Can I just finish this first?" Her long blonde hair blew in the gentle breeze. She tried putting booties on Candy, the family dog.

"No honey, take those things off the dog and come inside and leave Candy out."

"Ok, Daddy," Sonia huffed. She pulled at the bottom of her dress and stomped inside. "Hi Daddy," she said as John picked her up and swung her around the room. She squealed.

As they sat down for supper, Mary fixed a plate for Sonia. "How was your day, John?"

John forked a piece of chicken into his mouth. "Same old, same old. Did you hear about that terrible accident that happened just outside the city? A bus crashed and I think everyone was killed."

Mary's eyes widened. "No, I didn't hear that."

"I heard it on the radio," John said

"That's terrible," Mary sighed. She stared at her husband, how she loved him more than anything. Then she turned her gaze toward Sonia. Sonia was picking peas off her plate one-by-one and popping them into her mouth. She giggled. Her blue eyes glistened. Mary's heart swelled. She had never been this happy.

After supper John cleared up the dishes while Mary bathed Sonia and got her ready for bed. As was their regular routine, they sat on either side of Sonia and took turns reading a bedtime story.

Once the story was finished, Sonia's eyes got droopy and she slouched further under the covers.

"Goodnight, sweetie," both Mary and John said. They kissed her warm cheeks and went downstairs.

Mary went to make some tea before settling onto the couch to watch the news. The news covered the bus accident and the camera panned over the wreckage. There were three survivors: two children, a five-year-old boy and girl, and one gentleman. The news announcer went on to say that the gentleman was in very critical condition and the boy had a broken leg, but he was expected to be okay. The little girl did not seem to have any serious injuries other than some scrapes and bruises. The news announcers were speculating at whom the children belonged to. The paramedics had found the little girl scrunched up against a young woman. She was crying and in shock, and kept calling for her mother. The mother showed no signs of life. No names were released, pending notification of next-of kin.

"That is just awful," Mary said as she sipped her tea and placed her hand on John's. Her eyes were glued to the TV as she watched the paramedics carrying people from the bent-up bus. It was amazing that there were any survivors at all.

Suddenly, the camera panned across the little girl's face for a fraction of a second. Mary froze. Tears streaked the girl's face. Her matted blonde hair reminded her of Sonia.

"She looks so much like Sonia," Mary gasped. "That poor girl was probably travelling with her mother. She'll be an orphan now." Mary shivered. The thought of anything happening to Sonia made her heart ache.

"She does look a lot like Sonia," John said leaning forward on the couch. His voice trailed off.

"What if that was Anna-Marie and her daughter?" Mary asked.

John didn't respond right away. Sure, the little girl looked remarkably like Sonia, but it just couldn't be. But those eyes, those big blue eyes. So similar. He swallowed a lump in his throat. "Maybe it's time we told Sonia that she was adopted."

Mary paused and stared at her husband. She had thought about this for the past five years. How and when would be the best time to tell Sonia? Would Sonia understand or show resentment? Would she want to find her real mother? Would she still love Mary and John? "We can't, not now," Mary said as tears filled her eyes. "I know we have to, but she's still too young."

"You're right," John answered. He hastily picked up the remote and changed the channel.

As the night came to an end, Mary couldn't concentrate. She kept thinking about the accident and how much that poor little girl looked like Sonia.

*****

The next day, Mary took Sonia to her first piano lesson. She had been putting it off for a while, but after last night, a memory was triggered. She remembered Anna-Marie sitting in Sylvia's office on the day they first met. How Anna-Marie's big blue eyes lit up with excitement when she mentioned how much she loved playing the piano.

As time passed, Sonia kept taking piano lessons and she loved it. Sonia was also a very good student. She loved going to school and learning new things. One day, when Sonia was in second grade, Sonia's teacher, Mrs. Miller, called Mary at home.

"Sonia is very upset and I think you need to come to the school right away. I can't seem to get a response out of her." Mrs. Miller said.

When Mary arrived and saw Sonia, her heart dropped. She had never seen Sonia so upset. She was choking on her own tears and could hardly breathe. Mary bent down to embrace her daughter, but Sonia pushed her away.

"You are not real!" Sonia screamed.

Shocked, Mary didn't know what to say. "What are you saying, sweetheart?"

Sonia scrunched up her tiny face, balled her tiny hands into fists, and gritted her teeth. Then, she burst into tears again and sobbed. "Tony and Greg are saying that you are not my real Mommy, and that Daddy is not my real Daddy. They are saying that I don't have a real Mommy and Daddy."

Mary's heart sank deep into her chest. She and John were friends with Tony and Greg's parents, but she never thought that they would relay this information to their children.

"Oh, honey," Mary said as she took Sonia into her arms. "You are our very special little girl. Don't listen to what those boys have to say." Then Mary looked at Mrs. Miller and asked, "What happened here?"

"I'm so sorry. During recess Sonia seemed fine and then she got so upset and I couldn't calm her down. I tried to find out what was wrong but to no avail."

"Its fine," Mary said as she rocked Sonia back and forth. "I'm going to take her home."

By the time Mary and Sonia had arrived home, Sonia had calmed down a lot. Mary gave Sonia her favourite snack, animal cookies and chocolate milk. They sat at the kitchen table. Mary watched as Sonia shoved cookies in her mouth, trying to figure out the best way to explain the situation.

"Sweetie, you're very special to us and we're so happy to have you, you are our little girl. No one can take you away from us because we're a family and we are your Mommy and Daddy." Sonia paused for a moment then gulped down some chocolate milk. Mary continued, "We love you very much and don't ever forget that."

And then, as if she couldn't control herself, Mary explained how Sonia was adopted.

Sonia paused. "So you're not my real mommy?"

"Your real mommy loved you very, very much, but she wasn't able to take care of you. We loved you so much that we wanted to take care of you and love you forever." Sonia cocked her head to the side, as if trying to understand.

Mary continued, "You know that birthmark under your foot?"

Sonia nodded then hoisted her tiny leg onto the table. Mary pulled off her sock and gently rubbed the bottom of her sole. Sonia giggled.

"It's shaped like an 'S' for 'Special' because you're special," Mary said.

Sonia awkwardly grabbed her foot and ran her tiny fingers over her birthmark. "It does look like an 'S,'" she said.

Mary smiled. "That's right, 'S' for 'Special,' our 'Special Sonia.' We love you so much."

*****

Sonia grew up fast, too fast for John and Mary's liking. At first, she excelled in school, and practiced piano every day. As she approached adolescence, Sonia started to rebel. She often wondered why her birth mother gave her up for adoption. And, no matter how much love and support John and Mary gave her, she couldn't help but feel abandoned, as if she had been thrown away like garbage. Why did her birth mother not want her?

One evening, when Sonia was 14-years-old, she had planned to hang out with friends.

"You cannot go out on a school night. You have piano lessons and homework to do."

Sonia stomped her foot and hastily crossed her arms. She had grown into a beautiful young teenager. Long, flowing blonde, corn silk hair cascaded over her shoulders. She swept her bangs to the side. "I'm the only girl who isn't allowed out on a school night. It's so unfair."

Mary looked up from her magazine and smiled. But, before she could say anything, Sonia had stomped up the stairs to her bedroom. Just before she slammed the door shut she yelled, "You're not my real mother. You can't tell me what to do!" She threw herself onto her bed and burst into tears.

Mary swallowed the lump in her throat. If only Sonia knew how those words pierced her heart. Sure, teenagers were notorious for acting-out, but Sonia's words cut deep.

Mary slowly ascended the stairs and paused at Sonia's door. She could hear her daughter crying softly. "Sonia?" Mary said as she tapped the door lightly with her knuckle. "Can I come in?"

Sonia wiped the tears from her eyes. She felt awful about what she had said and she knew how much it hurt her mother. She loved her adoptive parents very much. "Come in," she whimpered.

Sonia's room was a bit in shambles – clothes were thrown over her computer chair and lay in heaps on the floor. Piano sheet music was spread out all over the place. Mary stared at her daughter sitting on the bed.

"I'm sorry, Mommy," Sonia whispered. "I didn't mean it."

"It's okay, sweetie," Mary said. She stepped further into the room, stepped over piles of clothing and paper, and sat on the bed. She placed her hand on Sonia's knee. "I know you didn't mean it."

"I just can't help but feel lost sometimes," Sonia said. "I know that you and daddy love me very much, but I can't stop thinking about my real mother and why she didn't want me. I mean, it's like, I don't know anything about her. I know you and daddy want to protect me, but I feel like I have a right to know."

Mary sighed. She couldn't even begin to imagine how Sonia felt. The rejection. The abandonment. She and John had given Sonia a very loving and supportive environment. Wasn't that enough? Shouldn't that be enough? "How about this…let me put on a pot of tea and you and I will have girl-time. I'll tell you all about your birth mother, Anna-Marie. Sound good?" Mary asked.

Sonia bit her lip to hide her excitement. "Yes, that sounds good."

As they headed downstairs and into the kitchen, Sonia felt nervous. It wasn't that her parents refused to tell her about Anna-Marie, but she always felt like they were hesitant to say anything. The only thing she knew about Anna-Marie was that she was young, 17 or so, and couldn't afford to raise a child. Everything else – how her real mother looked, how she dressed, how she carried herself – Sonia filled in the blanks.

Mary took a sip of her tea and dove into the story of how Anna-Marie got pregnant. "She was a very sweet and beautiful girl, just like you," Mary said as she twirled a strand of Sonia's blonde hair. "She loved you very much."

Sonia couldn't believe what had happened to her mother. How she was not that much older than Sonia herself. What was more frustrating was the information of how Anna-Marie got pregnant, and how she would never know her true father. Anger swirled through her, but it eased her mind knowing that Anna-Marie loved her very much and didn't abandon her.

"I understand why Anna-Marie gave me up for adoption. Do you think I can find her someday?" Sonia's heart leapt at the idea.

"When you're good and ready, I promise that I'll personally help you find your mother." Mary smiled. A burden had been lifted—after all those years—to finally reveal the story. She could tell that Sonia seemed relieved as well. But, what Mary didn't mention, for reasons she couldn't quite put her finger on, was that Sonia had shared the womb in Anna-Marie's belly.

CHAPTER 7

"Wow, she's fantastic! I haven't heard anyone play like that in years," Justin said turning to his cousin.

"Yes, and not only that, she's also very pretty," Kevin said.

Justin and Kevin were sitting in the first row as Kevin's father sat off to the side in a wheelchair. The view of the stage was perfect. They were there to represent Justin's father's company, Haines International. Justin's father, Simon Haines, was a very busy businessman, and he was also the mayor of Eastwood City. He was unable to attend the concert, so Justin was there on his father's behalf.

For the past ten years, Simon Haines sponsored annual charity concerts through his company. Every year it was for a different charity, and this year it was for their local Eastwood hospital. Different artists donated their time and talent. Typically, after the concert was over, Simon would say a speech, which would then be followed by a reception with food and drinks. This year, Justin was going to speak instead of his father. At just twenty-eight years old, Justin showed signs that he, too, was quite the orator.

As Justin watched Sonia Wells play the piano, his palms grew sweaty. She truly was beautiful. Her blonde hair glowed under the florescent lights, and her fingers moved rapidly across the keys. He'd heard about her from an employee; apparently she had played for a lot of charitable organizations, as well as professionally.

Sonia had fumbled, and then looked up at the audience with a shy smile and an apologetic look. The grand piano was positioned so that the audience could see her face.

"You know, she looks so familiar," Kevin said. "I just don't know where I've seen her before."

"It's probably just your imagination," Justin replied. "Familiar or not, she's a cutie." He could not keep his eyes off her. He was mesmerized by her beauty and her talent. After she finished playing, there would be two more acts, and then Justin would say his speech. Butterflies danced in his stomach.

As Justin made his speech, Sonia and the other acts stood off to the side of the stage. Sonia had noticed Justin in the audience when she played, and her eyes connected with his for just a moment. But, it had been long enough for Sonia to feel something electric and miss that key. He was a handsome young man with thick wavy, dark blond hair and a sharp jaw line. The son of the mayor. And there he was now, standing in front of her. A funny knot grew in her stomach. Everyone who performed was asked to come out onto the stage so Justin could thank them personally.

When it was Sonia's turn, she felt nervous and found it difficult to look Justin in the eyes. He handed her a bouquet of flowers, and she stumbled over her words. What was wrong with her? Sure, she always got nervous before playing in front of an audience, but now, because of one gorgeous guy, she had become a bumbling, stumbling idiot.

At the reception, Justin scanned the crowd for Sonia. And there she was. A sense of relief fell over him, but also nervousness. Justin had had a few girlfriends on and off before but he'd never really made it a priority—he was always too busy working for his father. But this girl was different. He couldn't pinpoint what he felt, but he knew he wanted to get to know her.

Sonia stood next to a middle-aged couple, probably her parents. Justin took a deep breath and decided to formally introduce himself. As he was approaching, he overheard the woman say, "I'm so proud of you, honey. You did such a beautiful job."

"May I introduce myself," he said. "I'm Justin Haines."

Sonia responded with a slight giggle in her voice. "Yes, I know. Everyone knows." She could feel heat rising to her face. She took a deep breath, hoping that he hadn't noticed the change of skin colour and shyly stated, "I'm Sonia Wells, as you know, and these are my parents, John and Mary Wells."

Justin extended his hand to John and Mary. "You have a very talented young lady here. You must be proud of her."

"Oh we are, thank you," Mary said with a big grin.

Justin turned toward Sonia and said, "I really enjoyed your playing tonight. It was just beautiful. Do you play professionally?"

Sonia bit her lip, an action of nervousness. "I, uh, play professionally sometimes, but mostly just for fun or charity events." She felt so embarrassed, and she didn't want to make eye contact, but she couldn't help herself. His big eyes sucked her in.

"Here you are," Kevin said as he approached them. "I've been looking for you. My dad wants to go home now." Kevin then noticed Sonia standing there. "Oh, I'm sorry for interrupting" he said extending his hand to Sonia. "I'm Kevin Haines, Justin's cousin. He shook hands with John and Mary as well. "Sorry to interrupt but we all came in one car and my dad wants to leave."

"Oh, that's okay," Sonia said, but she wanted to spend more time with Justin. He captivated her heart and she didn't want it to end. She looked around the room and saw that most of the crowd had already gone. "We should get going too."

Frantic, Justin hated the thought of leaving this gorgeous creature and never seeing her again. He bravely asked, "May I phone you sometime?"

Sonia was relieved. She could feel her face blushing again. Why was this happening? She was never a blusher. Not wanting Justin or her parents to notice, she buried her face into her purse as she reached for her notepad, hoping it was long enough for the redness to subside.

"Yeah, sure," she said, and took out a small notebook and scribbled her name and phone number. She shyly, but happily, handed the scrap of paper to Justin. They all said their goodbyes.

As John opened the car door he said, "He seems like a very nice young man."

Sonia's reply was nonchalant. "Yeah, he's okay." She did not want to let on that she really liked him, and that her heart was pumping so hard she was afraid her parents could hear it. She had to pretend that he was "just another guy," but she felt differently about this one. She couldn't describe it, but it gave her goose bumps. She secretly hoped he would call sometime soon. She had had a couple of serious boyfriends over the years, two in fact, the first when she was seventeen, for about 3 months, and the second when she was nineteen. And that lasted about a year. But she hadn't seen a possible future with either one of them.

She often wondered if she would ever find Mister Right. And now, at twenty-one years old, she wondered if this was love at first sight. Justin was all she could think about the whole way home. Her parents were talking about the evening, but Sonia didn't hear a thing. She was miles away in her thoughts.

*****

The next morning, Sonia had just walked into the kitchen to get some breakfast when the phone rang.

"Who could that be this early?" her mother said as she brought breakfast to the table.

Sonia sleepily went into the living room and picked up the phone. Her mother peeked around the corner and saw the look on Sonia's face. She knew instantly who was on the other end of the line.

"Oh-a-yah, I guess so. That sounds nice. Yes, I know that place. I'll see you then," Sonia said.

"Who was that?" Mary questioned with a smile after Sonia hung up.

Sonia answered looking a little shy, "That was Justin. He wants to have lunch. He wants to talk about my music," she said as if it didn't really matter.

Sonia was a bundle of nerves the whole morning. She spent most of the time going from the bathroom to her bedroom rearranging her hair, makeup, and clothing. She wanted to look just right. Sexy, but not slutty. Confident and casual.

When she walked into the restaurant, she felt very uneasy. She couldn't find Justin right away, but then she saw him sitting at a corner table.

He stood up and walked toward her. "I'm so glad you took me up on my invitation. I was afraid I would never see you again," Justin said. He placed his hand at the small of her back and led her toward the table. He pulled out Sonia's chair, and then sat down.

Sonia shyly smiled and said, "Thank you, I'm happy I came."

"What can I get you to drink?" he asked.

"Just some coffee, please," Sonia answered.

"Two coffees, please," Justin said to the waitress as she filled their water glasses. "The food is great here. I hope you don't mind, but I already took the liberty of ordering."

Sonia giggled. She couldn't stop staring into his big blue eyes.

Lunch was wonderful and went smoothly. Neither of them felt uncomfortable for long. They felt like they had known each other forever. The rapport between them seemed to be endless and enchanting. They were definitely not bored with each other.

Time flew. After almost two hours, Justin felt his phone vibrate on his hip. "I'm sorry," he said, but I need to head back to work for a meeting. I had a great time and want to see you again."

Sonia smiled. She knew that something special had transpired over the past two hours. The time had come to say goodbye, but not until they arranged another date.

CHAPTER 8

Sonia looked one more time in the mirror and felt satisfied. She had bought this dress especially for tonight. It was a light blue and white dress, the right half had white flowers embroidered all over it. The dress came just above her knee, and her lacey high-heeled shoes made her well-shaped legs look longer and shapelier. She wore a belt around her waist emphasizing her flat tummy. She looked like a Barbie doll. The neckline was cut just low enough to tease a little. She wore a silver necklace with a little pearl teardrop hanging just above the fullness of her breast.

Sonia smiled at herself. Justin had asked her to dinner and a show. She was so thrilled at the invitation that she went straight out and bought herself a dress. And now, Justin was waiting in her living room with her parents.

She only met Justin a week ago. Their lunch together still gave her goose bumps. She was so nervous. She carefully applied eye shadow to make her light blue eyes stand out. She took a deep breath, adjusted her dress and headed downstairs.

When Sonia entered the room, Justin's eyes widened. She got her good looks from her mother. She was the spitting image of Anna-Marie.

"Oh, honey, you look so pretty," Mary said and then turned to John.

John smiled and said, "Yes, you look very nice." He meant it, she did look beautiful, but he couldn't ignore his concern. His little girl was going out with a man he hardly knew. He couldn't object, though. After all, she was twenty-one-years-old and an adult. It seemed like yesterday she was playing in the sandbox in the backyard. John just had to trust that he and Mary brought her up right.

Justin had a very eager look on his face. His eyes were as big as saucers and as his mouth dropped he said. "Sonia, you look incredible." She was beautiful in every way. He knew from their luncheon how much he was turned-on by her personality. Although he didn't know her well, he was hoping to change that. At the moment, he was mesmerized.

"Well, you look really great, too," Sonia said shyly. Justin looked very dashing in his light gray suit, tailored to fit his toned body perfectly. His dark blond hair, blue eyes, and fit body looked like it came straight out of a swimsuit magazine. He was a tall man, at least five or six inches taller than Sonia's slender five-foot-seven frame. He towered over her. His smile was the most alluring, with perfect, straight teeth.

"Well, you two better go otherwise you're going to miss the show." Mary said.

John cleared his throat. "Behave yourself."

"Oh, Daddy," Sonia huffed. She was embarrassed by her father's protectiveness.

Justin knew what John meant. Justin had every intention of being a perfect gentleman. He certainly did not want to do anything to scare Sonia away. Justin had never felt this type of energy with anyone.

"I'll have her home before midnight," Justin said.

"You two have fun," Mary said as she watched her little girl walk out the door. Gone were the days of playing with dolls and coloring in books. Her little girl had grown up.

"How are we getting there?" Sonia asked as she noticed that there was no car out front.

"Oh, you don't like to walk, eh!" Justin said with a teasing smile.

"Oh-ah, I don't mind walking," Sonia said a little embarrassed.

But then, a limousine drove up and stopped right in front of her house. Sonia could not believe her eyes. "A limousine? I have never been picked up in a limousine." Her heart raced.

"There's a first time for everything isn't there?" Justin said.

"Well, I just hope you didn't steal it," Sonia laughed.

"Well, yes, I did," Justin teased, "but I'll bring it back when I'm finished." And then he explained, "This is one of my father's company cars, and I had permission, so you don't have to worry."

"Well, that's a relief," Sonia said. "I really didn't want to end up in jail tonight," she laughed.

Justin laughed to himself as he helped Sonia into the limousine. He had asked, Jack, his chauffeur, to hide the car so he could surprise Sonia with it.

It was about a forty-minute drive to the dinner theatre. Justin pulled a bottle of wine out of the little fridge and asked, "May I pour you a little wine before dinner?"

"Yes, that would be nice." Sonia said. She felt like a princess—she had to pinch herself to make sure she wasn't dreaming.

The drive was enchanting and exhilarating. Sonia was so captivated by Justin that she had a hard time concentrating on the show. She was feeling emotions for this man that she had never felt before. He was good-looking, funny, and a real gentleman. Quite frankly, he was sweeping her off her feet.

After the show was over, Sonia couldn't ignore the way her heart felt every time she stared into Justin's eyes. And when they approached Sonia's house, she couldn't believe that it was ending so fast.

The chauffeur got out of the limousine and opened the door for Justin. Justin then walked around to Sonia's side and opened her door. No man had ever given Sonia this much attention in her life. It felt good; she liked being treated like a lady. She could get used to this.

Justin walked her to the front door, and, for the first time all evening, they were both standing there not knowing what to say. Sonia broke the silence. "Thank you so much, Justin. I had a really great time."

Justin thought that Sonia was the prettiest woman he had ever seen. He was so smitten with her and desperately wanted to kiss her. "You're welcome, and I hope that you'll go out with me again sometime." His heart pumped so hard; this girl was making him crazy.

"Yes, Justin, I would like that very much." Sonia said. Her cheeks hurt from smiling so much. They stood there for what seemed like forever. She wanted him to kiss her. *Please kiss me,* she thought.

He inched closer. It was like a magnet pulled them together. And, suddenly it happened. He gently caressed her cheeks and kissed her. Sonia thought her legs would give out. It was a good thing Justin was holding her. She closed her eyes and allowed herself to be swept away in the moment, never wanting it to end.

Gently, Justin pulled himself away. "I'm sorry," he said.

"No, no, it's okay." Sonia said a little embarrassed.

"No, it's not okay." Justin said. "I promised your parents that I would be a gentleman." Then he kissed the top of her hand. "When can I see you again, Sonia?"

Sonia giggled and said, "As soon as possible."

"Until then," Justin said and kissed the top of her hand one more time. Sonia watched as he walked down her driveway, got into the backseat of the limo, and drove away.

She leaned against the front door for a moment then stepped inside. A goofy smile was plastered across her face. She stood in the hallway for a moment, reliving the kiss. Without realizing it, the words slipped out, "Ooh Justin."

"Oh, honey, is that you?" Mary asked from the top of the stairs.

"Yes, I'm home." Sonia answered, as normal as she could manage. She was hoping her mother hadn't heard her calling out Justin's name.

She walked up the stairs toward her room. "Goodnight Mommy," she said using their special term of endearment. She loved calling her mother "Mommy" - it always gave her a warm feeling knowing how much her mother loved being called that.

"Did you have a nice time, honey?" Mary asked her daughter.

"Yes, I had a great time. It was a fantastic show. I'll tell you all about it tomorrow morning," she said as she gave her mother a quick hug and slipped past her into her bedroom.

"Alright, sweetheart. Talk to you in the morning. Goodnight." Mary turned to go back to her own bedroom.

Sonia's mind was consumed by thoughts of Justin's kiss. She laid her head on her pillow and smiled. In her mind she saw Justin's irresistible sparkling blue eyes smile back.

CHAPTER 9

A week had passed since Sonia last saw Justin. All week, Sonia walked around as if floating on a cloud. Was this what love felt like? She did every task with a smile on her face, and when he called to see if she wanted to go to a dance with him, her heart leapt out of her chest.

John and Mary were very happy for Sonia. They liked Justin. He was friendly, polite, and came from a good family. He was also a good conversationalist and well educated. As Sonia got ready in her room, Justin waited downstairs with John and Mary.

Sonia finished the last touches of her makeup and headed downstairs. She still felt nervous, but not as nervous as the last time. She was getting to know Justin on a deeper level and their connection made her comfortable.

Clad in a beautiful red dress, Sonia descended the stairs. Her dress fitted her curves and was appropriate for dancing—the skirt flared out, and she couldn't wait to dance the night away.

A red Ferrari with a pure white interior sat in front of Sonia's house. This time Justin did not have a limousine.

"The limousine was just to impress you. How do you like this car instead?" He grinned.

Sonia looked at him and smiled. "What a beautiful car!" she exclaimed.

Justin, again, was the perfect gentleman, opening the door for Sonia, and as they drove away, Sonia thoroughly enjoyed the ride and the breeze tickling her face.

The dance hall was huge, with high ceilings and wooden walls. Different colored lights flashed to the beat of the music. There were people everywhere, dancing, laughing, and drinking. Sonia felt the magic in the air and the urge to get her feet moving.

Justin impressed Sonia with his dance moves. His body moved to the rhythm, his hips swinging back and forth.

"Where did you learn to dance like that?" Sonia yelled over the music. "You're fantastic."

"Well, you're not so bad yourself," Justin whispered in her ear. They danced all night long and drank a little. As the night progressed, the dances got slower and their bodies inched closer together. Justin wrapped his arms around her waist and pulled her closer. She felt his body tighten against her thighs. Her whole body tingled.

They had stayed at the dance hall until closing. Sonia wished it could have lasted forever. "This is exactly where I want to be," Sonia whispered as Justin gripped her tighter and kissed her softly on the lips.

After that night they saw a lot of each other. They visited museums and old churches. On sunny Sunday afternoons, they loved to sit on a patio and eat ice cream, or on warm evenings they enjoyed having a drink under the stars. They played golf, went bowling, or packed a lunch and went to the beach. Other times they would simply go sightseeing. Spending time together was all that mattered, and they always made the best of it.

After about a month of dating, Justin invited Sonia to his place for a home cooked dinner. He lived alone. It was a big house with a swimming pool, a sauna and a hot tub. Justin was a very wealthy man; he worked very hard, but he also made time for his hobbies, one of which was cooking.

The doorbell rang at Sonia's house. Justin had said that he was going to send someone to pick her up. When Sonia opened the door, a well-groomed man in a chauffeur's uniform stood in front of her. She recognized him as the chauffeur from the first time Justin had picked her up for the dinner and show.

He took his hat off and said, "Good evening, miss. I've been sent here by Mister Justin Haines, I'm Jack."

"Yes, I remember." Sonia smiled. "I'll just grab my jacket and purse and I'll be right there." She gathered up her things, locked up the house because her parents were out, and headed toward the car.

Thirty minutes later they pulled into a laneway. "Is this it?" Sonia asked, stunned.

"Yes, Miss, this is where Mr. Haines lives."

It was incredible. Blooming flowers stretched along both sides of the laneway varying in colours of yellows, pinks and purples. There were flowerbeds all around the house. She had never seen such an assortment of plants and bushes in all shapes and sizes. She had only ever seen gardens of this magnificence in magazines.

Jack got out of the limo and walked around the vehicle to let Sonia out.

"Thank you Jack." She said and then watched as Jack drove away.

As she walked up to the door, the smell of flowers filled her senses. Not only did this place look beautiful, it smelled absolutely wonderful. *Justin actually lives here?* It was even more beautiful than he had described. *Would the inside be just as wonderful?*

Before she had a chance to knock, Justin swung open the front door.

"Justin," she stammered, "this place is fantastic. You should have warned me."

"Why?" Justin asked. "You wouldn't have come otherwise?"

Sonia giggled and gave him a quick hug and kiss. Justin took her hand and led her inside.

"You may sit there," Justin said pointing to a chair, "If you promise not to interfere with my cooking."

"I won't," Sonia said. "It smells so good in here."

Justin poured two glasses of wine. They drank a toast to each other. Sonia was in awe of the place. The black granite countertop mirrored the pot rack hanging overhead. Justin had to finish up a few things. There was some sauce to be stirred, some fruit to be cut. Sonia just watched as he scurried around the kitchen.

When he finished, Justin gently took her hand and led her to the dining room. Sonia thought she'd died and gone to heaven. Justin knew how to romance a girl. Soft music quietly played in the background. The table was set with exquisite china, very delicate and elegant. There were two long candles and a short bouquet of flowers, all set on a beautiful white linen tablecloth.

Sonia just stood in amazement. "This is so nice I don't know what to say."

"So you like it then?" Justin asked.

"Like it! I love it! If your food tastes as good as your dining room table looks, then this evening is going to be the best!"

Justin blushed. "Sit down, and I'll serve you."

Sonia took her seat and relished in the moment. Justin had made poached salmon that was lightly glazed with a butter sauce, asparagus, and mashed potatoes. The food melted in her mouth.

Afterwards, they decided to take their dessert into the living room. Big fluffy couches sat facing the fireplace. They sat on the floor next to the fire.

As Sonia took a bite of her apple pie, Justin said, "You have some whip cream on your lip. May I wipe it off?"

Without thinking, Sonia went to clean her face with a napkin, but Justin quickly grabbed her hand. "Let me do it?" he said with a twinkle in his eye and a slight grin on his face.

He looked so cute Sonia had to smile. She felt her cheeks burn, and she knew it wasn't from the fire. "Okay," she said barely audible.

Justin scooted closer to her. "Did you say okay?"

Sonia nodded her head, closed her eyes, and let Justin kiss the whip cream off her lips. He then licked his own lips. "Your whipping cream is much sweeter than mine." He leaned in to kiss her again.

Her whole body went numb as their tongues entwined as one. The feeling was electrifying. Their lips were made for each other. He pulled her closer, and she wrapped her arms around his broad shoulders, her hands running through his thick hair.

Justin slowly unbuttoned Sonia's blouse. He gently kissed her neck and slowly moved toward her breasts. Her body jolted with excitement. His hands felt the soft roundness of her breasts. His manliness throbbed.

Sonia felt like she was floating on clouds. This was the first time any man had touched her so passionately. Something inside of her, nerves maybe, told her to slow down, but she didn't want him to stop. She desperately wanted him. His hands slowly unbuttoned her blouse further. It felt so good to be in his arms.

Reaching around her back, Justin unhooked her bra and let it fall to the floor. "Sonia, you're so beautiful," he whispered between kisses. His whole body was tightening up—the electricity going through his body could not be turned off. He slowly took the rest of Sonia's clothes off.

Sonia felt like her body was bursting into flames and trembled. She couldn't extinguish the flames or calm down the trembling. Awkwardly, Sonia took off Justin's clothes. She needed to feel his warm skin against hers. She couldn't wait any longer.

He gently laid her down and pulled himself on top of her. He entered her for the first time. Their passion exploded, and left them lying naked and spent on the floor.

When Justin got his breath back, he kissed her lips again and lovingly caressed her cheek. "Sonia, I know we haven't known each other for long, but I know I'm falling in love with you."

Sonia looked into Justin's eyes and saw kindness. "I knew I was falling in love with you the very first time I saw you at the concert. Remember when I fumbled the music? It was because of you. I looked up from the piano and I saw you, and was lost in the moment. I knew right away something felt different. I love you, Justin."

"I love you too, Sonia. I knew that I felt something for you that night. That's why I was looking for you after the concert, and I was so relieved when I saw you. I was afraid that I would never see you again and that tore my heart."

They just lay there for a while embraced in each other's arms. After a while, Justin picked Sonia up and carried her into the coolness of the moonlit night. He walked toward the pool and stepped in with her still in his arms.

They swam naked under the stars, holding onto each other, and wouldn't let go.

CHAPTER 10

Sonia and Justin had been together for over 6 months, and tonight was the night she was going to meet his parents. Sonia had seen Simon and Amanda Haines and knew who they were. Everybody in their city knew who they were. Simon Haines was the Mayor and a very well known man in the business world. She really wanted to make a good impression and make Justin proud.

When she arrived at Justin's parents' house, Sonia felt her stomach clench. She wrung her hands together. "It's okay," Justin said. "They'll love you."

"I hope so." Was Sonia's nervous reply.

They were greeted at the door by Simon and Amanda. Amanda was a beautiful woman with a great figure and short blonde hair. She had a gentle smile and piercing green eyes. Simon looked a lot like Justin—with thick dark blonde hair, and blue eyes that sparkled with kindness.

"Nice to meet you, Sonia. Justin has told us so much about you," Amanda said. Simon nodded in agreement.

"It's nice to meet you too," Sonia stumbled. Justin squeezed Sonia's hand, which gave her some strength. They headed inside and sat down at the table for some tea.

"It's nice to finally meet the girl who has made my boy so happy," Simon said. He smiled warmly at Sonia. She felt her cheeks blush.

"We hear that you are quite the pianist," Amanda said.

"Yes, I've been playing since I was a little girl. I love it. It makes me feel alive," Sonia said. She could feel her legs shaking from her nervousness. Was that the right thing to say? Playing the piano did make her feel alive, the way she could express herself through music, through her fingers.

"We'd love to hear you play," Amanda said. "We have a baby grand in the lounge. Would you be so kind as to play us a song or two?"

Sonia looked at Justin for reassurance. Playing would be a wonderful idea because then she wouldn't have to talk. "Of course," she said, "I'd love to."

When Sonia sat down at the piano, she held her fingers as if in a trance over the keys. Before she played the first note, she took a deep breath. Whenever she played, she entered into a different world. It was as if she floated in the air with the music. She played to her heart's content, completely oblivious to the fact that Justin and his parents were in the same room. When she finished playing, she emerged from her trance-like state and smiled.

"Wow," Simon said. "I'm thoroughly impressed. That was phenomenal."

"Thank you," Sonia said. She felt at ease.

On the way home, she asked Justin what his parents thought of her.

"Honey," Justin said taking her hand into his. "They liked you, and they will love you just as much as I love you."

*****

The next evening, Sonia was at Justin's house when the phone rang. He put it on speaker so she could hear the conversation.

"Hi, dear, it's Mom. I just wanted you to know that your father and I had a nice time last night. Sonia's a lovely girl, and so beautiful! Promise you'll bring her over again sometime."

Justin smiled and winked at Sonia. "Thanks, Mom, I think she's a great girl—beautiful, talented, compassionate, creative…" Sonia covered her mouth to stifle a laugh and playfully punched his arm. "We've been together six months now."

"Has it been that long already?" Amanda questioned. "I'm sorry we haven't met her sooner. We're always so busy, but we would love to see her more often and you too. Let's make a point of it, okay?"

"Sounds good, Mom, and Sonia will be very pleased to hear that you like her. She was so nervous meeting you both." He grinned at Sonia as she gently punched his leg for teasing her.

"Well, she has nothing to worry about. She's wonderful. Tell her we like her very much. I have to run, but we'll talk soon. Say hi to Sonia for us."

"See!" Justin said after he had said goodbye and hung up the phone. "They love you."

Sonia smiled then locked herself around him. She had never been so happy in her life.

*****

Another year passed and the love between Sonia and Justin grew stronger. Justin had asked Sonia to go on a cruise with him. She accepted. John and Mary were a little uneasy with it at first, but Sonia was a woman now and had her own life to lead. Their little girl had grown up and fallen in love.

The holiday was fantastic. Every day Sonia and Justin visited a different island. They bought gifts from some of the islands. Sonia especially bought little tokens for her parents.

There were many things to do on the ship. There was dancing every night, a movie or a show, and then there was talent night. Justin had, without Sonia knowing, put himself on the competition list for karaoke night. Justin could not sing very well, but it didn't matter.

The last one on the list was Justin and when they called his name, Sonia looked up in surprise.

"You're going to sing? I thought you couldn't sing. As a matter of fact, I know you can't sing. I've heard you sing in the shower," she laughed.

Justin smiled. "Just wait and see." He walked up to the stage and took the mike. "I first want to apologize to everyone because my girlfriend tells me I can't sing and she's probably right. But I'd like to try it anyway. I would like to sing something special to my girlfriend, that is, if you all let me?"

Everyone started cheering and clapping. Sonia was getting embarrassed, but silently she felt honored that Justin was going to sing something for her. She sat there stunned, waiting for Justin to proceed.

"Okay," Justin said clearing his throat. "Here it goes. I'm going to sing to "Edelweiss," but I've changed the words especially for my girlfriend, Sonia."

He looked at the DJ and nodded for him to begin the music.

I love you Sonia, dear,

Will you marry me sweetheart?

Please say yes, say you will,

Then you'll make me so happy.

As he sung, Justin stared into Sonia's eyes. When the song was over he said, "Sonia, sweetheart, I love you so much. I can't imagine my life without you. Will you marry me?"

The room erupted into thunderous claps. Sonia thought her heart would burst. Justin walked off the stage and as he approached her, Sonia didn't know what to do. She was in shock. She couldn't believe her ears. Justin had sung to her in front of all those people and had asked her to marry him. Her cheeks burned. She felt a surge of love for this man that was stronger than ever.

She stood as Justin came closer and they embraced. She answered with a soft voice into his ear, "Yes, I will."

"She said yes!" Justin announced to the crowd. He picked her up and swirled her around.

The room erupted again. People clapped and cheered. Strangers were congratulating them from every direction. Then Justin took Sonia by the arm and led her to the stage. She walked willingly with him, but wondered, *what is he up to now?*

Justin took the mike again and thanked everyone. "I would like everyone to celebrate with us and drink to our engagement, and your next drink is on me." A waiter walked onto the stage with two glasses of champagne on a silver tray. A little box sat between the glasses. Justin took the blue velvet box, opened it, and showed it to Sonia.

Sonia stood stunned. Her eyes filled with tears. The ring was gorgeous. She placed her hands over her mouth and squealed. "OHHHH Justin, it's so beautiful!"

Justin carefully slid the diamond ring on her finger. The diamond was huge, and tiny diamonds sat snuggly around it. The gold band had very intricate design work. It was the most beautiful ring Sonia had ever seen.

"Thank you, Sonia, for making me the happiest man on Earth."

Sonia couldn't hold back her tears. She was ecstatic. "You make me the happiest woman ever." As they kissed, the crowd cheered some more, but the newly-engaged, couple didn't hear a thing.

Justin picked up the glasses from the tray and handed one to Sonia. "I would like to make a toast to my fiancé." Everyone raised their glasses and toasted to the happy couple.

It was a beautiful evening, and after they said goodnight to everyone, Justin and Sonia went on the deck, cuddling and kissing the night away.

CHAPTER 11

Dameon Smith sat in the kitchen, still in his pajamas, sipping his morning coffee while reading the local newspaper. He flipped through a couple of pages and then nearly spilled his coffee upon seeing a picture of a young woman standing next to a young man.

That can't be Celia, he thought. Her hair was different. Celia's hair was messier and longer. He didn't usually pay much attention to the inmates. Pretty ones, however, always garnered a second look, and Celia definitely had the looks for him to notice.

Dameon stared at the picture again. The quality wasn't totally clear, but the young man looked familiar. Yes, he looked like the mayor's son. And the face of the young woman. He couldn't believe his eyes. Celia was in prison and there was no way it could be her. Being the warden of Eastwood City Jail, he knew it couldn't be her.

He read the caption under the picture:

Justin Haines, son of Simon Haines, to be married to Sonia Wells sometime next year. No date has been set. Their engagement party is to take place in the next couple of months. The date will soon be announced.

So, the young man was the son of Simon Haines, but who was that girl? He inched his face closer to the picture. The girl looked exactly like Celia. The similarities were uncanny. The same heart-shaped face, big round eyes, and dimpled cheeks. Thoughts danced through his head.

Suddenly, Dameon looked at the clock and realized he needed to get ready for work. He placed his coffee and paper onto the table and got ready, all the while thinking about that picture. Before he left for work, he tore out the picture and put it in his pocket.

When Dameon arrived at the prison, he searched for Ann, the head nurse, his on-and-off-again girlfriend.

He could summon Ann to his office, but he'd rather not for something like this. Nobody at work knew that they were in a relationship, and that was the way he liked to keep it. If he didn't run in to her today, he would invite her to a fancy dinner. He wanted Ann to be in a good mood when he presented her with his idea. He would need her help.

*****

Celia hummed to herself as she folded towels. For the past four years, this was one of her jobs—working in the laundry room, folding towels. She was incarcerated for killing her boyfriend when she was eighteen years old.

The odds were stacked against Celia since the beginning. Her single mom left Celia in the care of various babysitters while she earned a living. At the age of five, Celia and her mother were involved in a horrific bus accident, in which almost everyone had been killed, including her mother.

Celia did not remember much of the accident, but every so often, she would wake up panting. Nightmares. Her mother's face flashed before her eyes. A man in a funny-looking suit with a red helmet took Celia away. Flashing lights, people screaming, her mother not moving. Sometimes, Celia wasn't sure if her nightmares were real memories from her past or just her imagination running wild.

After the accident, no living relatives stepped forward to claim her, so Celia was taken into an orphanage and then into foster care. She bounced from foster home to foster home, and with each move she became a little more distant. At the age of twelve, she was finally sent to a group home for girls. At age fourteen, she walked out of the group home and never looked back. She started living on the streets, stealing to survive, got into drugs, then prostitution.

At eighteen, Celia got into a terrible fight with her boyfriend. He had lost his temper one night, and as usual, took it out on her. He often beat her senseless. That one night, though, she had had enough. She still didn't know exactly how it happened, but as he gripped her by the throat, she grabbed a knife and stabbed him, over and over. The one thing she did remember was how she called out for her mother. *Mother, please help me!*

Her boyfriend had died, and she tried running away, but didn't get far. She was arrested, and with her rap sheet, and because she was eighteen, an adult, the courts found her guilty and sentenced her to life in prison for first-degree murder. She was stuck in this hellhole. The best she could hope for was to get out on good behaviour.

She would try to appeal; it was self-defense in her eyes. She might be able to get out in seven or ten years, but that was still a long time. Four years had felt like a lifetime already.

A loud, honking bell rang out, which meant that Celia was finished with her work for the day. Relieved, she brought a towel to her face. She breathed in the scent of fresh laundry. It was the small things that kept her going.

She cleaned herself up and proceeded to the dining room for dinner. And, like most nights, after she finished eating, Celia would go off on her own. Book in hand, she sat in the corner of the recreation room and disappeared into the story.

*****

Celia's file sat on Dameon's desk. He had flipped through the paperwork over and over. He decided to do security rounds with the other guards to see if he could get a glimpse of Celia. He stood silently inside the large room searching for Celia's face in the crowd. And there she was, sitting in the far corner with her face immersed in a book. He held his eyes on her while he took the picture out of his pocket and studied it some more.

Celia could sense someone watching her. She glanced up and noticed the warden staring at her intently. Her stomach tightened. Why would he be staring at her? Did she do something wrong? It was normal for a prison guard to browse the recreation room, but usually the warden wasn't present. She wanted him to piss off. He was making her nervous.

The warden made eye contact, and Celia quickly looked to the floor. When she looked up, he was gone. She tried reading again, but she couldn't concentrate. There was something about the way he stared at her that left her feeling vulnerable.

CHAPTER 12

Dameon arrived at the restaurant at eight o'clock. Ann was already seated at the table. He waved, took his coat off, hung it up, and then approached the table.

"Hi, sweetie pie. How are you?" he asked as he leaned over the table and kissed her on the cheek. Then he placed a small box in front of her.

Ann looked at the box and smiled. "I'm fine, but honey, you don't always have to buy me a present. I do appreciate it though, thank you." She reached across the table and grabbed the box. Upon opening it, she exclaimed, "Dameon, it's beautiful." She embraced him in a hug and kiss.

"I'm glad you like it," Dameon said.

The little silver bracelet looked very expensive, but it wasn't. However, it was simple enough for Ann's taste. She loved how it sparkled in the light. "I really love it," Ann said again.

People thought that Dameon was a sweet, honest, and sincere guy. He was somewhat handsome, and when he turned on the charm, it was easy for people to like and trust him. Besides, he got his job with all the right qualifications. Faults or not, he also had a very quick wit and seemed to be able to talk his way into whatever situation he fancied. That was how he got the job at the jail in the first place.

What Ann liked about him was his creativity. He used to work as a freelance photographer. He was actually quite gifted as a photographer, and to feed his passion, he would often freelance his pictures to the local newspaper.

"How was your day?" Ann asked.

"I have to show you something," Dameon said with a smirk on his face.

As usual, Dameon's cell phone rang. He answered it, and began speaking in a different language. Ann looked around the restaurant nervously. She knew enough not to ask what the phone call was all about. Dameon could be very secretive; she had learned over the years not to question him. She didn't want to upset him. She knew that he had a few businesses on the side. At least, that was what he told her.

"What do you want to show me?" Ann asked once Dameon got off the phone. The words slipped out of her mouth. She knew him well enough to know not to pressure him. He could be really sweet, but he also had a nasty side. She didn't know much about his family, and Dameon simply didn't like talking about them. All Ann really knew was that he liked to make money. He had promised her that one day he would let her meet his family, but she would have to be patient. After all, he was a very busy man. He also had a problem with alcohol. She could already smell alcohol on his breath. When he drank too much, he became a totally different person, a real Jekyll and Hyde. That was usually when the fights started.

Ann often wondered why she was with Dameon, but after all this time, she had grown to love him, even with all his faults. There were complications, like with any relationship. Ann always mentioned her fifteen-year-old son, Mike to him, but Dameon showed no interest. He wanted nothing to do with Mike. That hurt her but she continued to hope that one day, things would change.

"We're going to have a good evening together," Dameon said. They had recently had a fight over another girl whom Ann thought he was having an affair with. This was nothing new; it happened a lot. They would often fight over his drinking, or Mike, but this time it was over another girl. Their relationship was so on and off that it was almost as if they looked for things to break up.

The make-up sex was amazing. Dameon promised that things would get better and he would give up everything for her. He had told Ann that this time he was really going to change—it was going to be for real—and she was the only one for him.

"I'm really happy you asked me out to dinner," Ann said. "I love you."

Dameon responded almost too quickly, "I love you too, sweetie pie."

Finally, the waitress came over. "Would you like anything to drink?" she asked.

"Yes, I'd like a beer," Dameon said.

Ann interrupted. "No, don't have a beer. Have a coke or an iced tea or something." Then she said to the waitress, "I'll have a coffee, please."

Dameon gritted his teeth. He hated when people told him what to do. "No, I'll have a beer. I can handle one beer."

Dameon waited for the waitress to take their orders before reaching into his pocket for the picture. He slid it across the table with a grin plastered on his face.

Ann picked up the photo and her eyes grew. "She looks exactly like Celia! But the picture isn't very clear. If this girl didn't have such a neatly-layered haircut, you would think it was Celia." But, she thought, that would be impossible.

Dameon took a sip of his drink and said, "It says here that the woman's name is Sonia Wells who is engaged to Justin Haines. Do you know who Justin Haines is?"

"Yes, I do. He's the son of Simon Haines, the big conglomerate king and our multi-million dollar mayor," Ann said.

"I've been thinking about Mike, Ann. You want to help Mike, right?" Dameon said. Ann's eyes lit up at the mention of her son. Dameon knew that Mike was a touchy subject. "Well, I have an idea to make some money for you and Mike."

Ann had no more savings left because she had been supporting her son, and Mike had been stealing from her left and right. But what could Dameon have in mind? She knew it couldn't be legal. She hesitated and then said, "Yes, of course I want to help Mike. I don't understand why you want to suddenly help me, but go ahead, I'm listening."

Dameon shifted in his seat. "You know that no one knows about us, the relationship we have. It's very important right now to keep it that way because I have a plan. I'm going to try and find out where this woman Sonia Wells lives. Then I can put my plan in motion." Dameon inched closer, his voice barely above a whisper. "I would like you to show this picture to Celia and see what her reaction is. Make sure no one sees you doing it, and then, tell her that you've found a way to get her out of jail. But make sure Celia doesn't blabber it around. Tell her that if she does, there will be consequences. Threaten her with something. I don't care what you do, just make sure that no one knows."

Thoughts raced through Ann's head. What was he planning, and how could this help her and Mike out? With a quizzical look on her face, she asked. "What is your plan then, Dameon?"

He simply responded, "You just have to wait and see."

"How am I going to show that picture to Celia, and how and why are we going to get her out of jail?"

Dameon sternly said, "I believe that Celia can help us to make some money, and well, you'll just have to leave the rest up to me. Just show her the picture and tell her what I told you. You're the head nurse, aren't you? You can make her visit you in the infirmary, can't you?"

Ann felt her stomach plunge. She did not like where this was going. What did Dameon have up his sleeve? She loved him, that much was true, but would she be willing to risk her career over something he wouldn't even disclose? And then there was Mike. God, how she loved her son. She had put him in therapy, in rehab, and none of it worked. Now, she was broke, living from paycheck to paycheck, and Mike was sucking her dry, financially and emotionally. She was desperate.

Ann opted not to pry anymore of Dameon's plan. She could tell by his tone that he was becoming somewhat agitated with her questioning. She hesitantly took the picture and put it in her purse. *As long as nobody gets hurt,* she thought.

CHAPTER 13

That evening Celia had decided to go to her cell after dinner. After dinner, the inmates got time for themselves. They could either go to the recreation room or go back to their cell. Normally, Celia would go to the recreation room to read, but this evening she decided to read her book and enjoy the alone time – her cellmate had just been released.

Suddenly, a female guard tapped the bars of her cell. "Get up! You have to come with me."

Celia, somewhat puzzled asked, "Why?"

"You have to go to the infirmary," the security guard said.

"Why would I have to go to the infirmary, I don't feel sick?"

With more authority in her voice, the security guard said, "I don't know, I was just told to bring you there."

Celia put her book down and followed the security guard to the infirmary. When they got there, the guard let her in, told her to wait, and locked the door behind her.

Celia sat down on a chair and noticed how the infirmary lacked in color just as the rest of the prison. All the walls were painted gray. How she missed a life outside in the real world.

A few minutes later, Ann stepped into the room and closed the door. "Hi Celia," she said. She stared at Celia's face for a moment before taking the photo out of her pocket. She examined the picture. It had to be Celia.

Celia felt uncomfortable, like she was in some sort of trouble. She took a deep breath and asked, "Why am I here? I'm not sick."

Ann replied, "I'd like to show you something." She hesitated for a moment, and then handed the picture to Celia.

Celia stopped breathing and straightened up in her chair. Quickly trying to recover her uncharacteristic reaction, she sarcastically replied with, "So, this girl looks like me, so what? Doesn't everybody have a twin somewhere?" She tossed the photo back to Ann.

This wasn't going to be easy, Ann thought. She remained calm. "It says her name is Sonia Wells. Have you ever heard of a Sonia Wells?"

"No!" Celia said, while rolling her eyes. "Why would I know Sonia Wells?" She felt her blood boil. "In case you haven't noticed, I've been behind these bars for over four years and I don't exactly hang out with people like that, do I?"

Ann maintained her stoic disposition. Dameon had some nerve. What was he thinking? "Well, I thought that you might have liked that picture because she looks so much like you."

Celia sarcastically laughed. "Is this some kind of a joke?"

At that moment, Ann felt sorry for the poor girl. It was rumored that Celia had murdered her boyfriend out of self-defense. There were other women in the prison who deserved to be there –

murdering their children, their husbands, their husband's lovers, but Celia's situation was out of self-defense. *Where was the justice?* Ann thought.

"I'm sorry to have bothered you," Ann said. "You may go back to your cell." She called for a guard and Celia left without saying anything.

When Celia got back to her cell she laid on her bed, book in lap. That picture. That girl. Her heart plunged. She didn't want to let on to Ann, but it had really surprised her that the girl in the picture looked so much like her. The name Sonia meant something, but she didn't know why. It kept on nagging her, racking around in her brain, until she fell asleep.

*****

The nightmares came. They always came. She was holding onto a leg of a bench. She was being banged all around in the bus, as it tumbled over and over, holding on for dear life. Fear raced through her. She thought she could hear her mother call her name. Her mother's voice was so soft she could hardly hear it. And then, she called out, "Mommy! I'm okay, but where are you?" Her mother didn't answer. Terrified, she kept on calling, "Mommy! Mommy! Mommy!"

She thrashed around in her bed and screamed. She was unknowingly disturbing the surrounding inmates from their sleep. They started yelling for her to shut up. They rattled the bars of their cells, cursing in Celia's direction.

A guard came in and turned the lights on. "Keep it down!"

One of the inmates yelled, "Shit man! She's always waking us up! Fuck, how would you like to be fucking woken up by some nutcase."

The guard replied with a lack of sensitivity, "Just be quiet and get back to sleep!" She walked over to Celia's cell and said, "Hey Winters, wake up."

Celia had already awakened with all the commotion and sat up. Annoyed, she quipped, "Yeah what?" her body still shaking from the nightmare.

"You were dreaming again!" the guard told her with annoyance.

"Sorry." Celia laid back down.

The commotion died down, and the lights were shut off. Celia lay in bed thinking about her nightmare. She was sweating. She had dreamt this before, quite a few times, but it had been a while ago. Where did it come from?

Mother, she whispered, over and over, as she usually did, to help her fall asleep.

CHAPTER 14

"It's such a beautiful dress, Mommy. You did a fantastic job! I love it!" Sonia beamed. She stood in front of the full-length mirror in her bedroom and twirled around.

"Hold still," Mary said with a chuckle. She was trying to put the last pin into the hem. "I'd like to make your wedding dress as well."

Mary was an exceptional seamstress. She had made all of Sonia's dresses when she was little. Sonia's favourites were worn at her piano recitals and graduation.

"I would be honoured! And quite truthfully, I wouldn't want it any other way," Sonia said. "I know you'll do a beautiful job. This one is fantastic, and it's just my engagement dress." Sonia hugged her mother. "Thank you so much," she whispered in her ear.

"Your father and I wanted to take care of the engagement party since Justin's parents are taking care of the wedding. We certainly can't afford the type of elaborate wedding they are planning."

Sonia had decided that if Justin's parents wanted to go with a large-scale wedding, it was fine with her. But her parents, however, wanted to give Sonia and Justin a special party, so they decided to throw the engagement party. Marrying into the Haines' family meant the engagement party would be, for John and Mary, like paying for a small wedding anyway. They had saved money since Sonia was young for her education and marriage, but they hadn't expected her to marry into such wealth. They knew their limitations and graciously accepted the invitation of Simon and Amanda Haines to cover all costs for the wedding.

The engagement party was to take place two months from now, a week before Sonia's twenty-third birthday. It would be as elaborate as they could afford.

Sonia stared at her dress again in awe. It was a light blue, long, chiffon dress with white trim around the neckline, and the cuffs were made from fluffy imitation fur. The dress hugged her bosom and flowingly fell to the floor.

"Well, that's it then," Mary said. "It's almost finished. Take it off now so I can sew up the last little bits for you."

After Sonia had changed into her regular clothes and met Mary in the kitchen for some tea the doorbell rang.

"Is that Justin?" Mary asked.

"I don't think so. He would've just walked in," Sonia said. Sonia ran toward the front door and was greeted by a handsome, well-dressed gentleman.

He introduced himself, "I'm Dameon Smith. I'm a freelance photographer, and I read in the newspaper about your upcoming engagement party. I was wondering if you needed a photographer. I would love to do it. I could show you portfolios of what I've done and I can keep the cost quite reasonable."

Any talk of the wedding always made Sonia's heart burst, but something about this man made her uncomfortable. Maybe it was the way he was staring at her.

Sonia hesitated, "I don't know. I'll call my mother, hold on a sec. Mommy!" she called.

Seconds later, Mary appeared in the foyer. She extended her hand. "I'm Mrs. Mary Wells. How can I help you?"

Dameon took her hand and said, "I'm pleased to meet you. I'm Dameon Smith. I would like to speak to you about being the photographer at your daughter's engagement party." Then he handed her his business card.

"I'm sorry, Mister Smith," Mary politely said. "I won't make that decision without my husband. You may come back this evening when he'll be home."

"I understand, thank you. What would be a good time for you?" Dameon replied. The excitement was building in him. The first part of his plan could be put into motion if he could get this job. But he had to compose himself. He had to look professional. His heart anxiously pumped in his chest.

Then Mary said, "Eight o'clock would be good, but we would like you to bring some more identification, some samples of your work, and some references that we could contact. Then we'll discuss prices. I have to let you know that we've been shopping around, but if all goes well, we'll certainly keep you in mind."

"Eight o'clock would be fine. I'll see you then, and thank you," Dameon smiled.

When Dameon left, Sonia said, "I didn't feel comfortable with that man. He gave me the creeps. He just kept staring at me."

"That's because you're so beautiful," Mary said. "He seemed nice enough. When your father gets home all three of us can sit down and talk, and then we'll see what he's like and has to offer. He just might be the person we're looking for."

*****

That night over dinner, Mary and Sonia told John about Dameon Smith and the appointment they had made for eight o'clock that evening.

"Well, it can't hurt to talk to him. We need to hire a photographer anyway," John said.

Soon after dinner, Dameon arrived. John greeted him at the door and they introduced themselves.

"Take a seat in the living room and I'll get my wife and daughter," John said.

"May I get you some coffee?" Mary asked upon entering the room.

"That would be nice, ma'am," Dameon replied.

"It will be ready in a few minutes. I just put a pot on," Mary said.

Sonia greeted Dameon with a polite smile and nod. Dameon could not believe his eyes. The likeness to Celia was so amazing; he tried very hard to stop staring.

"I think the coffee is ready. I'll be right back," Mary said. Sonia went with her to help.

Once she got into the kitchen, Sonia whispered, "I really don't feel comfortable around this man."

Mary looked a little puzzled. "What do you mean, dear?"

"I don't know. I just feel funny around him. He keeps staring at me," she said.

"Well, honey, he's a man and you're an attractive woman. Don't you worry."

Sonia rolled her eyes, grabbed the coffee, and headed toward the living room.

As they discussed the party, Dameon was very nervous but he remained composed. He pulled out his portfolio. He was a good photographer; they could easily see that in his work.

John felt good about Dameon; they hit it off right away. He also liked Dameon's reasonable prices. "We're still going to look around some more but we'll call you either way."

Dameon replied, "That's fine, I understand." He pulled out his camera from his briefcase. "But, can I take a picture of the three of you? That way, you will have a better idea of what I can do?"

"Why not?" John said.

Butterflies took over Sonia's stomach. *Why did she feel this way?* Without saying a word, she watched as Dameon walked around the living in search for the perfect light and right angles. He ushered the family toward the fireplace.

"I look awful," Sonia huffed. I don't even have any make-up on." She crossed her arms.

"You look fine," John said and Mary agreed.

Then Dameon said, "You're a natural beauty." Sonia shyly looked at the floor. "I'm sorry," he continued, "forgive me for staring, but you're exceptionally beautiful. I don't think you need any makeup, and your bone structure is perfect for the camera."

Sonia felt the tension in her shoulders ease. Maybe she was being a little harsh on this guy. If he was really that good, he'd be able to make her look perfect in the picture, and that was all she wanted – perfect photos for her and Justin's perfect day.

"I'll have this picture ready in a couple of days," Dameon said as he packed up his camera, "and I'll bring it over so you can see my work firsthand."

After Dameon left, the three of them sat in the living room discussing the issue further. John said, "I think we should take this guy. He seems like a very nice gentleman, his work is good, and his prices are reasonable."

Mary added, "I guess we'll see when he comes back with the picture, but I still think we should look around a bit more before we make a commitment."

Then Sonia interrupted, "I still don't feel comfortable with him, the way he kept staring at me. Good thing he apologized about staring at me, but still, it creeps me out!"

Mary said, "It's important that you're happy with the photos. Plus, you'll be so busy you won't even notice him."

*****

Two days later, Dameon showed up at their doorstep with the photo he had taken. It was amazing, even Sonia had to agree. She couldn't believe how great he had made her look, even without any make-up on. But Mary told Dameon that they were still going to shop around a little more. So, the following day, Mary and Sonia went to check out some other photographers. They visited three others, and found a steep difference in prices for the quality of work.

They were getting hungry when Mary suggested they stop in the nearby coffee shop. Sitting on the patio, Mary said, "I think we'll have to go with Dameon Smith, Sonia. He seems much more reasonable, and your father seems to like him. They hit it off right away, his work was really good, and with the references he got, I don't think I mind him either."

Sonia sighed. "Okay, we'll go with Dameon Smith because Daddy seems to like him. I guess it doesn't really matter who does the photography, as long as it's done right. And Dameon seems to know what he's doing. I did like how that photo turned out."

Sonia wanted to please her parents, and although it was decided that Dameon would photograph the engagement party, she couldn't ignore the weird feeling in her stomach.

CHAPTER 15

Ann came home from work exhausted. She took her mail and sat on the first chair she came across. It had been hard for her to talk to Celia. Celia's harsh reaction to seeing the photo had made Ann feel uncomfortable about telling her that she had a possible way of getting Celia out of jail. She was frustrated that she hadn't been able to tell Celia about that, and she knew that Dameon would be angry with her for not doing everything he had asked her to do. She was nervous now to tell Dameon about what had happened.

She heard the phone ring but was afraid it might be Dameon so she didn't answer it.

"There's some guy on the phone for you, Mom," Mike screamed from the other room.

Ann was surprised to hear her son's voice. She didn't think he was home. Ann worked late a lot, allowing Mike the freedom to come and go as he pleased. She felt guilty knowing that he got into trouble because she was absent so much of the time.

Mike handed her the phone. He didn't look well. His completion was pale. He probably needed a fix. But for now, she knew she'd have to deal with Dameon, who was likely the person on the other end of the phone. She walked with the phone into her bedroom so Mike couldn't hear.

"Mike's home, I can't talk now." Ann whispered into the phone.

"I'll be quick," Dameon replied "Come over tomorrow for dinner, and I'll order in. How did it go with Celia?"

"Okay," Ann said nervously. "I'll tell you about it tomorrow at dinner. What time?"

"Eight o'clock" he said, and hung up.

Ann sighed and walked back into the living room. Mike looked at her and asked, "Who was that?"

"Just a telemarketer," she replied.

*****

The next night Ann met Dameon at his place. Dameon brought home Chinese food.

"Hi sweetie-pie," Dameon said and gave her a passionate kiss.

She loved his tender side and would drink these moments in, always wanting more. While in his warm embrace, Ann said, "It sure smells good in here."

"Yup. We better eat before it gets cold."

They sat down at the dining room table. While Dameon poured her a glass of wine, he didn't waste any time with the questions. "How did it go with Celia? Did you get through to her? Is she interested in getting out of jail?"

Ann stayed silent.

"Well, Ann! Are you going to tell me?" Dameon sternly asked.

Then Ann told Dameon how Celia had reacted to the photo and that she hadn't mentioned the idea of getting out of jail to her yet.

"Well you'll just have to tell her tomorrow, Ann." Dameon ordered. "I have a new picture of Sonia. It's much clearer. Here, take a look you really can't tell the difference." He handed Ann the newest photo.

Ann was amazed; the resemblance was absolutely incredible. "How did you change her hair like that?" Ann asked.

"Trick of the trade," Dameon answered.

"How did you get this picture?" Ann asked.

"I took it." Dameon said. "I went to Sonia's house and I asked if I could take a picture."

"Just like that?" Ann questioned him.

Dameon chuckled and took a sip of wine. "Well, it wasn't that easy, but it wasn't that difficult either. Just take the picture and go to Celia again, and tell her what I told you."

He spooned some food onto his plate and told Ann to do the same. Without asking any more questions, Ann did as she was told.

*****

Celia was called to the infirmary again. This time she was in the recreation room when a guard came for her. It was not the same guard as the first time, but Celia had suspicions on why she was called there again. *What did that nurse want?*

Once she was in the infirmary, Ann came in handing Celia a photo.

Celia waved her off with, "I don't want that picture!"

Ann replied, "I know, but I have another one for you that you might be interested in."

Celia sighed and snapped the picture from Ann's hands. This time her stomach literally dropped to the floor. "Who is she?" she asked. "She looks just like me! It's as if I'm looking in a mirror." Not being able to take her eyes off the picture, she repeated again, "I can't believe it. This girl looks exactly like me. It's like she's my twin or something."

Then Celia turned as pale as a ghost, remembering her nightmare. "I had a terrible nightmare the other night and I remembered something. It was in my dream. Oh, God, I can't believe it. I might really have a twin. I remember my mother, when we were on the bus, saying something about going to visit my sister. That's when the accident happened. I must have blanked it from my mind all this time. Could it be? Could she be my sister?"

Tears formed in the corners of her eyes. Celia was so lost in thought that she'd forgotten Ann was in the room. She hazily looked up at Ann and asked, "Could I really have a sister?"

"I don't know," Ann said. She was trying to figure all of this out as well, but she thought of Dameon and swallowed. "Listen carefully to what I have to say, Celia," Ann said. She inched closer and lowered her voice. "I want you to think about this and don't, under any circumstance, repeat what I'm about to say."

Celia felt her heart race. She listened intently.

Ann inched closer. "I know a way of getting you out of jail."

Shocked, Celia sat back in her chair. *Was this woman nuts?* Then she replied sarcastically, "Yeah sure, you know a way to get me out of jail. How and why would you want to do that?"

Ann looked her straight in the eyes and said, "Okay, THE HOW, is up to me," even though she had no idea how Dameon was going to do it. "And THE WHY…well, there's something in it for me as well. Think it over for a day or two, then let me know if you want to get out of jail, and make sure you keep your mouth shut. If you say anything about this to anyone, then it's you who's going to be in trouble, not me. I'll just deny it, and nobody will believe you. So think about it, and if you're interested, tell the guard that you're sick and you want to see me in the infirmary, got it?"

"Whatever," Celia said nonchalantly; not really believing what Ann had just told her. She was thinking about the picture, and wondered if that could really be her sister.

*****

A few days later Ann was called to the infirmary because one of the inmates was sick. When she walked in, she saw Celia sitting there. "Hi, Celia, are you sick?" Ann asked.

"Yes, sick and tired of being in prison. So tell me about your plan. I'm in."

CHAPTER 16

The engagement party was a huge success. The weather was beautiful and there were a lot of guests. That was, of course, to be expected, with the number of influential people that Justin's parents knew. There were two tables full of presents, and a beautifully decorated gift box with a slit on the top that Sonia's bridesmaids had made, and it was full.

It looked and felt like a wedding. Sonia believed that she was in a dream. Her father was right, she had no time to worry about Dameon Smith because she was too busy entertaining all the guests. She hardly noticed him. Many of the guests were strangers to Sonia, but Justin introduced her to most of them. She was the centre of attention and felt like a princess. She felt beautiful in her blue dress that her mother had made.

Dameon was busy taking photos and videos. He overheard many conversations, and he secretly recorded a few of them with a hidden audio recorder in the breast pocket of his suit jacket. He skillfully talked to many of Sonia's friends, and a couple of women from the office of the fashion magazine that Sonia worked at.

Dameon appeared to enjoy himself while learning as much about Sonia that he could. He even got to talk to Sonia and Justin for a while. Justin, like Sonia's parents, thought that Dameon was a very nice and professional man.

Even Sonia had to admit that he didn't make her feel as uneasy as he did when they'd first met. *He wasn't so bad after all,* she thought.

*****

A couple of weeks later, the photos and videos that Dameon took at the party were developed and edited. He had done a fantastic job. He put in some text here and there, with pictures zooming in and out, as well as other effects he added. The whole party on the videos went by so smoothly, flowing seamlessly like a movie. Dameon definitely knew his stuff. He couldn't wait to give the Wells' family the finished products.

"Would you like some coffee, Dameon?" Mary asked.

Dameon shifted on the living room couch. "Yes, that would be very nice." Any excuse to prolong his stay would be an opportunity to get to know the Wells' family better.

While Mary poured the coffee, John said, "Let's see what you've got."

Dameon was very eager, so he took everything out of his briefcase and spread it out on the coffee table.

Sonia, John, and Mary were all wide-eyed as they flipped through the photo albums.

"It's fantastic!" Mary said.

"Everything and everyone looks so beautiful!" Sonia exclaimed. So overcome by the quality of his work, she blurted, "Would you like to take our wedding pictures too?"

Dameon was over the moon with excitement, but of course he couldn't show it. He smiled and said, "I'll have to get back to you on that. When exactly is the wedding?"

"Well," Sonia said, "we don't know the exact date yet, but as soon as we know we'll let you know."

"Okay, that's fine." Dameon replied and then continued with, "Oh, say, I just had an idea. If you'd like, I could make a whole movie from the engagement party up to the wedding. I mean, from all the planning. For instance, the writing out of invitation cards, and the making of the cake and buying the flowers and the dress." He flipped his hands in the air. "It was just a thought. Probably a crazy idea, right?"

"Well, I don't think it's a crazy idea, what do you think Sonia?" Mary asked.

Then Sonia spoke up. "I like that idea, and nobody has ever done that as far as I know. It would be unique. And then maybe you can also take some movies of our new house that we're going to build, I'll just have to make sure that Justin likes the idea as well."

Mary and John both looked at Sonia with surprise and asked simultaneously, "You're building a house?"

"Yes," Sonia said. She felt her cheeks blush. It wasn't as if she'd kept it a secret. She and Justin had been pondering the idea for quite some time, but they both agreed not to mention anything until it was firmly decided. "Justin and I just made up our minds yesterday. He's going to sell his house and we're going to build a new one for both of us. He wants us to start out new. I told him I didn't mind moving in with him, but he said that I would never really feel like it's my home. He thinks of everything. We were going to tell you together, but I guess I just blurted it out." Sonia grinned.

"Well, that's fantastic news," John said. "When are you going to start?"

Sonia told them that they didn't know yet and that they'd first have to find the right location.

Dameon added, "Well, if that's the case, then I could include that whole endeavour in the video. The engagement party first, and then the planning of the wedding and the building of the new house. First, the empty property and then the start of the build, and then the completion…" Dameon rambled on and on.

Sonia interrupted, "I love the sound of it! Would you mind doing all of that?"

"I would love to," Dameon said. "It would be fun, and would be great for my portfolio too. We can end the movie with a big finale: the wedding day. Unless you want me to come along on your honeymoon too," he chuckled.

They all laughed.

"Yeah, sure," Sonia laughed as she sipped her coffee, "that would be crazy!" She was starting to change her mind about Dameon; *he was not such a bad guy after all.* She went on to say, "It could work, from the engagement up to and including the wedding. I'll talk to Justin and see what he thinks about all of this."

Dameon felt like he was going to explode with excitement. So far, everything seemed to be going his way. He had planted the seed, and all he could hope was that it would grow the way he wanted it to.

The evening continued with laughter and coffee. Dameon inquired about Sonia's work, friends, and hobbies. Sonia thought it was nice that he paid attention to what she was saying—most men would have been bored. She was actually starting to warm up to Dameon.

*****

The next day, Sonia showed Justin the photos and videos. "I think I judged Dameon a little too harshly and too soon. My Daddy was right; he seems like a fine gentleman. He wants to film everything – from the engagement party, the building of our house, up to the wedding," she said, as the thought of Dameon coming along with them on their honeymoon entered her mind and made her laugh.

"Why are you laughing?" Justin asked.

Sonia giggled. "I was thinking about something Dameon had said. He was joking, of course, but it was kind of funny. He said he could come along on our honeymoon, discreetly of course."

Justin laughed and squeezed Sonia's hand. "Absolutely not," he said. "I'm going to want my new wife all to myself."

CHAPTER 17

"How are you sweetie pie?" Dameon said as he embraced Ann. Ann usually visited Dameon at his house because it was a safe place to get together. Dameon didn't like to meet at her house because Mike didn't know about their relationship and he wanted to keep it that way.

Ann sensed that something was going right based on Dameon's goofy grin. "Tell me about your plan," she said.

Dameon led her toward the couch. "What would you like to drink, sweetie pie?"

"Orange juice would be fine." She didn't want to encourage him to have alcohol.

Dameon fetched the orange juice and then took a seat next to Ann on the couch. "Remember that picture, Ann? The one with Sonia standing between her parents? The one I gave you to show Celia?"

"Yes," Ann said nonchalantly. *Of course she remembered.*

"Well," Dameon went on, "as you know, I went to Sonia Wells' house and asked if I could take that picture. But that was not the only thing...I went there because I wanted a job taking photos and videos for their engagement party."

"Oh, why?" Ann said as her voice trailed off.

"Here take a look, I've put them in my portfolio binder."

Ann straightened her posture. "You mean to tell me that you got the job and you already did it?"

"Yes," Dameon answered.

With a surprised look on her face she asked, "What are the photos and video for then?"

Dameon smiled greedily. "We need them so Celia can learn to act, talk, and do everything exactly like Sonia. I want her to get so good at it that she becomes Sonia."

Ann swallowed a lump in her throat. "Why would you want to do that?"

Dameon proceeded to tell Ann his whole plan. Ann's hands shook as she tried to sip from her glass. "I'm not comfortable with this," she said nervously.

"Come on, Ann, I'm not going to hurt anybody. I already have another plan to make it all right again after we have the money. And I want to help you, that way you can help Mike. Don't you want to help Mike?"

Of course she wanted to help her son and it was very tempting, but she didn't want to hurt anyone. She was feeling conflicted. Mike should be going to a rehabilitation center, but she had already tried that with him. Maybe, just maybe, the right kind of money could put her son in a successful rehabilitation center.

Dameon leaned forward and placed his hand on Ann's knee. "I have a really good plan to make it all right again, after we have our money, over a half a million dollars or so!"

Ann gasped and placed her hands over her mouth. "Ooh!" she exclaimed. With eyes as big as saucers, Ann asked, "Do you really think we can get that much money?"

"Yes," Dameon said matter-of-factly. "I really believe that, and they will never even miss that money. They have so much money, for them it's only a small drop in the bucket."

Even though Ann knew it was wrong, a feeling of excitement began to flow through her body. *That was a lot of money!*

"They hired me to do the photography on their wedding day as well, and maybe even for the whole year."

"What do you mean for the whole year?" Ann asked surprised.

"Justin and Sonia are building a new house for themselves and they want me to take footage of that also. I have pictures and videos from their engagement party, which is great, but once the whole year is over and their wedding is done, I will have a lot more. The more we have the better."

"Well," Ann said. "I don't know yet, Dameon. Let me think about it."

Dameon was getting frustrated with Ann's hesitation, but he needed to remain calm. He needed Ann; otherwise the plan wouldn't follow through. Gently, he rubbed her back. "Let me show you the video and photographs."

Over the next hour, Ann watched video footage of Sonia and Justin's engagement party, of their friends laughing and dancing, of their parents sipping wine. Ann couldn't believe the amount of video footage Dameon managed to obtain. And the photographs were gorgeous.

Sonia and Celia looked so much alike! She cleared her throat and decided to tell Dameon what Celia had told her in the infirmary. "Celia told me that she thinks Sonia might be her sister. She vaguely remembers her mother telling her something like that."

Dameon pushed the pause button on the DVD player. "No way," he said. "Really? That would be fantastic if that's true!" Originally, he'd hoped that Celia would make a good actress, but if they truly were sisters, then it should be easy. "Show Celia the videos on your computer and she'll know how she's supposed to act."

Then Ann said, "Hold on, Dameon, I didn't say I was going to help you. I told you I wanted to think about it for a little while."

Dameon gritted his teeth. "Come on, Ann, what's there to think about? Can't you see that we can make a lot of money? And I promise, I will make everything right again afterwards."

"But how are you going to do that?" Ann asked.

"Oh, sweetie, just leave that up to me," he said with a twinkle in his eye.

Dameon could be so sweet and convincing. His hand gently stroked Ann's back.

"But what about Sonia?" Ann asked. "We're going to hurt her in the process."

"No! No! It will only be for a couple of days. You'll keep her sedated. She will never know what happened."

Confusion flowed through Ann's veins. Everything about this seemed wrong, but if Dameon said that nobody would get hurt, then what was the harm? She bit her lip. "Okay then," Ann said, "but only because I need the money. You really have to make sure that Sonia and Celia won't get hurt."

"Of course, sweetie, you know me. I wouldn't hurt anyone. And now that you've made up your mind, I will make sure that you'll be okay too. The first step is to ask Celia if she can act when you see her next. Of course, we hope she can! Tell her our plan and start showing her the videos." Inching closer to her, he said, "Let's change the subject now." Then he sweet-talked Ann all the way into his bedroom.

*****

Two weeks later, Celia met Ann in the infirmary, pretending to be sick again. Ann really didn't want to help Dameon but she had promised and she really needed the money. There was no turning back.

"Can you act?" Ann asked.

Celia cracked her knuckles. *Of course I could act.* She'd been acting since the moment she got in this place, acting like a tough girl so the other inmates would leave her alone. "Are you fucking kidding me?" Celia said with a smirk. "I've been acting all my life. You know what it's like to be put in so many different foster homes? Shit, believe me, you learn to act. If you wanted something, you had to say and do what people expected just to survive."

"Okay, maybe we can start by cutting out the foul language. Sonia does not cuss."

"Well!! Soooorrrrry!!!" Celia said in a snotty way.

Ann ignored it, and like she was told, showed Celia photos and videos of the engagement party.

Celia's rough attitude almost instantly dissipated when she saw Sonia on the screen. *Holy shit, she looks exactly like me! She even sounds like me.* She could feel her heart beating loudly. *Is she really my sister?* Sonia looked so happy on the screen, as she laughed and hugged her friends, guests, and parents. Celia wanted to turn away but she couldn't peel her eyes from the screen. *It's not fair!*

"Celia, I want you to learn to act like Sonia," Ann said.

"Why would you want me to act like Sonia?" Celia asked as she stared at Sonia kissing her soon-to-be husband.

"Because that's part of our plan to get you out of jail," Ann whispered.

"Oh," Celia reacted.

"So you think you can do that?"

"Yeah, I know I can." Celia said.

"Good," Ann said relieved. "You'll have to come into the infirmary from time to time and learn how to act like Sonia from studying the DVDs. You'll also learn about Sonia's family and friends. You'll have to start acting like Sonia in jail. But not until I tell you to." Ann continued.

"Why would I have to start acting like her in jail?" A million thoughts raced through Celia's mind. "I can see where you're going...you want me to act like Sonia when you get me out of jail cause you probably want me to take her place or something, but why do I need to act like her while I'm in here?"

"You're right, to get out you'll need to take her place. So you'll need as much practice as you can get being Sonia before you get out, so you're truly convincing." Ann said.

"Fine." Celia replied.

Ann called for the guard to come in and return Celia to her cell.

In her cell again, Celia reflected back to all those nightmares, it was true: she had a sister. Sonia. Living happily in the real world while she was stuck behind bars. It just wasn't fair.

I can do this!

CHAPTER 18

A couple of months before the wedding, Sonia and Justin had all their plans in place. It was going to be a beautiful wedding, and Dameon was going to take the pictures and videos.

Dameon had done a fantastic job. He took a lot of footage while the house was being built. Sonia did most of the painting and decorating. Dameon made sure that the video captured Sonia's personality, how happy and alive she felt with a paintbrush in her hand.

The house was beautiful. It was huge and had all the comforts most people would die for—a large swimming pool, a hot tub, 6 bedrooms with walk-in closets, a dynamic kitchen: the works. Sonia felt so spoiled.

When Mary came to visit she could not believe her eyes. Mary and John lived on the other side of Eastwood City, almost an hour away. Mary was very impressed by how much work they had accomplished.

Both mother and daughter swam in the Olympic-sized pool, and then lounged on the lawn chairs basking in the sun. They certainly had not spared any money to build this house, and Sonia truly felt like a princess.

"Mommy would you like a little drink?" she asked.

Mary replied, "I don't know, I have to drive home."

"You don't have to go right away," Sonia pleaded. "You can stay for a little while, can't you? We certainly have something to celebrate: the wedding is all organized and the house is almost finished. Come on. Stay. Have just one little drink."

Mary finally gave in, and Sonia went inside to get some wine and a little snack. Carrying a plate of assorted cheeses and wine, Sonia said, "We'll have a maid soon. Justin and I are interviewing a few different people right now."

"Wow," Mary said. "I'm so happy for you, sweetheart, and I know that you're going to be very happy with Justin. He's a good man. I'm also very happy that we finally had an official visit with Justin's parents."

"Yeah, aren't they great?" Sonia said.

"Yes, they are." Mary agreed. "We had a great talk and learned a lot about each other. Did you know that they haven't always been rich like this? They started with very little, got married, then moved to Eastwood City and worked themselves up. In the beginning they only had enough money to buy themselves a secondhand car and rent a cheap, tiny basement apartment."

"Yes I know," Sonia said. "Whatever they have now, they deserve. Both Justin's parents have worked hard for it and still do. They're good people and they also give away a lot to charity. Did they tell you how they helped Mr. Haines' brother out?" Sonia continued. "He was in a bus accident and ended up in a wheelchair."

Mary listening with interest said, "That must have been Sebastian. I met him at your engagement party. He said he was Simon's brother. A nice man, but I didn't get to talk with him very much."

"Sebastian works with Justin's father in the office," Sonia explained. "Apparently, Sebastian had a nervous breakdown after his wife died when Kevin, his son, was still very young. So Justin's father had asked Sebastian to work for him, to help him cope and give him a change of scenery. But on the way up to Eastwood City, Sebastian and Kevin had been involved in a horrible bus accident. Sebastian had been barely alive when the paramedics found him and was in a coma for over six weeks, and Justin's parents had taken Kevin in. So Justin had an instant little brother."

Sonia continued, "After Sebastian got out of the hospital he stayed with Justin's parents while he was going through rehabilitation. Then when Sebastian was well enough, he found a place close by for him and Kevin. He started working for Justin's father, as was the intent in the first place, and has worked for him ever since."

Sonia took a sip of her wine as she pushed back a wisp of her hair that had fallen over her eyes.

"That sure was nice of them." Mary said. "They really are lovely people. I'm glad to have finally met Simon and Amanda. I feel good about them being your in-laws."

Mary sat up and squinted in the sun. "Well honey, this place is gorgeous! But I better get back home so I can work some more on your dress."

Sonia giggled like a five-year-old. "I can't wait to try it on! I'll be home tomorrow. Thank-you so much Mommy for making my wedding dress!"

Mary smiled. "I wouldn't have it any other way for my special girl,"

*****

Mary finished the dress to Sonia's overwhelming delight. Everything else had been taken care of by Justin's parents.

Sonia was starting to get nervous. She just hoped that everything was going to be perfect.

When the big day finally arrived, Sonia thought she would faint from excitement and nerves. The weather was perfect – the sun peaked out over one solitary, big, fluffy cloud, and the rest of the sky was pure crystal blue.

The church was filled to the brim with people from all over the city to see the mayor's son get married. Daisies lined the pews of the church and a string quartet played classical music.

Sonia stood outside the doors, waiting for her cue. Her beautiful white gown trailed along the floor. Her hair was pinned up and wisps fell loosely around her face. She held a bouquet of white roses, her heart pounding, and her hands shaking. The biggest moment of her life was about to happen.

As the music started, Sonia took a deep breath. Her father gently grabbed her arm and whispered in her ear, "You are a gorgeous bride and I love you so much."

Sonia felt her eyes moisten. She couldn't cry yet! She didn't want to ruin her makeup. "Are you ready, Daddy?" she asked.

As they slowly made their way down the aisle, Sonia couldn't focus on anything but Justin standing at the altar. His smile said it all – that she was the most beautiful thing he had ever seen.

Sonia took Justin's hand as she looked up into his eyes. He was the most handsome, compassionate, and loving person she had ever met, and she thought her heart would burst. She thanked her lucky stars and squeezed his hand.

As the ceremony started, Sonia couldn't help but focus on anything else but Justin. This was it, the big moment. He shakily placed the ring on her finger and she returned the favor. "I do" was said two times.

"You may kiss the bride."

With that, Justin swept Sonia into his arms and kissed her. The crowd cheered and wept. This was the wedding Sonia dreamed about.

The reception was even more phenomenal, like something straight out of a fairy tale, and Sonia was Justin's princess. Ice sculptures stood in every corner. Colorful flower arrangements were set on each table. There was a variety of food, fruit baskets, and desserts spread out on a long table. Justin, Sonia, and the majority of the guests danced the night away.

When the night came to a close, Justin and Sonia sped away in a limousine to their new house. Justin carried Sonia in his arms over the threshold. After making love, they lay in each other's arms and fell asleep for the first time as husband and wife.

The next day Justin and Sonia took it easy. All day long they made love, relaxed by the pool, and thoroughly enjoyed just being with each other.

Because of Justin's work, they weren't able to go on their honeymoon right away. It would be another month before they left.

Sonia ran her fingers through Justin's hair. After all the planning and organizing for the wedding, a honeymoon was definitely a treat that she couldn't wait to enjoy.

CHAPTER 19

"Why are you bringing your laptop?" Sonia asked as she busily packed her suitcase. They were almost ready to go to the airport. Their honeymoon awaited.

"My father asked me to bring it. I may need to do a conference call," Justin said.

Sonia stopped packing and stared at her husband. "We're going on our honeymoon! It's crazy for your dad to think that you'll work on our honeymoon!"

Justin pulled Sonia closer and gave her a kiss on the cheek. "How cute," he said. "We're having our first fight."

Sonia forced a smile. "No we're not. I just don't understand why your father would expect that."

"I told my father that I want to keep it to a minimum. He knows it's our honeymoon, but I also understand, and I hope you do too, that I'll be gone for a month, and that's a long time away from the business."

Sonia sat on the bed defeated. "Okay then, I guess." she said with disappointment in her voice. "I would have liked it if you had told me that before."

"I know. I just didn't know how to tell you because I didn't want to spoil the fun for you. You were so excited about being together, just the two of us, for a whole month. I just didn't have the heart to tell you that I might have to work a little."

Sonia had thought that nobody would call them on their honeymoon and there would not be any errands or assignments. It would just be the two of them. Of course, they had already gotten settled into their own house, but she was still looking forward to their honeymoon with no distractions.

She clenched her jaw to keep from sounding too angry. "How often will you be working?"

"Only a couple of hours a week, not much, I promise. And when I'm working, you can take that time to go shopping or see the landscape." Justin added sheepishly.

"All right." Sonia resigned, she couldn't help but feel a little crack in her heart.

CHAPTER 20

"Hi Tom, come on in," Dameon greeted Tom as he entered Dameon's office.

"I'm all set to relieve you." Tom said.

"Great," Dameon said, relieved that Tom was perfectly on time, and then went on with, "because I need to show you what you will be doing while I'm gone." Dameon had everything ready and lined up for Tom to take over for a month while he was gone on vacation. He just wanted to go over some last minute details, and more importantly, Dameon wanted Tom to be sitting in his office when the phone rang. The phone call he was waiting for which he expected any minute.

Today was the day he was going to get Celia out of prison. The phone rang. He picked it up and said, "Warden Smith here."

On the other end of the line, Ann was nervous but tried to sound as normal as she could. "Hello Warden, Nurse Sutton here."

"Yes, Nurse Sutton, what can I do for you?" Dameon asked even though he already knew. They had it all rehearsed; they knew exactly what was going to happen next.

"I have an inmate who needs to go to the hospital," Ann said. "She has a lot of pain in her stomach and I think it's her appendix."

"Who's the inmate?"

"Celia Winters; her number is 89257, and I will need a wheelchair for her."

"Okay," Dameon said, "go ahead and start the paperwork. I'll make sure you get the papers from the office, and I will notify the hospital and find a security guard to escort you and the inmate."

"Thank you," Ann said and hung up.

Dameon sat there for a moment. He was pretending to contemplate the situation. Playing it cool, Dameon said, "Well, Tom, we have a situation here. An inmate is sick and needs to go to the hospital. So here's your first task. You can escort her to the hospital."

"Sure." Tom replied, ready to take over from Dameon.

"Great, just call the hospital that you are on your way. You'll have to escort the inmate together with Nurse Sutton. I'm finished here. I'll leave it all in your capable hands. Here are the hospital release papers for you to sign." Dameon handed Tom the papers he took out of a filing cabinet drawer. "Good luck," he smiled.

Just as Tom was about to sign the papers for the legalities, Dameon said, "Oh, wait a minute, on second thought, I may as well escort the inmate myself. I'm all finished here anyway. I still have three hours before I need to be at the airport and that way you can get yourself settled in here. I might as well finish it off with a drive to the hospital and back." Dameon chuckled.

"Are you sure?" Tom asked

"Yeah no problem" Dameon said, "I'm sure. As long as you're all okay here?"

"Yes," Tom said with confidence.

"Good, then I will sign the papers." Dameon took the papers back and signed them. He then turned to leave but before he closed the door behind him he turned to Tom and said, "I'll look in on you when I'm back from the hospital and before I go on my holiday just to make sure you're okay with everything."

"Go already, I'll be fine," Tom said.

Dameon left the office and went to get a wheelchair and meet up with Ann in the infirmary. He handed Ann the papers.

"It's ridiculous how many papers they want you to sign," Ann said.

"Not really. It's a prison after all. That's the government for you - lots of paperwork."

Ann stared at Dameon with a worried look on her face. The plan was in action. She had to go through with it now.

Because she was the head nurse, Ann had the authority to sign people out to go to the hospital when needed, and she would be the one authorized to take the inmate there. But a security officer would have to accompany her with the inmate to the hospital. They had it all figured out. Dameon would be that security person. He made sure that it would be the last working day before he was going on holiday.

Celia was the one who had to start it all. At a prearranged time, she pretended to be incredibly sick. She howled in pain, grabbing her abdomen.

Dameon had the wheelchair ready and ordered Celia to sit in it. He still couldn't believe how much she looked like Sonia, especially after spending so much time with the newly-weds.

Celia looked pale. She feigned sickness. She leaned over and whispered, "How am I supposed to get money from this Justin guy?"

"Don't worry about that yet. I'll tell you when the time is right," Dameon said. "Right now, all you have to do is keep acting sick. Tell the doctor that you're in excruciating pain, and ask him to give you something for the pain."

"Yeah, yeah," Celia said, "I know it all. Ann has told me everything."

Then Dameon said, "Okay, let's go then."

After getting through a bunch of security, they left the prison walls. There was a prison van waiting for them. Dameon put Celia in the backseat behind the bars, and then climbed in the front behind the wheel, with Ann next to him and drove off.

On their way to the hospital Dameon told Celia, "You're going on a honeymoon with Justin, so you have to make sure that you really act like you're his wife."

Celia looked out the window at the passing trees and houses. It had been so long, five years to be exact, that she had ventured out into the real world.

"Are you listening to me?" Dameon said with agitation in his voice.

"Yes, uh, sorry. I was just noticing how blue the sky looks," Celia said mesmerized.

"This is no time to worry about how blue the sky is! You need to worry about acting like Sonia!" Dameon brought Celia back out of her thoughts.

Then the reality of the situation kicked in. "What if I don't like the guy? He might notice that something is up!" Celia demanded.

"You don't actually have to like him. You just have to make sure that you act like you like him, and I don't think you have to worry about not liking him. He's very handsome and loving. You might even fall in love with him. Just give it time."

"If you say so," Celia said. "At least I'll be out of prison and rich," she finished with a satisfied smirk.

"I'm coming along with you on your honeymoon," Dameon continued.

Celia laughed. "That will be a first, having a chaperone along on a honeymoon. I bet Justin will love that!"

Dameon glared at Celia from the rearview mirror. He didn't like her attitude. He needed her to take this more seriously. He huffed and said, "Sonia and Justin don't know that I'll be there. I found out where they were going, and I booked my own vacation. They will be surprised to see me at the airport. I'll just tell them I'm off on a business trip. And then when I bump into them on the same island, I'll make it out to be a huge coincidence. You'll have to meet up with me from time to time while you're on the honeymoon. Do you understand? Call me the very first opportunity you have. Ann will make sure you get Sonia's cell phone and she'll program in my number for you. You know what to do; we have gone over this many times. I will carry my phone with me at all times. Whenever you are in a public place excuse yourself to go to the washroom, that's the safest place, Justin can't overhear your conversations there."

Ann squirmed in her seat. This whole thing made her so uncomfortable, but she was too far in it now. She felt sorry for Sonia and Justin, but the money shone like a beacon of light; if, of course, the plan worked out.

As they approached the hospital, Dameon chimed, "Start acting sick, Celia."

On cue, Celia grabbed her abdomen and moaned in pain. Dameon pulled up to the emergency entrance and parked. "This is it," he exclaimed.

Both Ann and Dameon got out of the van and escorted Celia with handcuffs strapped around her wrists through the entrance. There were people already waiting to escort them to the doctor's office. Ann was the only one who was allowed to go in with the prisoner; Dameon had to stand outside the door. He was nervous, hoping that everything went the way they rehearsed it.

It did.

The doctor told Ann that it was not appendicitis, so it must have been something she ate. He told them that if it got worse, to come back. Ann asked the doctor if he could give Celia something for the pain. Celia pretended to swallow the pill but kept it tucked tightly under her tongue. The doctor dismissed them, and they walked back to the doors with Celia in handcuffs.

Once in the van, Celia spit the pill out into a little plastic bag that Ann had given her. Dameon started to drive, knowing that the hospital would notify the prison that they were on their way back. He called the prison and got Tom on the phone.

"Hi, Tom, we're on our way back."

"Yes, I know," Tom said. "The hospital has just notified us."

"It might take us longer than expected; there's been an accident up ahead and we're just sitting here in traffic."

"Thanks for letting me know," Tom said. "Just give me a call when you get through so I can make note of it."

"Will do," Dameon said and he hung up. And, instead of heading back to the prison, they made their way toward the airport.

About halfway there, Dameon drove onto a little side road and then onto a driveway. At the end of the driveway, there was a little shack and a car sat behind the shack. Dameon parked the prison van beside the car.

Ann was surprised she didn't know about this little hideaway. She wanted to ask Dameon about this place, but he'd already gotten out of the van and started to get the wheelchair out. "Get Celia out of the van," he said in a rushed tone. Ann knew not to ask any questions.

Dameon gave Ann the keys for the handcuffs and told her to take Celia's handcuffs off. He opened the trunk and took out a trench coat, gave it to Celia, and told her to put it on to hide her prison clothes. Then he told them both to get into the car. Ann was relieved that Dameon had thought of changing the prison van for a car.

As the women sat in the car, Dameon put the wheelchair in the trunk and pulled out a suitcase. He changed clothing right then and there, and Ann watched through the mirror. *This man thought of everything.* Although she was still hesitant about the whole plan, she found herself relaxing in the front seat. Maybe the plan was really going to work out.

Celia couldn't help but smile from the backseat. She rubbed her wrists; the handcuffs were gone. Soon, she would be Sonia, but more importantly, she would be free.

CHAPTER 21

Sonia and Justin walked into the airport hand-in-hand, each pulling a suitcase behind them.

Dameon spotted them and quickly caught up. "Fancy meeting you two here," he said. "How are the lovebirds doing?"

Sonia and Justin turned around and were surprised to see Dameon.

"Uh, hi," Justin said. "What are you doing here?"

They couldn't believe their eyes. "Yes, what *are* you doing here?" Sonia echoed.

Dameon had his hands full, a suitcase in one hand, a tripod under an arm and a hot coffee in his other hand. "I'm here on business," he said as he put down his luggage and shook Justin's hand. "I don't have much time, I have to meet someone. But what a coincidence! I happened to see you two walking in, so I ran to catch up with you to wish you both a great trip. Are you off on your honeymoon?" As he went to shake Sonia's hand, he tripped over his tripod and spilled his coffee all over her shirt.

Sonia jumped back and squealed. "Ouch!" Her shirt was stained with coffee, and the skin on her chest started to turn red from the hot liquid.

"Oh my God, I'm so sorry!" Dameon said as he handed her his napkins. Justin tenderly wiped his wife's shirt clean. Sonia bit back tears.

"Are you okay, sweetie," Justin asked concerned.

"It really hurts," Sonia cried, "and my shirt is ruined. Where's the bathroom?"

Dameon pointed toward the bathroom while Justin made a gesture to Sonia's suitcase. "We've got some time," he said. "Why don't you change and then we'll check our luggage.

Sonia weakly smiled. Justin bent over and gave his wife a comforting kiss on the cheek. She turned to walk to the bathroom.

Dameon was left there standing with Justin. He apologized again, "I'm so sorry about that. I just wanted to wish you guys a nice trip, and now look what I've done. I hope she'll be okay. I'm so sorry. I have to rush off, I'm already late. Please give Sonia my sincerest apologies and have a great time."

"I'll do that for you." Justin said, "She'll be fine. I'll tell her how badly you feel and we'll see you again sometime in better circumstances," Justin laughed.

As Dameon walked away, he was bursting on the inside – everything was going according to his plan.

Ann nervously paced around in the washroom. She pretended to comb her hair, wash her hands, just to waste some time. Celia waited quietly in the handicap stall. Finally, the bathroom door opened and Sonia walked in.

As she stood by the sink blotting her shirt and skin with a wet napkin, Ann stood in awe but made sure that Sonia couldn't see her face. She couldn't believe how much the girls looked alike. Ann took a deep breath and counted to ten – the time was now.

Pretending to put perfume on her handkerchief, Ann held up the cloth soaking in chloroform and grabbed Sonia from behind. She quickly forced the cloth over Sonia mouth and nose. Sonia struggled, but not for long. She was out cold as she fell into Ann's arms. Ann then dragged her into the handicap stall where Celia was waiting. She took out a needle and injected Sonia in the thigh. The chloroform would not keep Sonia out for very long, but the injection would last for hours.

In a state of awe, Celia managed to help Ann change Sonia into her prison clothes and hoist her into the wheelchair. Celia quickly went through Sonia's suitcase and chose an outfit. She wanted to make sure that every stitch of clothing that she wore from now on was Sonia's, including her jewelry and undergarments.

Celia didn't bother to waste any time, but when she was dressed, she paused and stared at Sonia. It was like staring in the mirror. She cautiously touched Sonia's face.

"Hurry up!" Ann said in a loud whisper.

Celia took off Sonia's wedding ring and let out a squeal. "Look at this!" she said.

"Be quiet and hurry!" Ann said again.

While Celia finished up the last touches, Ann put Sonia's coffee-stained clothing in the suitcase.

When Celia saw herself in the mirror, with her hair cut exactly like Sonia's and wearing Sonia's clothes, she was just amazed at how identical they were. "Wow, I look just like her, but I better put on her makeup, just like she has."

"Do what you have to, but hurry up," Ann sighed. She rummaged through Sonia's purse, and found Sonia's cell phone and then programmed Dameon's phone number into it.

When Celia was finished, she stared at herself mesmerized.

With a worried look on Ann's face, she handed Celia Sonia's phone. "I've put Dameon's cell number in here. Make sure you call him as soon as you can once you're on the island."

"You didn't have to program it in," Celia huffed. "We've gone over his number so many times, and you know that I memorized it. But, I'll give him a call as soon as I can."

Ann was a bundle of nerves. "You're Sonia now," she enforced. "Justin will be waiting for you outside the washroom; you know what he looks like from the pictures. Act surprised. Ask where Dameon went. Tell Justin that you wanted Dameon to take some pictures of you at the airport. Make it sound like a joke. Tell him that you were hoping Dameon could take pictures before he spilled coffee on you again."

"Yes, yes I know," Celia said impatiently.

"And one other thing," Ann continued, "give Justin a kiss, first thing, just like Sonia always does."

Celia said annoyed. "I know what to do; I've been practicing for a whole year. I feel like I'm Sonia, and from this point on, I am Sonia. I can do it."

Ann was getting even more anxious. "Okay, then go on," she said as she pointed to the door. The only thing she could hope was that everything would go smoothly.

Celia took a deep breath. Her heart pounded. She picked up the suitcase and Sonia's purse and walked out of the washroom. She saw Justin standing there and recognized him immediately; looking at all those videos had paid off. She smiled as she made her way toward him.

"There you are," Justin said. His eyes beamed. "You look beautiful."

"Thank you, Justin," Celia said as she gave him a kiss. "Where is Dameon?"

"He was in a hurry to meet someone," Justin informed her. "He wanted me to tell you how sorry he was and he wanted to wish you a nice holiday."

"I was going to ask him to take some pictures of us," Sonia laughed and continued, "Before he spilled coffee on me again. But, I guess no pictures." Celia smiled as rehearsed. "I was just kidding anyway." She grabbed Justin's hand.

As they walked toward the luggage drop-off, Celia asked, "What was he doing here anyway?"

"I think he said he was here on business," Justin replied.

Celia inched closer to Justin and watched their suitcases being taken away.

*****

Dameon hustled to his car as fast as he could and drove to the entrance where he knew Ann would be waiting with Sonia passed out in the wheelchair. Together, they lifted Sonia into the car. Then Dameon put the wheelchair into the trunk, and they drove off to where they had hidden the prison van.

Once they got to Dameon's little hideaway, they switched cars again, and Dameon changed back into his prison guard uniform. Before they reached the prison, the phone in the van rang.

"Hi, Dameon," Tom said. "Where have you been? I called you fifteen minutes ago and there was no answer."

"Yeah, I know," Dameon replied.

Ann couldn't believe how calm Dameon was. She was a nervous wreck.

Then Dameon said in a relaxed voice, "We had some technical problems here. I could hear you, but you couldn't hear me. Sorry, Tom, I tried to call you back but that didn't seem to work. We're about three minutes away. You might as well get your guys to the door because we're just about to drive onto the grounds. We'll need some guards."

"Will do," Tom said, and they hung up.

After they made it through security, there was a lot of paperwork waiting for Dameon in his office. Tom had to sign as a witness. Ann just had to sign one form before Dameon sent her to put the inmate back in her cell. Nobody was suspicious.

"She didn't have appendicitis," Dameon told Tom. "The doctor didn't know what was wrong with her. He gave her some drugs for the pain and she'll probably be drowsy for awhile."

Dameon tied up any loose ends with paperwork and said to Tom, "I'm leaving for my holiday so no more last-minute errands for me. I'm going to clock-out now. I'll see you in a month."

*****

With the help of Kim, another guard, Sonia was carried into Celia's cell.

"You look tired, Ann," Kim said.

"Yes, I know," Ann answered. "I've been up all hours of the night with my son. He's been sick," she lied.

"Well, you should take some time off to take care of your son and yourself," Kim said.

Ann sighed. "I know, but I can't afford that." She tried to be as strong as she could. She didn't want Kim to know that she was nervous, so she quickly said, "I'll be fine. You can go back to your regular post."

"Are you sure?" Kim said as she looked at Sonia. "I can stay here for awhile until she wakes up."

"No, that's okay. I'm sure this girl isn't going to wake up for a while," Ann said as she walked out of the cell. "You can lock up now. I'll keep an eye on her."

"Okay," Kim said, and then locked the door.

As Kim walked away, Ann shouted, "I'll call you as soon as she wakes up. Then you can unlock the cell for me so I can examine her."

Ann went to her office and plopped herself onto her chair. She leaned her elbows on her knees and with her face leaning into her hands she said aloud, "Oh my God, what have I done?" She felt like crying, but she knew she couldn't fall to pieces now. Her shift wasn't over for a couple more hours, so she had to stay focused. After a few minutes, she decided to get up and do something to take her mind off things. She headed down to the infirmary.

Everything in the infirmary was quiet, so Ann ordered supplies and finished up some paper work. Every so often, Ann checked to see if Sonia was awake yet. Finally, after more than an hour, she woke up. Ann's shift was almost over, but she wanted to make sure that she was still there when Sonia woke up.

"How are you feeling?" Ann said to Sonia after Kim had let her in the cell.

"I'm okay." Sonia said, still a little drowsy. "What happened? Where am I?"

Ann could hardly hear Sonia; her voice was very weak. "The doctor gave you something for the pain."

"What pain?" Sonia asked still very weak. "I was going to change. The coffee didn't really burn me. It wasn't that hot."

"What is she talking about?" Kim asked.

"I don't know," Ann said. "I think she's hallucinating again. She's hallucinated before."

"Yes, I know," Kim answered. "I think everybody knows that she's a little nuts."

Sonia sat up and rubbed her eyes. She stared around the room and didn't recognize anything. It was cold. She shivered. The woman that was talking to her was friendly, but the woman standing by the barred entrance looked stern and wore some kind of police uniform. As the fog began to clear from her mind, she started to panic. "Where am I?" Sonia wailed. "And where is Justin?"

Kim said, "You're in your cell, Celia, where you belong, and don't pretend that you don't know that."

Sonia shook her head. "Why are you calling me Celia? My name is Sonia." She looked at Ann for some sort of explanation.

Ann scrunched her forehead and gently took Sonia's hand. She felt terrible guilt burning a hole in her stomach.

"Yeah, yeah," Kim said, "we know and you have a boyfriend named Justin."

"Yes," Sonia said with some hope in her voice. "Yes," she said again, "but he's not my boyfriend anymore. He's my husband now. We got married a month ago and we were going on our honeymoon. Where's Justin?" she asked. "Is he okay?" And then even more in panic Sonia asked, "Did the plane crash?"

Kim laughed. "Yeah, the plane crashed." She turned to Ann and said, "Her stories are getting better every time I see her."

"Yes," Ann said, "she seems to be getting worse."

Sonia started to get more upset, wondering if she had a memory lapse. Did they get on the plane? Did it crash? She didn't remember going on the plane. All she could remember was the hot coffee being spilled all over her and going to the bathroom to change.

Sonia started to rock back and forth. As she cried, she choked on her tears as they fell down her cheeks. The staff at the prison was used to Celia's hallucinating because she had been pretending to be Sonia for more than a month now, just to make everybody believe that she was going crazy.

Sonia didn't know where see was. She didn't like the woman in the uniform. Fear flowed through her veins. She kept repeating, "Justin where are you? Mommy, Daddy, where are you?" She called them over and over again.

Ann swallowed a lump in her throat. She couldn't believe she had agreed to do this and suddenly felt hatred toward Dameon. "I'm going to get something to calm her down. I'll be back in a minute."

As Ann stormed down the hallway to the infirmary she couldn't believe how she was coerced into Dameon's plan. She wanted to help her son and their financial situation, but at what cost? She grabbed some medicine and headed back to Sonia's cell.

"Please, Celia, take it," Ann pleaded. She held out two tiny pills in her palm.

"Stop calling me Celia. My name is Sonia."

"Okay," Ann said apologetically, and then with a soft voice she went on. "But please take this. It's for your own good. Everything will be fine, but right now you need some rest. Please take it."

Sonia couldn't see clearly through her tears but she popped the pills in her mouth. Maybe this was all a bad dream, she thought. Her eyelids felt heavy, and she struggled to keep them open. She called out for Justin one more time before she fell into a heavy sleep.

CHAPTER 22

The flight went smoothly, and when they arrived at the airport in St. Martin, Celia thought she would cry of happiness. As they waited for their luggage, Celia couldn't help but feel like her heart would burst. She pinched her arm to make sure she wasn't dreaming. She had heard that St. Martin was supposed to be a beautiful island.

"This is going to be amazing," Justin said as he pecked her on the cheek.

Celia felt her cheeks blush. Justin didn't seem to notice anything different. This was going to be easier than she thought.

She was in paradise! But, she needed to remain focused.

As soon as Celia and Justin entered the hotel room, Celia clapped her hands together and screamed, "Oh honey, this is so beautiful!" just like she'd seen Sonia do a million times in the videos.

They walked over toward the window and were in awe of the view. The crystal blue ocean stretched out for miles and palm trees sprouted every few feet.

"I love you," Justin said. He grabbed Celia around her waist and kissed her on the lips.

It had been years since Celia had been intimate with anyone, and she wasn't complaining. She understood her sister's attraction to Justin. He was handsome, charming, and romantic. She could get used to this.

"We need to hang up your suits and my dresses first before they get too crinkled," Celia said. Justin agreed and they started to unpack their suitcases and hang up some clothes.

Suddenly, Celia felt the urge to use the bathroom. Should she close the door or leave it wide open? What would Sonia do? She started to panic but realized it wasn't that big of a deal. She decided to leave the door unlocked in case Justin felt comfortable enough to walk in. Justin never did come in, but when Celia came out of the bathroom Justin was standing there stark naked.

As a natural reflex, she looked away, but then realized that Sonia would not react that way to her husband. "Oh, you're already undressed?" she said coyly.

With an excited boyish smile and a twinkle in his eye, Justin said, "Yes, I am!" He walked toward Celia. "And you're not. Here, let me help you."

Celia's heart pounded so loudly. She was nervous but at the same time she was excited. It was a good thing that Justin was deliciously handsome. This made it easier for Celia to be like a wife. Overall, Justin had been very nice to her on the airplane and she liked him as soon as she saw him.

On the plane, Justin had occasionally stolen a kiss from her. It was good that the flight was long so Celia could get used to Justin. But now they were alone, and Justin was standing naked in front of her.

His strong hands slowly unbutton her blouse. She felt her excitement race through every inch of her body. She hadn't had sex in over five years and the anticipation of what was to come was taking over. Even though he was a married man, she didn't care at this moment. After all, she was in his eyes, his wife.

Taking clues from Justin, she helped him to take off her clothes. Sonia may have been a little more reserved or even proper in the bedroom, so Celia had to make sure to control herself at times. There were moments; however, that she felt she couldn't contain herself. The touch of his tongue tracing around her body was heavenly, and she couldn't help but get totally involved. She decided to go with the flow and let Justin's warm touch carry her away.

Afterwards, they lay snuggled together as the air conditioner blew over their naked, spent bodies.

"Wow, sweetheart, I have to take you on more honeymoons. Remember our first time together, at my place, after I made dinner for you?"

Celia nodded with a smile and pretended that she remembered. "Yes, honey, I remember."

"I still remember the cream on your lips." Justin chuckled, "We had so much fun that first night, it was amazing, but this, Sonia, was out of this world."

Celia just smiled and gently rubbed his chest. *Did I overdo it? I'll have to calm down a little next time.* It had been so long since she had been intimate with a man that it had been hard holding herself back. Lying in Justin's arms felt so good.

Justin stroked her hair. "Let's take a shower and get dressed. We can go for a walk and have a little look around before dinner."

"That sounds nice," Celia replied. Suddenly, she was not worried about taking a shower with Justin. She was surprised how quickly she felt comfortable with him. They washed each other in the shower. Celia loved all the attention. What a different life compared to her life in prison.

After their shower, they did some sightseeing before going out for dinner. After dinner they decided to go to a show, and when they got back into their hotel room, they didn't waste any time undressing each other. To Justin it was lovemaking, but to Celia it was just great sex.

"I love you," Justin said.

"I love you too," Celia lied as she fell asleep with a smile on her face.

***

The next day, Celia woke up in dread from the last traces of her regular nightmare and wondered what she was doing in this comfortable bed. Then she realized where she was. It was heaven, to wake up here instead of in her jail cell; she had no more reason to continue those awful nightmares.

Smiling, she stretched out her arms and felt for Justin, but he wasn't there, so she sat up and looked around the room. He was sitting at the desk in front of a laptop. "What are you doing?" she asked.

"Oh honey, you woke up," Justin said with a smile on his face. "I thought I'd send my father an e-mail to let him know that we arrived okay and he already e-mailed me back. He needs me tomorrow for a conference call."

"Huh?" was Celia's reaction. She was still a little sleepy and had no clue what Justin was talking about.

"Yes, honey, don't you remember? I told you that I would have to work a little on our honeymoon," Justin explained. "I promised my father I would."

Celia looked a little puzzled, but suddenly realized that Sonia must have known about Justin doing work on the honeymoon. She sat up quickly and said, "of course, honey, I'm sorry. I forgot for a moment. I'm still a little sleepy," she laughed softly.

"Why don't you go shopping and just enjoy yourself tomorrow while I'm on that conference call," Justin suggested. "It'll probably be a long one; we have a big project to discuss."

"Okay, honey" Celia smiled.

Justin shut his laptop, jumped on the bed and cuddled with Celia. They made love for the rest of the morning.

That afternoon they went to a quaint little restaurant down the block from their hotel. Celia knew she had to find an opportunity to phone Dameon, so at the restaurant she excused herself to go to the ladies room. As soon as she was in the washroom, she phoned Dameon. He picked up after the first ring. He was obviously waiting for her call.

"Why didn't you phone me earlier?" he asked anxiously. He had been worried, and had expected a call from her the day before.

"I'm sorry but this is my first opportunity," Celia lied. She could have phoned him when they were at the show last night, but she didn't feel like spoiling the evening with Justin by talking to Dameon. "Right now we're in a little restaurant. You could accidentally bump in to us here." She gave Dameon directions

"Okay," Dameon said and hung up.

When Celia returned from the washroom, Justin stood and pulled out the chair for her.

"Thank you," Celia smiled. Justin was treating her like a queen, and she loved every moment of it. She felt a little guilty deceiving him because he was a nice guy, but she couldn't do anything but to go on with their devilish plan. Otherwise, she'd be back in jail.

When they were almost finished with their lunch, Dameon walked in. Justin saw him and was dumbfounded. Celia was relieved to she him but she had to look just as surprised as Justin.

"Small world," Dameon said as he walked closer to them. He pretended to be in shock. "This is some coincidence. I hope I'm not interrupting."

"No, no, please," Justin said flabbergasted. "Join us for some coffee." Justin motioned to an empty chair. He looked at Dameon with wide eyes. "First, at the airport and now here. Why didn't you tell us that you were coming to this island? You said you were going on business, but you never told us where and what kind of business."

Hanging his camera bag over the back of the chair Dameon sat down, "I didn't realize that you guys were going to the same place as I was, plus I was in a hurry. I had to meet someone to get instructions for a video shoot that I have to do here on Maho Beach. And then I spilled my coffee all over you," he said as he looked at Celia. "And, after that, well you know the rest. I'm still so sorry about that, Sonia. Did you get burnt?"

"Oh, I'm fine," Celia said, "but I'm very surprised to see you here." Then, with a catty smile she changed the subject. "It's nice to see you. Is Maho Beach where we flew over?"

"Yes, it is, and it's beautiful," Dameon continued. "It's really a unique beach. The airport runway is so close to it that the planes only fly in one direction. They come in the same direction as they go out. Every time a plane takes off, it has to taxi first to the end of the runway, which is just a few meters from the beach, and then it takes off as fast as it can and veers sharply to avoid hitting the mountains. So, when the plane takes off, all the parasols, beach towels, floating chairs, hats, etc., fly into the ocean. It's kind of funny because the tourists don't realize what will happen when they set up their beach stuff. This is what my client wants me to video for a film he's making. Cool huh?" Dameon laughed.

Justin and Celia sat with open mouths listening to Dameon. Justin was fascinated and Celia was amazed at how normal and relaxed Dameon sounded. She wasn't the only one who could act.

"Well, now that you're here, have some dessert with us?" Justin said.

"No dessert for me, but thank you. I need some lunch first," Dameon said. "I would love to sit here while you eat dessert and I have my lunch."

Justin and Celia ordered dessert while Dameon ordered a turkey-club sandwich.

"Isn't it incredible that we ended up at the same island," Dameon said. "If you want, I'm more than willing to do some video on the beach of the two of you. Just let me know, I can schedule you in before or after my shoot." Then Dameon wrote down the information where he was staying and handed it to Justin. "Here's my contact info while I'm on the island, just give me a shout if you want to take me up on it."

Dameon couldn't help but wonder how everything was going, but based on Celia's wide smile, he figured everything was going smoothly. Justin seemed to be in very good spirits, so he obviously hadn't noticed that the woman he was with was not his wife. Celia must have made him quite happy last night. Dameon felt a pang of jealousy. He wouldn't mind Celia for himself; she was a very attractive woman.

As they were finishing their coffees, Justin excused himself to go the bathroom.

When Justin was gone, Dameon asked, "So, how did it go last night?"

"Not too bad," Celia whispered. "You were right. Justin is very handsome and loving. It surely beats being in jail," she commented with a smirk.

Dameon could feel the heat rise to his cheeks. He was surprised at how jealous he was getting. "Just leave out the smart remarks! Has Justin noticed anything? Could he be suspecting that you're someone else?" he added with a whisper.

"No," Celia said. "To him, I'm Sonia, so don't worry. Believe me, I will do it right. I don't want to go back to jail. I have no choice but to do it right."

"So what did you do last night?" Dameon asked.

"We had a great time, went to dinner and a show and... well, you know... do I have to spell it out for you? Do I detect some jealousy in your voice?" she said with a cute smile.

"No, of course not," Dameon made a gesture with his hand as if to wave the comment away. "You just do your acting right," he said. "But let's be serious because Justin will be back soon. Make sure you call me every chance you get. And if the opportunity arises that you can be alone with me, make sure I know about it."

"Well, I think we're in luck," Celia whispered. "I just found out that Justin wants me to go shopping tomorrow. He brought his laptop with him. Can you believe that? Bringing a laptop on our honeymoon, and apparently Sonia knew about it."

Dameon was surprised and thought it very strange for Justin to bring work along on his honeymoon.

"He said he has to be on a conference call," Celia continued. "So, I think I can see you tomorrow. I'll call you and let you know what time." This was the perfect opportunity for Celia and Dameon to get together.

"Good," Dameon nodded. "But for now I want to come along this afternoon to take pictures. Do some sweet talking."

Then Dameon and Celia noticed Justin coming back to the table and quickly switched their conversation.

"So it was a good show then?" Dameon began his act.

"Yeah, it was the best, you should go see it." Celia fell right back into her role.

"See what?" Justin interrupted as he joined them.

"Oh, honey, I just told Dameon about the show we saw last night. It was great, wasn't it?"

"Yes, it was, but let's get going now. We want to see a lot today. Are you ready Sonia?"

"Sure," Celia said as she wiped her mouth with her napkin. Then she turned to Dameon and asked, "What are you doing this afternoon?"

"I think I'll just lazy around," Dameon answered. "I can't do anything until I see the film producer tomorrow."

"Hey, why don't you join us for a little while," Celia said, turning to Justin she continued, "if you don't mind honey, cause then Dameon could take some more photos of us to add to our wedding collection." Then she turned back to Dameon, "that is, if you don't mind. I see you have your camera with you."

"We may be imposing on Dameon, sweetie," Justin responded.

"Oh no, it wouldn't be imposing at all," Dameon said kindly. "It would be fine, but are you sure you want me to tag along?"

"Yes, that's okay," Justin said. "We would like to see a lot today and since you're here, we might as well take advantage of it." He playfully smacked Dameon's arm. "I'll make sure you get paid well for it though."

"Oh you don't have to worry about that," Dameon said. He grinned. This was working out better than he had ever imagined.

After the bill was paid, the three of them walked around the coast, stopping here and there for Dameon to snap pictures. After sightseeing for three hours, Celia and Justin said their goodbyes and headed back to the hotel room. The day had left them both exhausted. They fell asleep in each other's arms, and for the first time since Celia could remember, she was genuinely happy.

***

The next day, Justin got a call from his father to confirm the time for the conference call that afternoon.

"I'm so sorry I won't be able to spend the afternoon with you sweetheart. I thought I'd have enough time to have lunch with you first but I'm afraid not, the call will be earlier than I expected. Hope you don't mind." He looked at her with puppy dog eyes.

"It's okay," Celia sighed. "I might have a bite to eat at that nice big mall we saw yesterday and then go shopping there for a while." she replied.

"You're not angry with me?" Justin asked with an apologetic smile.

"No," Celia said. She moved closer to embrace him. "How long do you think your conference call will take?"

"I wouldn't be surprised if it lasted up to two hours. So take your time with shopping, don't rush on my account. I'll do some other paperwork in the meantime. I'll text you when I'm done. Hopefully I can get a lot of work done today and not have to do much more on the rest of our honeymoon."

Celia pretended to be disappointed but understanding. "Okay, I'll do some shopping and have a bite to eat at the mall, but it won't be the same without you honey."

"I know sweetheart." Justin sighed.

"What are you going to have for lunch?" Celia asked acting concerned.

"I'll call for room service when I get hungry," Justin replied.

Celia gathered her purse and sun-hat and gave Justin a kiss and a hug goodbye.

Justin retuned the kiss and smiled, "Have a great time and get something nice for yourself."

As Celia headed out the door, she couldn't help feeling jealous toward her own sister. How Sonia had lucked-out with a fine husband while she rotted behind bars. But no more. This was Celia's new life.

CHAPTER 23

Dameon and Celia met at the same restaurant where they had lunch the previous day. Celia had phoned Dameon as soon as she walked out of their hotel. As they sipped their coffee, Dameon said, "You're going to have your own bridal fashion boutique business."

"What?" Celia sputtered, "What do you mean I'm going to have my own bridal fashion boutique business? What the shit do I know about business or bridal fashion for that matter?"

Dameon shifted in his chair. "Watch your language, will you? You have to be more careful. If you use that kind of language in front of Justin we're going to be found out. That's not Sonia's character at all."

"Oh, don't worry," Celia responded sarcastically. "Whenever I'm with Justin, believe me, I'm totally Sonia, sweet and innocent. I've been practicing for a year and you obviously thought I was ready."

Dameon answered, "I know you're doing a great job of being Sonia, but I worry that if you use that kind of language in front of me, you might make a mistake and slip in front of Justin."

"Well, you don't have to worry about that," Celia huffed, "because I don't want to be found out either. I can be Sonia all the time." She fiddled with her napkin and stared out the window. "I am Sonia, I am Sonia," she repeated.

The waitress brought over two plates of eggs and hash browns.

As Celia stared at her food, fear gripped her stomach. The words spilled out of her mouth, "I don't know anything about business."

"That's fine," Dameon said. "I'll tell you what to do."

Dameon went on to explain what he expected of Celia. Of course, she was somewhat upset knowing that she'd have to run her own business. She had dropped out of school when she was fourteen and lived on the streets until she ended up in jail when she was eighteen.

Dameon said patronizingly, "Don't you worry your pretty little head. Let's order a drink." He called the waitress over and ordered a beer. Celia just had a cup of coffee.

Celia was suspicious that Dameon had already been drinking. The smell of it on his breath was a tell tale sign. Being a street kid, she could usually spot the drinkers right away. In the little time she had spent with him, this was the first time she actually noticed that he was drunk. Professional or not, an alcoholic was an alcoholic. She had no idea what kind of man Dameon was. All she knew was that he was a good conman, not the kind of man that Justin and Sonia would associate with if they knew what he was really like.

But regardless, for an older guy, he certainly was a good-looking man, and she was just as wrong for playing along with him. Sonia's face popped into her head. For the first time, Celia felt sorry for

Sonia. How Sonia was slumped in the wheelchair when Celia stole her identity. How could she do that to anyone, and her sister? She shook her head to wipe away those thoughts. As awful as the situation was, she would do anything to live a beautiful life with Justin and not go back to prison.

Dameon interrupted her thoughts. "I know a small store in the middle of town that's going to be available for rent in a couple weeks. It's a perfect place for you to have a bridal shop."

Celia began to protest but Dameon cut her off. "Just hear me out, will you? I'll coach you along, and by the end of the month, I want two-hundred thousand dollars."

Celia spit her coffee back into her cup and stared at Dameon wide-eyed. "Are you kidding me? Two hundred thousand dollars? That's a shit-load of money!"

"Watch your mouth!" Dameon said louder than he wanted. He tapped the table with his fork. "Believe me, it's nothing for Justin. It's a drop in the bucket, and he'll be happy to give it to you so you can start something of your own. He'll be supportive of you. If you do your part right, he'll give you anything. He's madly in love with you 'Sonia'." Dameon winked.

"Yes," Celia said in a daze. *Was this really happening? Could it really work?* For the past year, she did what she was told without asking any questions, but this seemed a little ridiculous. "Justin doesn't suspect anything, but do you really think this will work?"

"If you do your job right, it'll work out for all of us. Ann and I will get the money that we want. You'll have your freedom, a handsome husband, and money. It's perfect, and we'll all be happy."

Dameon inched closer. "Now, listen to me closely. I don't really want to tell you this, but I have to. If you ever think of running off with the money before giving it to me, I'll have you back in jail so fast that you'll never even know what hit you. And if you try to snitch on us, rest assured you'll regret it. The courts will never believe you—a jail junky—over us."

"Do you think I'm stupid?" Celia asked dumbfounded. She knew the ropes; she grew up on the streets after all. She bit her lip. "I was just starting to like you. But now, fuck you." She flashed him the middle finger. "Do you think I'm going to cheat you guys?"

Dameon sneered, "Like I already said, watch your language because one of these days, you'll get angry with Justin and you better hold your tongue. Sonia would never use that language even if she were mad. And no, I don't think you're going to cheat on us because that wouldn't be very smart." He looked at her sternly and continued, "To tell you the truth, I was starting to like you, but I have to make sure I can trust you. I have to be careful. For all our sakes, we have to be able to trust each other."

"Well, you can trust me," said Celia. "I don't want to go back to jail, believe me."

"Good, now that we understand each other, can we just be adults about it?" He reached out his hand.

For a split second Celia wanted to punch him, to scratch his eyes out. What a cunning bastard, but she had signed up for it, and there was nothing she could do but play her part. With some hesitation she shook his hand. "Okay, we can be adults."

"Let's forget about this conversation and focus on our plan. You haven't eaten anything," Dameon stated noticing her untouched plate of food.

"Lost my appetite," Celia spat.

"That's fine with me, if you want to be that way," said Dameon, "but you have to understand that I had to be sure about you."

Celia crossed her arms and leaned back in her seat. "Well, don't you think that I've earned your trust by now? I could've taken off right away when I came out of the washroom at the airport."

"Yes," Dameon said, "but it wouldn't have been a smart move because then you would've been hunted down as an escapee and would eventually be back in custody."

Celia shrugged her shoulders. "I know. That's why I didn't run off. So just tell me what you want me to do next. Like I said, I don't want to go back to jail."

While Dameon ate, he told Celia how his plan was going to work. Celia was nervous, but agreed it might work. After lunch, Dameon told Celia that as soon as she had an opportunity to see him again to give him a call. Celia promised to do so. They each went back to their own hotels, but Celia made sure she went by the mall to buy a purse so she could prove to Justin that she went shopping.

*****

The honeymoon was going well, but Justin had to work more than he had anticipated. Celia took advantage of that and saw Dameon every chance she could. The time away from Justin allowed her to let her guard down a little. Justin promised that he would make it up to her, and he kept his word by taking her to fancy restaurants, fabulous shows, and sight-seeing, quiet walks, anything she wanted. They had also taken Dameon up on his offer to make a video of them on the beach. He shot a lot of footage.

While at the beach, Justin's father phoned.

"I'm sorry," Justin said as he put his phone back in his beach bag. "That was my father. He has another thing for me to do. I know it's a kind of crazy, but I promised him, and he really needs me right now. A big project came in. Wrong timing I guess."

Dameon pretended to be very sincere. "Sometimes things can't be helped, I understand that. We're finished here, anyway. I think we have enough video for me to make a nice movie."

"I have to get to my computer," Justin said guiltily. "I'm so sorry, sweetheart."

"That's okay, honey, I'll go with you," Celia replied.

"No," Justin protested. "You stay here and enjoy the sun a little more. I'll be back in thirty minutes."

"I'll keep her company if you don't mind Justin," Dameon said.

"That would be great. I'll be back us soon as I can."

"This is working out great," Dameon said as soon as Justin was out of eyesight. "I can tell Justin that I would be honored to show you around the island while he works."

*****

In the second week, Dameon and Celia really started to enjoy each other's company. Celia had pushed away the conversation they had on their first meeting and they started to trust each other a little more. Celia even started to like Dameon; he was very handsome. Dameon was amiable to Celia, hiding his own unscrupulous reasons.

They were at a point in their scheme where they couldn't do much more until closer to the end of the honeymoon so on their next meeting, they decided to go to a matinee. After the phone call at the beach, Celia always made sure to tell Justin where she was going. He knew that she was spending time with Dameon. There was actually a feeling of security for Justin knowing that his wife was not alone and was in the company of a man that he now considered a friend.

What Justin didn't know, was how much Dameon and his wife were becoming closer. Justin appreciated how understanding his wife was, regarding his work, and while he was grateful to Dameon for entertaining her he had noticed a slight change in Sonia's behavior. He couldn't quiet pinpoint it, but there were moments when things weren't exactly right. He attributed it to her being unhappy with him for working while they were supposed to be on their honeymoon.

After the movie, Dameon brought Celia back to her hotel room. Justin was sitting at the table and papers were spread all over the place.

"Hi, honey, we're back," Celia said as she walked over and rubbed Justin's shoulders.

"Perfect timing, I just got off the phone," he said. Justin turned to Dameon. "Thanks for bringing my beautiful wife back. Now that you're here, would you like to go with us to the museum? You could take some pictures if you feel like it."

"Sounds good to me," Dameon said, "but I have to go to my hotel to pick up my cameras."

"No problem," Justin said, "we'll go with you. Your hotel is on the way."

The three of them left, Dameon walking in front and Justin and Celia linked arm-in-arm behind.

CHAPTER 24

By the end of the second week, Justin's father had promised that once he finished the project he was working on, he could have the last two weeks off.

"I'm sorry," Justin said to Celia as soon as he was off the phone. "My father wants me to work again, but he promised that this will be the last time. The rest of our holidays I'm free."

"That's okay, honey," Celia said with her beautiful, well-rehearsed loving smile. "I'll go for a nice long walk. The weather is beautiful. Maybe I'll go and see if Dameon is at his hotel and has our movie from the beach," she continued, "or should I wait until you can see it too."

Justin sighed. "It's okay. I need to concentrate, go ahead. I'll try to finish so we can go out tonight, I'll pick you up at Dameon's before we go to dinner."

"Okay, honey," Celia said, and before she picked up her purse, she seized Justin in a warm and tender embrace.

*****

When Celia arrived at Dameon's hotel, she went to the front desk and asked the clerk to tell Dameon that Sonia Haines was there to see him.

A surge of dread overcame Dameon when he heard the name Sonia Haines. Did they find out that he was using Celia as an imposter? He paced around his hotel room and told himself, "Don't be foolish, it's Celia showing up unannounced." But why would she show up without phoning him first? He told the front desk to send her up.

When Dameon opened the door, Celia was shocked to see him standing in nothing but a bathrobe. What surprised her even more was how sexy he looked. "I didn't expect you to open the door in your bathrobe," Celia muttered.

"Well, I didn't expect you to come knocking on my door either," Dameon said. "Does Justin know that you're here?"

"Yes, of course," Celia said. "You know I always tell Justin where I am. I'm here to see what you've done with our videos from the beach." She smiled.

"Well, come in then," Dameon said. He closed the door behind her. Dameon pointed Celia to a chair. His hotel room was not as luxurious as hers; her hotel room was quite a bit more luxurious with three rooms—a living room, a large bedroom and a sumptuous bathroom—with the main focus being the heart-shaped Jacuzzi. But both rooms were beautiful compared to anything Celia was used to.

"I better get the videos," Dameon said.

"Yes, if that's okay with you, unless you had other plans."

"No," Dameon said, "I don't have any other plans. You know that." He smiled deviously.

As Celia looked Dameon over from head to toe, she commented, "You might get dressed first."

Dameon smiled. "Why? This is my hotel room and you came unexpected. Besides, I'm comfortable in my bathrobe. But now that you're here, can I get you something to drink? I have a bottle of wine in the fridge with your name on it."

"I guess I could have some, why not?" Celia said. She just had to make sure to control herself. She didn't want Justin picking her up if she was drunk. He would get suspicious.

Dameon poured two glasses of wine and handed one to Celia. He sat on the edge of his bed, close to the chair that Celia was sitting on. He raised his glass to Celia and toasted, "To our plan; that it may continue to go smoothly and bring us a profitable return."

Celia smiled. "The future looks bright."

They both laughed. He stood up and walked over to the window and closed the curtains. "This will block out the sunlight so it will be easier to see the videos. And if you come and sit next to me, you can see it better."

Celia stood from her chair and sat down next to Dameon on the bed. "I feel funny," she said, "with a glass of wine in my hand and you sitting there in your bathrobe."

"Well, I can take it off if you like," Dameon said with a naughty smile.

Celia didn't know how to interpret Dameon's comment. She knew that he found her attractive, but wouldn't this deviate from the plan and make things complicated? He was flirting with her and it was working. He was tantalizingly handsome and she felt a strong sexual vibe floating around the room. She ignored her feelings and said,

"Come on, let's be serious. I'm here to watch those videos and Justin will come and get me when he's finished with work."

"What time will that be?" Dameon asked.

"I don't know," Celia answered. "He told me he would pick me up before dinner, so a couple of hours, I assume."

"Good then," Dameon said as he made himself more comfortable by shifting up to the headboard and stuffing pillows behind his head and back. He fluffed up pillows for Celia, encouraging her to get more comfortable. She hesitated a little, but moved up to sit beside him.

Dameon pressed the start button and they proceeded to watch the video. It was very good; Dameon had incorporated some special effects, and it flowed like a real movie.

Celia commented, "You seem to get better with each film. The videos I saw in the infirmary were very good. It was easy to learn how to act like Sonia from those videos, but this one is even better."

"I know," Dameon said. "I want to keep Justin happy with my videos. The more videos I make, the closer I can stay to you."

Celia felt her heart pound. "That's a good idea. It makes me feel a lot better knowing that you'll be close by."

Dameon's hand grazed Celia's fingers. "You know you have nothing to worry about. I'll be here to help you, and I know what I'm doing. All you need to do is continue doing what I've told you. You work on Justin and I'll do the rest."

Sensing a little apprehension, Dameon took her hands in his and looked her straight in her eyes. Celia's eyes were a striking blue and mesmerizing. Without warning, he blurted out the words, "You're beautiful."

Celia swallowed a lump in her throat. "You're not so bad yourself from what I can see."

"Well, thank you," Dameon said. "You better finish watching the videos." He stood and walked over to the small fridge. "Can I get you another glass of wine?"

"Yes, please," Celia answered.

While Dameon refilled both wine glasses, Celia finished watching the last of the video. He handed Celia a glass and placed his own on the bedside table. He fiddled with the radio until he dialed in on a station with soft background music, then he sat on the bed.

When the video finished playing, he picked up the remote and turned off the TV. He turned to Celia and said, "Drink up." He took a sip of his wine and stared at Celia, holding his glance for a long time. She was, in that moment, the most beautiful creature he had ever seen.

She did not turn away, but stared back at him. Her piercing blue eyes bore holes into his skin. As he inched closer, Celia didn't budge. She knew what was about to happen and she welcomed it. She carefully placed her glass on the table.

Within seconds their lips were locked in a ferocious hunger. They quickly tore off each other's clothes and threw them in every direction. There was no tenderness. The passion between them was raw, wild, and uninhibited. Celia enjoyed her lovemaking with Justin, but compared to Dameon, Justin was too much of a gentleman in the bedroom. Dameon was stronger and more forceful. She liked his bad-boy ways.

From the first moment Dameon had laid eyes on Celia in the prison recreation room, he'd wanted her. He loved women like her. She had lots of energy just like Ann, which was why he went back to Ann all the time. But Celia's sexual energy was too much to ignore.

Their climaxes both came after a while of heavy sweating, at which point they lay sprawled out on the bed.

Dameon rolled over and looked into Celia's eyes. "I think I'm falling in love with you, Celia."

Celia instantly changed the subject and said, "I thought you weren't going to call me Celia anymore."

"Yes, I know," Dameon said, "but this is different, Celia, because it's you that I'm falling in love with."

Celia knew that Dameon was a conman, but the way he looked at her told her that he was serious. "You can't fall in love with me. What about Ann? I thought you and Ann were together."

Dameon placed his hand on Celia's face and stroked her cheek. "Ann and I are on and off. She doesn't want a relationship. I won't see her anymore, if that's what you want."

"Why would I want that, Dameon?" Celia asked. Suddenly, this seemed to take a turn for the worse. What about their plan? "I have Justin, so I can't have you on the side, can I?"

"Why not?" Dameon said. "You're not married to Justin even though he thinks you are. Sooner or later he might find out who you really are."

Celia pushed him away and shot up to a sitting position. "Are you trying to scare me, Dameon? What do you mean, 'he might find out who I really am?' Is that part of your plan?"

Trying to calm her, he replied. "No, but something could give you away. Right now you're on your honeymoon and everything is fine, but once you get back to Sonia's normal life, you'll have to see her parents and friends."

Panic shot throughout Celia's body. Wasn't that part of the plan? That Celia would act like Sonia even around parents and friends? "I can do it. If I can fool Justin then I can fool anyone, don't you think?"

"I know you're doing a great job," Dameon replied, "and your acting is incredible but we can't expect it to last forever. We have to come up with a way out."

Celia angrily jumped from the bed and gathered up her clothes. As she was putting on her undergarments she asked, "Well, what's your plan then, Dameon? You always have a plan! I'm getting sick of constantly being told what to do."

"First things first," Dameon said, as he laid back into the pillows with his hands behind his head, "make me happy with what I've already asked you to do, and maybe we'll find more time to do what we just finished," he added with a smile and a wink. "I promise to make sure that you'll be happy and safe."

Every sort of emotion raged through Celia. Now Dameon wanted her to sleep with him on the side? Was this some sort of blackmail? Unfortunately, Celia had no say in the matter. She felt like she was being pimped by Dameon because if she didn't listen, she would be back in prison. Her heart ached.

"I know you will take care of me. I feel safe with you," Celia said robotically. And just as she kissed Dameon on the forehead, they heard a knock at the door.

CHAPTER 25

As Justin finished up the last of his work, he couldn't help but feel agitated. Sure, he had told Sonia that she could watch the videos without him, but part of him wanted to be there. In a way, he would have liked it if Sonia had waited for him.

She had been acting a little different lately. Before they were married, she always waited for him to do anything. She even felt a little guilty going out with her girlfriends without him. But now she seemed to have no problem going out with Dameon. But what could he expect? He was the one sitting at this stupid desk doing work on their honeymoon. He was the one not spending time with his wife.

At home, she had things to do when he was busy—work, friends, family, and piano. Here she had nothing else to do, so of course she was taking advantage of Dameon's company.

Anxiety surged through his veins. He shuffled around the paperwork, took a quick shower, got dressed, and called for a taxi. As he grabbed his wallet and locked the door behind him, he couldn't shake the feeling of worry. He trusted Sonia, but did he trust Dameon? All sorts of horrible scenarios popped into his head as he paced the sidewalk. He took a couple of deep breaths to calm down.

When the taxi finally arrived, he quickly got in. Upon arriving at Dameon's hotel, he handed the driver a tip, and got out of the taxi as fast as he could. He walked past the desk clerk and straight to the elevator as he already knew which floor Dameon was on from the last time when Dameon had picked up his camera for the museum. As he watched the elevator floors light up, he told himself to calm down, that it was not fair to accuse Dameon and Sonia of anything. This was the first time he'd felt any sort of jealousy and it bothered him greatly.

The elevator stopped on Dameon's floor, and as Justin stepped out into the hallway, he told himself to calm down. *Walk slowly, take deep breaths.* All of a sudden, he felt like he was spying on Sonia, but then he reassured himself. Sonia was expecting him. She knew he was going to pick her up.

The walk down that hallway seemed like the longest walk of his life. But finally he was standing in front of Dameon's door.

CHAPTER 26

Sonia awoke extremely drowsy and her back was hurting. She had had an awful dream that she was in some sort of jail cell. She sat up and rubbed the sleep out of her eyes. As her vision cleared, she realized that she was in some kind of confinement room with bars. She was sitting on a narrow, hard, cot. Fear burst through her. *This can't be real. How did I get here?*

Panic started setting in as she called out, "Is anybody there? Please answer me. Does anyone know where I am?"

It was 6 o'clock in the morning and the other inmates were starting to wake up. A guard would be there soon, and the bells would go off any minute for everyone to get out of bed. Sonia heard women screaming. Their profanities were directed at her. Why was this happening? Why were these people cursing her? She had never hurt anyone.

Sonia stood up, walked to the door with the steel bars, and tried to open it. But it was locked. Then she realized that the other women were also locked up. She saw them across the hallway. Fear was gripping her insides as tears ran down her cheeks. She started to call out for Justin and her parents.

"Oh, shut the fuck up, you bitch," the woman across the hall shouted.

Her fear was paralyzing her. Terrified, she didn't know what to do. She managed to walk back to her bed and sat down as quiet as a mouse. She was scared speechless. All she could do was cry, taking great pains to muffle her sobs with her hands. The women were still yelling at her, so she covered her ears hoping that she would wake up from this horrible nightmare.

There was a sound of heavy footsteps and a whistle being blown. Too scared to look up, she heard a woman's voice yelling, "Get up, you lazy bunch."

There was some moaning and shuffling going on. Still sitting against the wall on the bed, hugging her knees with her elbows, her eyes tightly closed and her hands still cupping her ears, Sonia didn't really register her.

"Hey, that means you too, missy!" the guard yelled through the bars.

Sonia removed her hands from her ears and looked up at the woman.

"What's wrong with you, Celia? Get up."

There it was again, someone calling her Celia. Didn't they know that her name was Sonia? *Where am I? Where is Justin? Is he okay?* All she could remember was being at the airport but not what happened after that.

She managed to get up as ordered, too fearful not to do as she was told. The tears continued to flow. The guard looked very stern and tough. Her hair was tied tightly in a bun on the top of her head, and her face was in a constant scowl.

Sonia recognized the uniform, but couldn't place where it was from. She knew she had seen it before. All of a sudden, the cell doors automatically opened. Sonia stayed put—frozen—not knowing what to do. She watched as the other women stepped out of their cells. Sonia had no choice but to follow them. She was like a zombie—this whole situation was too surreal. She could feel herself getting weaker. Her vision was getting black in front of her eyes, and she couldn't stop herself as she fainted.

*****

Ann woke up early. She couldn't sleep because Sonia was playing heavily on her mind. She couldn't forget the panicked look on Sonia's face, and felt horrible about what she had done. *Why did I let myself get talked into doing this? Was this really worth the money?* Guilt and remorse consumed her. She couldn't tell anybody about it. She couldn't give herself up because she would go to jail. It was hard enough working in a prison, never mind living in one. No one could know what she had done. She had to convince herself to stick to the plan and everything would be okay. Sonia would be okay.

What Ann really needed was Dameon's reassurance. She wouldn't see him for a month. She knew it would be the hardest month of her life because she had to deal with this on her own.

As she let the shower water spray over her face, she couldn't stop thinking about Sonia. How frightened she'd looked when she woke up behind bars. Ann knew she was the cause of the girl's misery.

When Ann finished showering, she turned on the TV as loud as she could to drown out her thoughts. She left the TV on until she went to work. She didn't want to go because she would have to face Sonia again. On the other hand, she wanted to go early to keep an eye on Sonia, to almost try and protect her somehow.

When Ann got to work, Nancy, the nurse on duty, told her about Celia's fainting spell that morning.

"Where's she now?" Ann asked.

"She's back in her cell. I left her there because she was hallucinating again, telling everyone that she was Sonia. And this time, she was really convincing. If you didn't know any better you'd almost believe her."

"So, what did you do?" Ann asked.

Nancy said, "I gave her some relaxers to calm her down."

"Okay," Ann said, "I'll look in on her."

"Good luck," Nancy said as she left.

Alone in the office, Ann thought about going to see Sonia right away, but then decided against it, pondering the notion that it was probably not a good idea. The other inmates might see it as favouritism and make life miserable for Sonia. Ann surely didn't want anything to happen to Sonia. The poor girl had enough to cope with.

She could go to the security office and have a look on the monitor to survey the girls without anyone knowing, but then Tom would ask too many questions. The least amount of attention drawn, the better, especially with Dameon not being there to cover for her.

Ann stared at a pile of papers on her desk and waited.

CHAPTER 27

Justin stood at the door holding his breath. He knocked again. Why was it taking so long for someone to answer? What were they doing in there?

"Hurry," Dameon said quietly as he walked to the bathroom with his bundle of clothes. Celia quickly straightened the covers on the bed, and then threw her sundress over her head. She tiptoed to the wall mirror and ran her fingers through her hair.

Another knock on the door.

Celia took a deep breath and headed toward the door. As she opened the door, Justin stood on the other side. She smiled. "Oh honey, I'm so glad you're here. Now you can see the videos. They're beautiful." She grabbed his hand and led him inside, ignoring the weary look on his face.

As Justin glanced around the room, he asked, "What took you so long?"

Celia answered very innocently, "What do you mean?"

"Well," Justin said, "I knocked twice before you answered. And where's Dameon?"

"Oh, I'm sorry." Celia said with a sweet apologetic smile. "I only heard you knock once. I guess the video was too loud. Dameon's in the bathroom." She kissed him again.

Justin felt guilty but relieved at the same time. He was just letting his emotions get in the way. There was no way that Sonia would cheat on him. He knew that she loved him more than anything, and he just needed to trust her. He felt embarrassed and just hoped that his emotions didn't read on his face.

"Well, I've missed you while I've been working but now I'm free for two weeks with no more interruptions from my Dad. He really promised this time," Justin said. "I can take all the time I want to see those videos."

A smile beamed across Celia's face. "I'm so happy you're done with work! Let's watch the videos now. I want to see them again with you!"

Just then, Dameon stepped out of the bathroom. He glanced over at Justin and acted surprised to see him. "Oh, hi Justin. Did you finish your work?"

"Yes," Justin said. "I'm totally free from work, so now I can concentrate on my honeymoon, and we might as well start with the videos. Sonia tells me they're fantastic and she doesn't mind watching them again."

"Of course," Dameon said. He glanced at Celia and raised his eyebrows, as if to say, *Justin hasn't noticed a thing.*

Celia knew exactly what the look on Dameon's face meant. She flashed him a smile of relief, while paying sweet attention to Justin. "Come, honey, sit on the bed, that way you can see the videos."

Justin's heart jumped out of his chest when he noticed that the curtains were closed and that there were two wine glasses out, one half full and the other one sitting empty on the bedside table. "Why are the curtains closed?" he asked. He couldn't contain his suspicions.

Dameon stumbled, "Oh, yes, we have them closed so you can see the movie better. The sun was shining into the room and we couldn't see it very well."

Justin nodded. "Of course, that makes sense." He hesitantly sat on the edge of the bed. Celia sat down in the chair. She nervously watched as Justin stared at her wine glass on the table.

Quickly, she said, "Dameon offered me some wine. Would you like some, too?"

"Oh yes, Justin, I'm sorry, where are my manners. Can I get you something to drink?" Dameon asked.

Justin looked at Celia's glass and said, "Well, I can't have Sonia drink alone, can I? And your glass is empty. I guess I'll have to have one too."

Dameon poured some wine into a glass for Justin. "Can I top yours, Sonia?"

"No thank you, Dameon. One glass is enough for me," Celia said politely. "I still have half a glass left. That's plenty for me, thank you."

Dameon was in awe of the way Celia changed so quickly to Sonia; it was really remarkable. He refilled his own glass as well.

Once the glasses were filled, they toasted to a beautiful rest of the honeymoon with no more interruptions from Justin's father.

"Shall I start the video then?" Dameon asked, trying hard not to show his disappointment at not being able to be alone with Celia anymore during the honeymoon.

Justin nodded. "Can you see okay from there, sweetie?" he asked.

"Oh yes, I've been sitting here the whole time, but I have to admit that it hurts my neck a little."

Justin patted the bed signaling for Celia to sit. She moved over to the bed and sat next to Justin. Dameon took the chair instead. As Celia was sitting next to Justin, she was thinking about the last two hours with Dameon. How they had started by sitting on the edge of the bed, then moving up to the headboard, and when the video finished, what they did after that. Sexually, Dameon was a better match than Justin. Justin was a good lover, but Dameon was wilder, rougher, and that was the way Celia really liked it.

"It's really good, don't you think, honey?" Celia quickly said coming out of her thoughts.

"Yeah it is. What are you thinking about with that silly smile on your face sweetheart." Justin asked.

Celia quickly responded. "I was thinking how lucky I am to have you."

Justin just smiled at her and felt the same way. He knew that he was the luckiest man on earth to have such a wonderful girl for his wife, and he shook all his earlier jealous thoughts away.

Once the videos were finished, they said their goodbyes and Justin and Celia headed back to the hotel room to get ready for dinner.

After dinner, Justin and Celia curled up on the bed and made sweet love. Justin felt so badly about letting his crazy thoughts run away with him. He loved Sonia and there was no doubt in his mind that she loved him. How silly of him to think that something was going on with her and Dameon.

*****

On the last few days of the honeymoon, Celia thought it was time to work on the plan. It was Sunday evening, and she and Justin had just come back from dining out. They had had a lovely dinner, complete with a violinist playing at their table. As soon as they were back in their hotel room, Celia turned on some soft music and Justin opened a bottle of wine.

Celia was starting to undress herself in front of Justin and Justin followed suit. He filled the enormous heart-shaped bathtub, and Celia added some aromatic lavender bath oil. They slipped into the bathtub with their wine glasses in hand.

After their glasses were empty, Justin stroked Celia's breast and nibbled on her nipples. Celia wanted to give Justin a good time, so she started out by kissing his chest, and then moved lower. Justin's manhood grew, and after awhile of fondling each other, they moved to the bed to finish their lovemaking.

As they lay in each other's arms, Celia rested her head on Justin's chest. She knew that this was the perfect opportunity to set the next step of the plan into motion. "Honey," she said quietly, "what would you say if I wanted to quit my job and start my own business?"

Justin was a little surprised but then said, "I think that's a great idea. But what about your job and the people you like working with so much? You're sure you want to leave that?"

"Yes, I do," Celia responded. "Of course, I'll miss the people there, but I would really love to have my own business." She softly ran her fingers over his chest. "I've been thinking about this for quite some time now, but I didn't want to mention it because I need a lot of money for what I want to do."

"So, you want me to give you some, eh?" Justin said with a cute smile.

"No, no, honey," Celia was quick to respond, "but I was hoping you could lend me the money that I need."

With a quizzical look on Justin's face he said, "Lend you the money!" And then he continued, "You're my wife. I don't lend you money. My money is your money. We're married so everything is ours now. You should know that by now."

"I know, honey, but I didn't want to take advantage of the fact that I'm your wife," Celia explained nervously.

"How much do you need?" Justin asked.

Celia hesitated for a moment. "It's going to cost quite a bit. That's why I didn't know how to ask." She lifted her head and smiled. It had been almost four weeks being with Justin. She knew she could get anything from him; Justin would melt by seeing her smile. He was so in love with his wife that he would give her everything, and Celia took advantage of that.

She kissed his stomach then moved closer to his face. She nuzzled her nose into his neck, her legs entwined with his. She could feel him getting aroused again, and before long, they were making passionate love once more.

When they were relaxing afterward, Justin asked, "How much money do you need?"

Celia looked at him with a question mark on her face pretending that she didn't know what he was talking about.

"Well, how much?" Justin repeated.

"Oh, that!" Celia responded with a little giggle and then became nervous. "Oh, um, ah, a lot."

"Well, tell me how much? How can I give you what you need if you don't tell me how much it is?" said Justin. He felt slightly annoyed because he was quite willing to give her whatever she wanted. Didn't she know that by now? He sensed a slight change in her, but quickly attributed it to the fact that she felt awkward asking him for money.

Celia started to tell him her plans about the fashion bridal boutique, and she was surprised that Justin thought it was a great idea.

"You'll be good at that, honey," Justin said. "You already know all about fashion since you worked at that fashion magazine, so that should be a natural for you. And a bridal shop, well, that shouldn't be too hard either since you had the prettiest bridal gown I have ever seen," he laughed. "So, yes, I'll support you. Just tell me how much you think you'll need to get started."

"Well," Celia said, "I already have a store in mind where I can have my shop."

Justin sat up surprised. He felt a little crushed that this was the first time he was hearing this information. "You mean to tell me that you've already been looking for a place without telling me?"

"Yes, I'm afraid so," Celia said, "but I was only dream shopping. I've been thinking about it for a long time, and just before we left on our honeymoon I found this quaint little store. It would be perfect! I'm sorry I didn't tell you sooner, but I didn't think it was that big of a deal because I wasn't sure of anything. I didn't know if I really wanted to do it. But now that we're almost home, I thought of seeing if it's still available."

Then Justin said, "You know, you don't need to work at all if you don't want to. You can just enjoy being my wife, go shopping or go to social clubs, see your friends or have dinner parties."

Celia remained silent. How she would love to do those things, but she needed to stick to the plan. "Okay, okay already," Celia laughed. She started to tickle Justin. He grabbed her by the hips and tossed her to the other side of the bed. They playfully teased each other.

Justin got out of bed and poured himself another glass of wine. "Sonia, sweetheart, would you like some more wine?"

"Yes, please," Celia responded. "I'd love some more."

Justin sat on the edge of the bed and handed Celia her glass.

"Let's toast to my new business adventure," Celia said.

"Yes, to your store," Justin agreed. "Now tell me what you need, what your plans are, and don't be shy about it."

Celia excitedly smiled. "I'll probably need about two-hundred thousand dollars to get started." She waited for his response.

Justin furrowed his brow and was deep in thought. "How did you come up with that figure?"

"Well," Celia said, "the rent, the renovation of the place, the inventory. And then I'll need some assistants, and a bookkeeper, and money for advertising." Celia spoke until she was out of breath.

"Honey," Justin giggled, "calm down." He kissed her cheek. He loved how excited and motivated she was. After her explanation, her quoted price seemed reasonable. "As soon as we're home, I'll set up a business account. How does that sound?"

"Would you really do that?" Celia asked.

"Of course I would," Justin said. "I love you."

"Could it be separate from my regular account?" Celia asked.

"I wouldn't have it any other way," Justin said.

Celia felt her heart pound. This was just too easy. "I love you too," she said as they finished their wine.

CHAPTER 28

The plane landed smoothly. As Justin and Celia waited for their luggage, Celia gripped his hand tightly. The easy part was over; now she had to act like Sonia around Sonia's parents and friends.

Dameon had boarded his plane a few days earlier. Justin was quite impressed with the beach video that Dameon had made, and after he got over his distrust, he had invited Dameon to come alone with them a few more times to make some more videos and pictures. Dameon expressed how he enjoyed spending time with them and he would be in touch very shortly about the developed videos and photos.

In the meantime, at the little opportunities that they had, Dameon had told Celia what to do. First, she had to set up her own business account with the money Justin was going to give her. Then, she had to go into the office where Sonia worked and tell the boss that she was going to quit. Celia was worried, but she knew she had to do it. She just hoped that everything would go smoothly.

Celia knew that everything would be very different now. The honeymoon was easy, but Sonia's regular life was going to start again, and she needed to be convincing.

*****

It was only a minute after Dameon had stepped into his house and closed the door before the doorbell rang.

He opened the door and was surprised. "Ann! What are you doing here?" he asked.

"Well," she said, "I knew you were supposed to be home around this time. I'm anxious to hear how it all went."

Dameon scowled. He was definitely not in the mood to see Ann and he was tired from all the traveling. He just wanted to crash on the couch, maybe watch some TV and hit the sack early. "Ann, I'm so tired. Can't this wait until tomorrow?" he asked.

"No," Ann insisted, "I want to know now. I want to see and hear all about how things went. You left me alone for a whole month and I had to cope with Sonia for all that time. That was not what we had talked about. It was only going to take a few days, and then you were going to make everything right again. That's what you told me. You lied, and I trusted you. When are you ever going to be honest with me?" Ann felt her heart race.

"Come on, Ann, I'm too tired to argue right now. We'll get together tomorrow." Dameon was still holding the door open and was hoping that Ann would turn around and walk away.

But Ann wasn't that easily persuaded. She felt that she had more than a right to know what was going on, so she stepped further into the doorway. Dameon had no choice but to let her in.

"Come on, Dameon, we'll make some coffee and talk." Ann usually wasn't this forceful with Dameon because she was always afraid that he'd flip out, but this time she was not afraid. She wanted him to know that she was not happy with the situation.

Dameon didn't want a scene, so he made some coffee. He needed Ann to trust him and take care of Sonia. He didn't want her to do something stupid like report him. He couldn't take that chance.

After making coffee they sat down and Dameon told her all about Justin and Celia's honeymoon. Of course, he left out the intimate moments with Celia. He told her that everything went smoothly and according to plan. All he was going to do now was develop the last of the pictures and videos. He would meet with them again as soon as they were finished.

"When are we going to get the money? You promised that we were going to get money out of this."

"I know," Dameon nodded. "I had to change the plan a little. I'm sorry but it's going to take a little longer than I first thought, so you'll have to have a little more patience, and as soon as I have more info I'll update you."

Ann gritted her teeth. After one month of dealing with Sonia crying, wailing, and fainting, that was all Dameon had to say? That she'd have to wait? "What am I going to do with Sonia?" she spat.

Dameon started to perk up a little from the coffee. He could see that Ann was not happy. He placed his cup down and looked at Ann with a concerned look on his face. "How did you do with Sonia? Tell me how she's doing. Did you have any problems with her? I hope everything went well."

Ann had the sudden urge to punch him. While he was out gallivanting in beautiful St. Martin, she was stuck taking care of Sonia. "It actually didn't go very well," Ann said. "The beginning was pretty tough. Finally, after four weeks, she settled down, but you have no idea what I've been through. Because of all the drugs we've given her, she seems to now think that she belongs in jail. Poor girl."

Ann stayed silent for a moment. She couldn't get Sonia's sad eyes out of her mind. "Every now and then she asks if she can call her parents and Justin. The staff just laughs at her..." Ann's voice trailed off. She couldn't stop the tears.

Dameon pulled her close and held her in his arms. He needed to show compassion, but in all reality, he could care less about how Ann felt. He was content in knowing that everything was as it should be and that the staff didn't suspect a thing.

Ann pushed Dameon away. Her eyes were puffy from crying. "I actually feel awful for Sonia. It's hard for me to pretend that she's Celia. All the medication we've given her has sedated her and she's calmed down. She doesn't say much at all anymore. It's like she's a different person. I can't wait to go home everyday so I don't have to see her. I don't know how long I can keep going."

"Ann, you can't start thinking like that," Dameon said worried. "If we give up now, people will find out, and we'll be in big trouble. We have to keep going. We have no choice right now."

"I know," Ann said, "I just wish I never agreed to this. All I wanted was the money."

Dameon took Ann in his arms again and rocked her back and forth. "It's going to be okay. Celia knows what to do and we'll have about one-hundred thousand dollars in a couple of days."

"One-hundred thousand dollars," Ann asked a little upset. "I thought you were going to get a lot more than that."

"Yes, I know," Dameon clarified. "We'll get that, but that's going to take a little longer."

"Why?" Ann asked annoyed.

Dameon explained his plan further, and how he threatened Celia that if she bailed on the plan, he was going to turn her in. She had no choice but to follow the plan.

"But if we give her up, we're going to give ourselves up," Ann said with a worried look in her eyes.

"I know," Dameon said, "but she doesn't realize that. She's just worried that she'll have to go back to jail. Trust me; she won't do anything to expose us. She'll do everything in her power to make sure that we get the money. Don't you worry; it's going to work out. I know it will."

Ann felt her body relax in Dameon's arms. He could be so convincing.

Dameon held Ann closer and said, "We've gotten ourselves this far. We can't turn back now. Everything will be fine. Come upstairs with me. We'll have some fun."

Ann wasn't really in the mood to go upstairs with Dameon, but followed him anyway. She couldn't help but think about Sonia sitting in her cell, curled up in a ball, crying herself to sleep.

CHAPTER 29

Celia was standing in her exquisite, modern kitchen, pouring herself a cup of coffee. She and Justin had been home a few days since their honeymoon. She just couldn't believe her good fortune. Such a beautiful house; with all this lovely stuff. After her breakfast she would dive into the pool. She had her freedom.

She also talked to Justin about her bank account.

"Of course you have to have some money if you want to start that store," Justin had said. She reassured him that she really wanted to do it. So, Justin had gone with her to their bank and opened a bank account in her name and deposited two hundred thousand dollars. As long as she kept Justin updated on the store's progress, she would have no problems.

As Celia stared out the window daydreaming Justin walked into the kitchen. "Good morning, sweetheart," he said as he leaned toward her with a tender kiss. "How are you this fine morning?"

Celia returned his sweet greeting. "Oh great, honey, I'm doing fantastic. As much as I loved our honeymoon, it feels good to be home." The photos and videos that Dameon and Ann showed Celia did no justice. The house was gorgeous and she couldn't believe her eyes.

"Everything just looks more beautiful than I remember. I'm so happy, Justin. Thank you so much for everything."

"We'll, don't just thank me," Justin said, "thank yourself, too. You've done so much work in this house. Don't you remember?"

"Yes, of course, I remember, but I'm still amazed." Celia had to be more careful with her words because apparently Sonia had done a lot of work in the house. Justin took her hand and they went into the breakfast room. The maid shuffled back and forth with plates of eggs, fruit, and bacon. Fresh-squeezed orange juice sat on the table in a pitcher. Celia still couldn't believe this was actually happening.

"Have you gone to your store yet?" Justin asked.

Celia took a sip of orange juice and wiped her mouth with her napkin. "I'm going to look at it this afternoon to see if it's still available. If not, then I'll find another place."

"Well, let me know how it works out and come visit me at my office when you're finished," Justin said.

Celia felt her stomach plunge. She didn't want to visit Justin at his work because there were so many people there that knew Sonia well. Some of them might notice something to make them suspicious, and that worried Celia. It had been difficult enough when she went the day before to Sonia's workplace and spoke to Sonia's boss regarding her resignation. The boss didn't believe her at first because Sonia apparently loved her job, so Celia had to be convincing.

"Okay, honey. I'll do that," Celia said.

After breakfast, Justin gave Celia a kiss and went to work. Luckily, Dameon had phoned later that day and asked if they could get together to see the last of their finished pictures and videos. This was a way for her to get out of visiting Justin at work.

She immediately dialed Justin's number. It only took a couple of rings for the receptionist to say, "Good afternoon, Haines International, how may I help you?"

"Can you please connect me to Justin Haines office?"

"Who may I ask is speaking?" the receptionist said.

Celia replied, "His wife." It sounded strange to her ears, but it made her feel kind of important at the same time.

"Of course, Mrs. Haines," the receptionist said. "I'll connect you."

"Thank you," Celia said. Suddenly she was worried. Should she have referred to herself as Sonia rather than Justin's wife?

As soon as Justin came on the phone Celia said in a sweet voice, "Hi, honey, how are you?"

"Good," Justin replied, "nice to hear your voice." Justin had wondered about Sonia's voice lately. It seemed to have changed a little, not much, but just enough for him to notice over the phone. He shook the thought out of his mind. "Are you coming to visit me?"

"No, I'm sorry, honey, I can't make it. Dameon just phoned and told me that he was finished with all our pictures and DVDs. I asked him to come over. You don't mind, do you?" she said as sweetly as possible. "And Justin, I have to go to the store as fast as I can. I have an appointment there at three o'clock."

"Don't worry sweetheart," Justin replied. "Do what you have to do. I'll be home around four-thirty."

"You know what, honey? I just thought of something. I'll give Dameon a call back and see if he can come later this afternoon so he'll be here when you get home. I'll see if I can go to the store earlier, and then by the time I get home, you'll be here. That way we can see Dameon's finished work together," Celia said.

Justin thought that was a considerate offer, much more like the Sonia he knew and loved. Every so often, he had a feeling that Sonia was changing, but he couldn't quite put his finger on it. But then when she did things like this, being considerate of his feelings, he knew why he fell in love with her in the first place.

Celia knew that Justin would approve of her proposition. Little did he know that she was going to see Dameon anyway. "Well, honey, I'll see you when you get home. Try to get home as soon as you can."

Justin felt good after he hung up the phone. A huge grin overtook his face as he buzzed Gwen, his secretary, to ask her not to book anything for him after four o'clock. He planned on getting home as soon as possible.

*****

After lunch, Celia took Sonia's purse and car keys and walked into the garage. She opened the car door then started the ignition. She was very nervous; the last time she'd driven a car was when she was sixteen. As Celia sat in the driver's seat, she couldn't help but think about Jimmy, her old boyfriend. She was sixteen and Jimmy was nineteen and wild. He taught her to drive, illegally, of course. He had a nice car and loved to go out for drives in the country, so he took her along and let her drive often. They had a lot of fun together, but after a while, Jimmy decided that girls his own age where more exciting. Celia hadn't thought about him until now.

She quietly thanked him for teaching her to drive, but wondered if she could still do it. After all, she hadn't had any experience since then and it had been a long time ago. She took a deep breath and drove carefully out of the garage and down the laneway onto the road. All she had to do was drive two blocks to Cedar Plaza and Dameon would be waiting. He'd promised to give her some driving lessons. She would have rather met a little farther away because she was afraid of anyone seeing her with Dameon, but she was too scared to drive so they decided to meet closer to her home.

Celia managed to get to the plaza without any incident. She was shaking by the time she arrived. When Dameon approached her she started to get out of the car but Dameon told her to stay behind the steering wheel because she needed to get over her fear.

Celia, clearly upset, snapped at Dameon, "I thought you said you were going to drive me."

"No," Dameon said. "I never told you that. I told you I was going to go with you to the store and for you to meet me here at this plaza."

"That's not fair," Celia said angrily, still shaking.

But Dameon insisted, "You need to be able to drive with confidence."

Celia realized that she had no choice, so she slid back behind the steering wheel. She was still shaking, but she felt more comfortable with Dameon next to her.

By the time they got to the store she felt a lot better and more comfortable with her driving abilities. Dameon had promised to take her out for a drive as many times as they could get together. He was actually pretty amazed at how well Celia drove. "Who taught you to drive and when?" he asked surprised.

"My ex-boyfriend Jimmy," Celia explained. "But it only lasted for about six months and then he left me for someone else. I never got enough driving experience, so I'm surprised at how well I did," she said with a relieved but proud smile. She parked the car in the little plaza in front of the store.

They had arrived about ten minutes early, which gave them some time to talk about the plan. Dameon didn't want anything to go wrong. He knew that sooner or later Celia was going to be found out. Somebody was going to be suspicious. She was going to do something that would be totally out of character for Sonia. And Sonia's parents might know that Sonia had a sister, probably a twin. So, Dameon wanted to get as much money out of this scheme as soon as he could before they were found out. He didn't want to frighten Celia by telling her this. They hadn't had an opportunity to talk about their plan for the last two weeks.

Celia was getting really anxious to find out more about his plan. She had been worrying about it, and worrying about where she was going to get the inventory she would need for the store. And, she had no idea how to even run a store.

Dameon had told her not to worry and that he would take care of everything. She just needed to stick to the plan.

At three o'clock they walked into the store to meet the owner.

"Good afternoon, sir. This is Mrs. Haines," Dameon said reaching out his hand. He purposely didn't introduce himself. "She's interested in leasing your store."

"I'm pleased to meet you," Celia said as she reached out her hand. "I brought my friend with me. I hope you don't mind. He knows a little more about leasing a store than I do. This is a first for me."

"Oh, nice to meet you. I'm Jerry," the storeowner said. "Let me show you around and then if you like it we can sit down and discuss the terms."

Celia actually loved the place. It was big and airy, and had beautiful display windows. This was a perfect location. After some negotiating, she signed the agreement.

On their way back to Cedar Plaza, Celia drove again. While in transit, Dameon said, "I expect some money soon. I need to give some money to Ann. She's getting anxious. I can't hold her off too much longer because she's not going to trust me, and that could be dangerous for us. So Celia, see that you get some money soon. You shouldn't have any problem because you can just take it out of your business account. Take out five thousand dollars."

Celia felt her nerves kick in. "Are you sure they're not going to ask me any questions?"

"Absolutely," Dameon said confidently. He could see that Celia was getting nervous and he didn't want that while she was driving. "Don't you worry," he said, "that's why I only asked for five thousand for now, because five thousand or anything less, they won't ask questions. We could go to the bank right now, but I'd rather you talk to Justin first to make sure he doesn't interfere in your business dealings. That way, you make sure he never sees your bank account. Withdraw the money a day or two after you talk to Justin."

"I'll do my best," Celia said.

She pulled into the plaza and dropped Dameon off at his car. Celia drove herself home feeling pleased, about her driving skill, but nervous about Dameon's request. As soon as she pulled into her driveway and parked her car in front of their garage she saw Jack, their chauffeur. Celia stepped out of the car. "Hi, Jack, could you wash my car and then put it back in the garage, please."

"Sure, Mrs. Haines, will do," Jack answered.

Then Celia turned to Jack with a big smile. "Please, Jack, call me Sonia."

"Of course, Sonia," Jack said lifting his hat.

Celia went inside and about a half an hour later, the doorbell rang. It was Dameon, just as they had planned.

"Come in, Dameon," she said with a meaningful smile. "I've been waiting for you. Have you got everything ready? I'm anxious to see it all." She spoke loudly so the maid who was standing behind her could hear. Celia wanted to make sure that nobody had any reason to suspect anything.

"Can I offer you something to drink?" Celia asked.

"Yes, that would be nice," Dameon answered, "some tea, please, if that's okay?"

"Sure," Celia said and sent the maid to fetch some tea. Celia led Dameon into her office, and while they were looking at the pictures and videos, Justin walked in.

Celia stood as she saw him and excitedly hugged him. "Oh honey, I'm so happy you're here so we can see the videos and photos together. They're really fantastic," she said. Then she continued, "Dameon made it into a whole movie for us. Come have a look, honey."

Justin greeted Dameon with a handshake. He was glad that Sonia was so happy with the videos. He couldn't say anything bad about them; they were really good.

After they finished watching the movie, Justin said, "Sonia, sweetheart, how did it go this afternoon with your store?"

"Oh, really good, honey," Celia said excitedly. She took the lease out of her purse. "I got the lease agreement right here."

"You signed it already!" Justin said surprised. "I could have helped you with the negotiating. I probably could have gotten you a much better deal."

Celia looked apologetic. "I'm sorry, honey, but I really want to do this all by myself, if you don't mind. It's a challenge for me. I want to see if I can do it. But I promise that if I need help, you'll be the first to know."

Justin glanced at Dameon. "We'll talk about this later. Let's not bore Dameon with this."

But then Dameon asked, "I'm just so surprised you're going to have your own store? What kind of a store?"

Celia clasped her hands under her chin. "It's going to be a bridal shop with the most fashionable dresses for the bride and bridal party."

"What a great idea! I think it's great for you to have your own business, Sonia, if I may say so," Dameon said with a smile.

"Thank you, Dameon. You know what?" Celia asked. "Maybe you can take some videos of that as well. But, on second thought," she then quickly said, "no, forget it. I can't afford to pay you for that. It's going to be expensive enough."

"I could do a short documentary for my own portfolio, and when your store is a success, as I know it will be, you can pay me then," Dameon said.

Celia squealed. "Oh, really? Dameon, would you do that?"

Dameon nodded and looked at Justin.

"We'll talk it over," Justin said.

Dameon stood up figuring that he had been at Justin's house long enough. It was time for him to leave Celia alone with Justin so she could do her thing. He knew he would hear from her tomorrow to tell him how things went.

Dameon picked up his jacket from the back of his chair. "Okay, you guys, I think it's time for me to leave. Sonia, good luck with your business. Let's keep in touch and I'll send you my bill for the videos and pictures."

Justin replied, "Yes, Dameon, just send us the invoice and I'll send you a cheque, or if you want, you can pick it up here."

"That's really nice of you. Thank you. I'll be in touch."

After Dameon left, Celia gave Justin a big hug and kiss. "I love you, honey."

Justin took her in his arms. "I love you, too, sweetheart, and I know that your store will be a big success."

"It will," Celia said, "and I hope you don't mind if I want to do everything by myself."

Then Justin protested and asked, "Why don't you want me to help you? Don't you think I can be a real asset to your business? Let me help you."

Celia took Justin's face in her hands and looked him straight in the eyes. "Please, honey, do me a big favour, and let me do this my way. I want to prove to myself that I can do this."

Justin took Celia's hand away from his face and said in a serious tone, "I don't doubt it. I'm sure you can do it by yourself, but what's wrong with a little help?"

"Nothing, Justin," Celia said, "but I had my heart set on this. I really wanted to do it all by myself. I would appreciate it if you gave me the opportunity to see if I can do it by myself. I want you to let me be free in this whole thing, and even more, I was hoping I could surprise you when it's all done. This means that you won't even come and have a look at the store until I'm all finished with it. Promise?"

Justin crinkled his brow. "You mean to tell me that I gave you money and I'm not allowed to see it?"

Celia stared at him long and hard. "Yes, that's what I mean. It's not about you honey, it's about me. I just need to know that I can do it all by myself. If I fail then you can help. Okay?"

Justin couldn't get angry with Sonia, he loved her, but this was the first time since they'd been together that he felt hurt. He loved her so much and he admired her determination to try and prove to herself that she could do it all by herself. He respected her for that, but wished that she wanted him to be a part of it. "Okay, sweetheart," he whispered. "But if you need help, please don't hesitate to ask me."

"I won't." Celia hugged him closely and smiled to herself. She had him wrapped around her finger.

CHAPTER 30

The doorbell rang and Sonia and Justin's maid, Martha, answered the door.

"Good afternoon," Dameon said politely. "I'm here to see Mrs. Haines."

Martha left Dameon in the front hall while she went to get her. It didn't take very long before Celia was there and asked him to follow her into her office.

Dameon knew the house inside out, but it still boggled his mind at how gorgeous it was. He could only imagine how much money had gone in to it to make this place so phenomenal.

"Can I take your coat?" Celia asked.

"I'm not planning on staying very long," Dameon replied.

Celia gestured for Dameon to take a seat as she sat down behind her desk. "Won't you stay for tea?"

Dameon winked. "Well, I came here because you told me you had a cheque for me." He watched as Celia twirled her hair around her finger. He made her weak at the knees.

Celia stared at Dameon and thoughts about their rendezvous in St. Martin flashed before her eyes. She blushed. When she went to see the store with Dameon the thought of being intimate with him didn't cross her mind. She was too preoccupied. But now, she was more relaxed and she would love to be in Dameon's arms again. Of course, she had to behave herself.

"Yes, Dameon, I have your cheque right here." She handed him an envelope while Martha watched and waited to be dismissed. Celia wanted to make sure that Martha saw her hand Dameon the cheque. "Martha, would you mind fetching us some tea?" she asked politely.

As Martha left the room, Celia took out a second envelope from her desk drawer. The envelope was much fatter, and she handed it quickly to Dameon.

Dameon placed the envelope inside the pocket of his jacket. He knew it contained the five thousand dollars in cash he had requested. He whispered quietly, "Can you get away tomorrow?" He smiled and shot her another little wink.

Celia grinned. She knew she had to see Dameon every time she could, and, surprisingly, she wanted to see him for more reasons than one. What Justin didn't know couldn't hurt him.

"I'll see what I can do," she said seductively.

CHAPTER 31

As soon as Dameon got home he phoned Ann with the news that he had the money. He was just in time; she was almost ready to go to work.

"Oh Dameon, that's fantastic. I don't know what to do with Mike anymore but at least the money will help. Thank you. When can we get together?" Ann asked.

"You can come to my place after your shift is over. I know we both have crazy hours and I know you'll be late. You just can't stay too long. I have to get to bed early because my shift starts at four in the morning."

"That's okay," Ann said happily. "I won't stay long."

After Dameon hung up, Ann sat in her living room for a moment. She wondered how much money he had for her. She was happy that she was finally going to get some money, but she wasn't sure anymore about what she had done to Sonia. She hated seeing Sonia in jail. Sonia was quieter as time passed, but she still cried a lot and had nightmares. The entire staff thought that Celia had gone mad, and Kim had told Ann more than once that she thought they should report it and take her behaviour seriously.

"Maybe they'll put her in a mental institution. That might be better for Celia," Kim had said.

But Ann continued to tell Kim that she thought Celia was just craving attention. She hoped Sonia wouldn't be emotionally damaged forever; however, Ann knew that it wasn't the case. Dameon promised to make "everything right," but did he even consider the emotional state of Sonia? If she went into a mental institution, she'd have less of a chance of ever getting out. Ann was worried, but she had no choice. She had to keep giving Sonia medication to keep her sedated.

Sometimes Sonia went to the laundry room to help fold towels, and when she seemed in a particularly good mood, she was allowed to work in the kitchen for an hour or two.

Money was money, but Ann couldn't help but feel drained by the situation. She wondered if she would live in guilt forever.

The phone rang.

Ann straightened in her chair and felt her heart pounding. She listened to Kim, the security guard, as she frantically rambled on the other end.

"I'm concerned about Celia," Kim said. "She has a fever and I brought her to the infirmary. I know your shift doesn't start for another hour, but could you come in a little earlier today and have a look at her?"

"Where is Nancy the grave shift nurse?" Ann asked.

"She had to leave," Kim said. "Something about a family emergency."

"Okay then, I'll be there as soon as I can." Ann said. She hung up and rubbed her temples. Would this insanity ever end? She grabbed her coat and keys and headed out the door.

As Ann entered the infirmary, Kim looked stressed and pale. "It's no wonder that Celia is sick again. She hardly eats anything anymore. Most of the time, she never touches what we give her."

Ann frowned. She wanted to slap Dameon across the face. Was the money really worth the sanity of an innocent girl? Sonia had been sick a lot lately. She seemed to have given up hope that she would see Justin and her family again. She barely called out for them anymore.

"I'll call for you when I finish examining her," Ann said. Kim nodded and left.

Sonia lay on the table. Her lips were pale and her eyes were wet from crying. She looked thinner than ever. A piercing pain ripped through Ann's heart. She felt so sorry for the girl. She stared at her for a moment and watched as Sonia quietly talked to herself. Ann could do nothing but pray that Dameon would make everything right again as soon as possible.

Ann cleared her throat. "Hi, Celia," she said with a fake smile. "You don't look so good. I hear you don't eat much anymore. You need to keep your strength up."

Sonia stopped talking to herself and glazed at Ann. "Why? I don't want to eat, why should I eat? I don't know who I am. I don't know why I'm here. I don't know why everyone calls me Celia. I thought I was Sonia, I just don't understand. Please Ann help me." Sonia burst into tears.

Ann watched as the poor girl heaved and sobbed. She wanted to comfort her and mend her broken heart, but what could she possibly do? Ann gently placed her arm around Sonia's shoulder and allowed her to cry. "I believe you," she whispered.

Sonia stopped crying and rubbed her face with the back of her hands. She stared at Ann with her big, blue eyes, which were red and wet from crying. There was hope in those eyes. Could it be possible that someone actually believed her? Sonia felt her heart swell.

Ann swallowed the lump in her throat. She needed to stay on track with the plan. "I know you believe that you're Sonia, but I think I know what's wrong with you. You are suffering from a split personality condition. You're hiding behind a made-up person you call Sonia."

Sonia pulled away from Ann. "But Ann," she said through her tears, "that can't be true, I don't think I'm Celia, I feel like I'm Sonia, the name Celia just doesn't make any sense to me."

"I know you think you're Sonia, but it's all in your head. Your brain can do funny things, even making you believe that you're someone else. You made up Sonia because you don't want to be Celia anymore. You don't like what you've done. You killed your boyfriend, and you're trying to reinvent yourself as someone else to forget your past."

Sonia was so confused. She couldn't remember any of that. She got off the table and wandered aimlessly around the room. Who was this Celia person they spoke of? She didn't think she could ever kill anyone, and she couldn't even imagine killing Justin. Why would she kill Justin? She loved him too much. She cried out, "That's not true! It can't be true! You don't know what you're talking about! Why do I remember all the good times I had with Justin and my parents…" her voice trailed off.

Ann sat down so she wouldn't faint. "Because you've convinced yourself that you're another person. I'm going to give you a sedative to calm you down a little and something to get your fever down. Please think about what I've said. You have to believe me, Celia. You have to let Sonia go. Don't hide behind her anymore. If you want to become a whole person again, you have to let Sonia go and realize that you really are Celia. You had a traumatized youth. Your mother died when you were five years old and you lived in foster homes. You didn't get the love that you needed and that's why you fabricated a person who had a normal family life. And now, you believe it so much that you think it's your reality." Ann stood and grabbed a syringe from a nearby table.

But Sonia protested, "I have dreams that are so real, and I can see my mother and my father and Justin, and they're so real. I couldn't have made that up. How can it not be real if it feels so real?" Her voice cracked. She felt like she was on the verge of another breakdown.

"Sweetie, just trust me," Ann said as she stuck the needle into Sonia's arm. She didn't know what else to say or do. She felt hopeless.

Sonia cried and then her eyelids got heavy. She slurred her speech; the sedative was working. Ann called for Kim and another guard to take her back to her cell.

"Make sure you eat, Celia. You'll feel better," Ann said as the guards hauled Celia's limp body out of the infirmary.

Ann let the silence of the room overtake her thoughts. She sat down and leaned her head against the wall. She needed to talk to Dameon. After all of this, the money just wasn't worth it. Not even for her son, Mike.

She glanced at her watch and noticed she had spent too much time with Sonia. She needed to do some other work, but didn't feel like it anymore. Ann felt ill and actually decided to use it to her advantage and go home sick. She felt some relief as she walked out of the building. The fresh air did her good. As she got in her car, anger swirled through her body. She screeched out of the parking lot and knew exactly where she was headed: Dameon's house.

Ann parked the car crooked outside of Dameon's and stomped up the driveway. She pounded on the front door and waited for him to answer.

"Ann?" Dameon said in a shocked tone as he opened the door. He didn't expect her until later that evening.

"Let me in," Ann spat. "We need to talk." She didn't wait for Dameon to invite her in. She stormed past him and plopped on the couch.

"Sonia's not doing well. She's withering away to nothing. She's losing her mind. Did you even consider what this would do to her? What are you going to do about it?" Ann crossed her arms. Enough was enough. She needed answers.

"Calm down," Dameon said. He placed his hand on her knee. "Everything is going to be fine." He flashed her a smile. "I'm so sorry to put you through all of this, and I know it must be difficult seeing

Sonia every day, but everything is going to work out. I promise. Trust me; I don't want Sonia to be in jail any longer either."

Easy for him to say. He didn't have to see Sonia in her misery, Ann thought.

Dameon scooted closer to Ann on the couch. "Plans have changed a little, and I can't do much right now—"

"What do you mean plans have changed?" Ann asked with indignation.

Dameon chuckled to lighten the mood. Ann was upset, but he needed to ease her concerns. He rubbed her back. "I can't explain right now. Just know that I'm doing the best I can. I got you some money, at least." He searched through his briefcase and then handed her a thick envelope.

Ann grabbed the envelope with shaky hands. She flipped through the bills. Five thousand dollars. It was a lot of money, but Dameon had promised her a lot more. "Where's the rest?" she asked.

"Please, sweetie, have some patience. I'm still working on it, and the rest will come. You just need to have patience."

"When Dameon?" Ann snapped. "When do you think we'll have the big money?"

"I'm working on it Ann," he replied, "but it's not as easy as I had first thought." He patted her hands as she held the envelope full of money. "Trust me, it will come, and I managed to get five thousand dollars for you, didn't I? So, please, give me a little more time."

"Fine," Ann said. "But how long do you think it's going to take, and how long do I have to contend with Sonia in jail?"

"I don't know exactly," Dameon said, "it could be a couple of weeks or maybe even months."

"Months?" Ann questioned with astonishment. "I can't keep this up for that long."

"You have to, Ann," Dameon demanded. He tried not to sound irritated, but he couldn't help himself. "You have to. I will try to get it as fast as I can, but if I try too fast, people will get suspicious."

Ann saw that Dameon was getting upset and she didn't want to anger him knowing what he was capable of when he was consumed by anger. If she had to put up with Sonia to keep his anger at bay then she would, as hard as it would be for her to do so. "Okay Dameon," she said calmly. "Thank you for the money. I'll wait for the rest, but please understand what you're putting Sonia through."

She didn't wait for Dameon to respond. Instead, she stood up and walked out the front door without saying goodbye.

CHAPTER 32

Dameon met Celia at her new store. Celia had driven herself there; she was nervous, but the more she drove by herself the better. It was important that she felt comfortable behind the wheel. And, meeting at the store was safer because Justin wouldn't question her whereabouts. Celia would mention how Dameon was there to videotape the store's progress. It was a brilliant plan.

"How was driving here by yourself? Were you okay?" Dameon asked as Celia unlocked the door to her store.

"Yes, fine," Celia said a little shaky. "Did you bring your video camera?"

Dameon held up his bag. They entered the store. He wanted to make a video of the empty store so he had proof that he was there to videotape.

"From now on I want to meet here because if someone happens to see us, they won't be suspicious if they see us at your store."

Celia grinned. "Perfect."

"I'm working the morning shifts at the prison for the next few weeks, so I'll have the afternoons off to be with you." Dameon said.

"That's great." Celia said with a sigh of relief. She knew she needed as much driving practice as she could and she liked the idea of spending time with Dameon.

Dameon smiled and held up a driver's booklet. "I have just the thing for you. I want you to study it so you know what all the signs mean. But don't bring this booklet home because Justin might find it and wonder why you have it. Make sure you keep it here, and if Justin ever sees it, tell him it was left in a cupboard or something." Dameon took her in his arms.

"I will," Celia said as she flashed Dameon a seductive look.

Dameon knew that look and was more than willing to satiate her. Within minutes they were rolling on the hardwood floor. It was not comfortable, but neither of them seemed to mind.

Afterward, Celia giggled and looked around the empty room. She stared at the blinds on the windows. "Next time, promise me a hotel or a motel room, and make sure it comes with a bed."

Dameon laughed and kissed her cheek. There was something about this girl that was different than anyone he had ever been with. He shook the thought from his head because he needed to focus. "It's time for us to organize how we're going to get the most money out of Justin. This is my plan. I have a couple of connections. I can have this store made into something really nice for almost next to nothing, and then after that, I can get the inventory that you need at a major discount."

"How? Where are you going to get that?" Celia questioned.

He sweetly smiled. "Oh, sweetie pie, just leave that up to me." He held her warmly against him. "I need your bank account number and password."

"Why?" Celia asked surprised. "I should be the one writing out the checks don't you think?"

"Yes, you should and you will, but I want a backup plan just in case something goes wrong."

"What do you mean?" Celia asked with concern.

"Don't look so worried," Dameon said. He softened his voice and continued. "Everything's going to be fine, but you're impersonating Sonia and we have to keep in mind that someone could find out, and then we have to be ready for that."

Celia felt a twinge of distrust. "You told me that no one would ever find out because I'm such a damn good actress. So what do you mean someone might find out?" She glared at him, her blue eyes piercing.

"Don't look at me like that," Dameon said. "I'm almost getting the feeling that you don't trust me. We just finished making love. I'm starting to feel very close to you, and I wouldn't let anything happen to you. You have to believe me." Dameon paused for a moment and with the most convincing voice he said, "I think I'm falling in love with you."

Celia felt her heart stop. Never in her wildest dreams did she ever think that Dameon would actually mean those words. She thought she could clearly see that this time he was telling the truth. She didn't know what to make of it; she was starting to feel strongly about

Dameon as well. The sex was definitely superb—it was much better than with Justin. Because of her past, it was hard to trust anybody. She had to admit; Dameon had been very good to her and had not shown any disloyalty whatsoever. It was true; she was falling for him too.

"But what are we going to do if someone finds out?" Celia asked. "If I give you the bank account number then you can just take off with it, and no one will know that you were involved."

"Oh, believe me," Dameon said, "Everyone will know I was involved. Don't forget that Sonia saw me before we swapped her with you. You don't have to worry about me taking off on you. I wouldn't do that."

Celia tried to make sense of everything. "Okay then," she agreed. She wrote out the bank information and handed it to him.

"You have to tell Justin," Dameon said, "that you found out that things are a lot more expensive than you first thought. Tell him that the remodeling of the store alone will be over a hundred thousand dollars because of the materials. Just tell him that you didn't realize the materials were that expensive, and you want to make it a real chic boutique. Also, tell him that you looked into the cost of the most updated and fashionable bridal gowns and that you may have to go to Europe to get the latest fashions. Tell him you'll need accessories like handbags, hats, shoes, and jewelry. So, in other words, you need a lot more than you first thought. You need to ask him for another three hundred thousand dollars."

Celia huffed. "Wow, Dameon, I can never do that. That's asking a lot." She looked at him in disbelief. He really expected her to ask for all of that and fear balled into her stomach.

Dameon insisted. "You know that's why we got you out of jail. I want to get at least half a million dollars and I promised a large chunk of that to Ann. We have to go through with it, because if we don't, Ann might go to the authorities. She's coping with Sonia everyday and she says it's not easy. If Sonia gives her a hard time, then Ann might be tempted to go to the authorities if we don't come up with the money. If it was only up to me, then I would take you away from all this and we'd hide somewhere and start a new life together. But we can't do that. Because of Ann, they can find us, and then we're in real trouble. I have faith in you. I know you can sweet-talk Justin into giving you that money."

Celia was getting worried; she took a deep breath and then said, "You really think I can do that?"

Dameon took her back into his arms. "I really think you can. You're an incredible actress. I've seen it over and over. I know you can do it."

Celia suddenly felt comforted by Dameon's words. She had Justin in the palm of her hands, and he'd do anything for her as long as she played her cards right. "Okay," she said. "I don't want us to be found out. I'll do it tonight."

"That's my girl," Dameon said. He kissed her long and hard. "We better get going before the traffic gets too busy." They locked up the store, and each of them went into their own car and drove off.

*****

When Celia got home she parked the car in the garage herself. She was very pleased with how her driving was coming along. Usually she'd leave the parking for Jack, but this time no one was around, so she decided to try it herself and made it without a scratch.

As she walked into the house she heard Justin's car drive up their laneway. She was happy she got home just before him. Not that it mattered; she would have told him she was at the store. But now she could greet him like a good wife. She wrapped her arms around him and gave him a loving kiss. Justin was happy to see her and he welcomed the embrace.

Celia asked in a caring tone, "How was your day?"

"I'm tired," Justin said. "I've had a busy day. Something went wrong and we had to fix that first, and that took time away from what I was supposed to do. But it's all fixed now. I'm glad I'm home."

Celia gently rubbed his back. She wasn't sure if tonight would be the best night to ask Justin for more money. He didn't seem to be in the best of moods. So she told the cook to make Justin's favourite dinner—Hawaiian chicken with all the trimmings. She had found out it was his favourite meal on the honeymoon. It would certainly cheer him up a bit.

After dinner, Justin was more rested and relaxed, so Celia encouraged him to go for a walk with her. It was a beautiful evening, the sun was low on the horizon, and there was a gentle breeze rustling through the leaves on the trees. Celia sensed that Justin felt the happiness and love in the air.

They walked quietly hand-in-hand enjoying the beautiful evening and the peace and quiet. "How's the store coming along?" Justin asked.

Celia looked excitedly at him and said, "I'm so glad you asked! I'm so excited about it, but I've run into some difficulty. When I first started, I hadn't figured out all of the things that I needed. I never knew it was going to cost so much." She took a deep breath and squeezed his hand tighter. "Can I borrow more money? Like three hundred thousand? I know it's a lot, but I can make this work. I'll pay you back."

Justin remained silent for a moment. "Paying me back is not the important part. What's important is that you're happy. Are you sure you need more right away?"

"Oh yes, honey, I really want it to be just perfect when I open the store. I want everything ready to entice my customers to buy, buy, buy!" she said with a great big smile full of enthusiasm.

Justin looked at her with love in his eyes. "I'll give you the money, as you need it," he explained. "Just give me the bills as they come in and I'll write a check out for them."

Receipts! Celia hadn't thought of that. She needed to remain calm. She said in a soft voice, "I really appreciate that, honey, but then I still won't feel like this is my project. I really want to do this all on my own. It's very important to me. I want to prove to myself that I can do this. I know it's a lot of money, but I know I can do it and I'll pay you back with interest."

"All right then," Justin said with hesitation, but he gave in. He actually thought it was kind of cute that she was so adamant about doing everything on her own. "Okay, I'll transfer the money to your account tomorrow when I'm at work."

Celia squealed and spun around allowing her skirt to flare out. She giggled and fell into Justin's arms.

Justin kissed her lightly. "Make sure you don't overpay for things, and if you're not sure about certain things, please ask me. It might even be worth it to hire a project manager. He or she could save you a lot of money when you're building the interior of your boutique."

Celia hugged Justin tightly. "Thank you honey, that's a great idea. I'll look into hiring a project manager, and I promise to keep you up-to-date with what I'm doing." She kissed him on the cheek. "I love you, and I'm grateful for what you're doing for me. Thank you."

"Well," Justin laughed teasingly, "I'm not only doing this for you Sonia, but I'm doing this for me, too."

Fearing she got caught in a lie, she asked, "What do you mean, for you?"

He raised his eyebrows and winked at her. "Well, that's no secret is it? I want you to be happy so that you can make me happy."

Relieved, she fluttered her eyes. "Why Mr. Haines, are you trying to seduce me?"

"Now you're talking," Justin said as he picked her up and swirled her around.

"Okay, okay," Celia giggled, "Let's go home."

Justin put Celia back on the ground and they walked home. When they got home and to their bedroom, Celia put on some soft music and lit some candles while Justin made a drink for both of them. As she unbuttoned her blouse, she decided to show Justin just how happy she could make him.

CHAPTER 33

"Have you called your parents yet?" Justin asked.

It had been about a week and a half since the honeymoon, and Celia was very busy with the store and also unknowing to Justin, with Dameon. She was startled by Justin's mention of Sonia's parents.

"Was it today that they were coming home from their cruise?" he continued.

Celia froze and drew a blank. Suddenly she remembered that Sonia's parents were coming back today. Dameon had already explained to her that Sonia's parents were going on a cruise. They had booked it about a year ago, even before they knew about Justin and Sonia's honeymoon.

Mary would have wanted to be home when her daughter and new son-in-law got back from their honeymoon. She was even ready to change the cruise to some other time, but Justin and Sonia had insisted that they kept their date—it was going to cost them a cancellation fee and they didn't want them to do that.

Celia has known this from the beginning, but hadn't given it anymore thought because she was so preoccupied with everything else. She felt her heart pound in her chest. She tried to act casual. She wrapped her arms around Justin and said, "Yes, I know isn't it exciting? I'm anxiously waiting for their call, but they haven't called yet."

"Well, maybe you should call them," Justin said. He crinkled his brow in puzzlement. Why hadn't she done so already? "I think they'd probably like to see you," he said. He thought it strange; Sonia would usually go see or at least phone her parents right away. But she'd never even mentioned her parents at all, not on their honeymoon or since they came home.

He had noticed changes in Sonia. One thing he found odd was that she hadn't bought anything for her parents while they were away. She always bought them something. Maybe she was too preoccupied by the store to think about anything else. Still, it seemed odd.

"You're right," Celia said. "I should call them, but I don't have time right now because I have to go to the store. I'll do it when I come back."

"You have to go to the store now? Justin questioned. "It's almost six o'clock!"

"I know, honey," Celia said in her sweetest voice. "I know it's late, but I have a meeting with the contractor for the cabinets. This was the only time he could meet me, otherwise I'd have to wait another month, and I want to get it done. I really have to go, but I'll talk to my parents later, and maybe we can see them this Sunday." She pulled Justin closer.

Justin smiled and washed away his strange feelings. "Okay sweetheart, we'll give them a call when you get back from the store."

After giving Justin a quick kiss, Celia picked up her purse and walked toward the door. It was a good thing she had this appointment because now she had time to think, and she could talk to Dameon. It had totally slipped her mind, but of course she had to go and see Sonia's parents. She couldn't wait any longer. She was afraid of not being able to pull it off, that Mr. and Mrs. Wells would see that she was an imposter. So far she had fooled Justin, but could she fool Sonia's parents? She just had to make sure that visits would be short.

She turned around and said, "I told Martha to have dinner ready at nine o'clock. I should be back long before that, so we'll have time to call my parents before dinner." She winked and blew a kiss. "I love you honey," she added as she walked out the door.

*****

Celia met Dameon at the store. There was another man there, Vince, the cabinetmaker. Vince was taking some measurements and as soon as he was finished he left. When Celia and Dameon were finally alone, they eagerly fell into each other's arms, and kissed.

"I missed you," Dameon whispered.

"Me too," Celia answered sincerely. She was, however, a little less carefree than normal. Her thoughts were drifting back to meeting Sonia's parents. The drive over had her wondering if she was in over her head. "I got the money," she said, "and I had no problem getting it. It was like taking candy from a baby."

"That's great news," Dameon said relieved. "Ann is getting impatient. She's wondering why she only got five thousand dollars. I had promised her a lot more, so I need you to give me more money soon. Here's how we'll do it. You write out your first check for fifty thousand dollars. It's for a down payment for the store fixtures. Write the check out to Store Works, a business that I established a couple days ago. It's a business that helps people set up their own businesses from beginning to end. In other words, Store Works will manage everything for you, from building the interior, to decorating and buying the inventory."

"Wow," Celia said. "Is this a legit business?"

Dameon laughed. "I just made it up, but I set this business up legally." He conveniently didn't mention what name he used to start the business. Then he continued, "And you're my first customer."

"You're a genius, Dameon! Justin actually suggested I hire a project manager, so this is perfect!" Celia said.

"That's wonderful!" Dameon smiled.

"You made my day," Celia continued. "At least you took away one of my worries."

"What's the matter?" Dameon asked. He noticed that something was up with Celia when she entered the store. She didn't seem to be herself today. She was preoccupied with her thoughts. Looking intently at her, he started to grin.

"What are you smiling about?" Celia asked.

"You seem a little uptight and I was thinking that you're not your usual self today, but I guess you haven't felt like yourself for six weeks now." He laughed.

"Yeah, yeah you think you're funny," Celia said, "but I don't feel like joking right now." She turned her gaze away from him.

"What's up?" Dameon was sincerely concerned.

Celia swallowed a lump in her throat and stared at Dameon with her big, blue eyes. "I have to see Sonia's parents. I'm worried. Plus, I haven't felt very well the last few days. I've been sick a few times; my nerves are going crazy. My stomach and head hurt. And now Justin is pushing me to see Sonia's parents, and I just don't know if I can do that."

"Of course you can," Dameon said with confidence. "If you can be intimate with Justin and fool him, then seeing her parents should be a breeze. You've been doing great so far. Just stay in character and you'll be fine."

Then Celia said with a sigh, "I guess you're right."

"So far everything is going according to plan. And I promise that as soon as we feel someone getting suspicious, I'll make sure that your money is secure in an offshore account and we'll vanish. We'll disappear together." Dameon stroked her hand.

"We?" Celia asked. "But what about Ann? What are you going to do about her?"

"Don't you worry your pretty little head about that, just leave it up to me and I'll worry about Ann. You just concentrate on visiting Sonia's parents and convincing them that you're Sonia."

Celia nodded. She wrote out a check to Store Works and handed it to Dameon and then they left the store. On the drive home, Celia couldn't help but be consumed by her thoughts. She had made it this far, but meeting Sonia's parents made her stomach ache. She pulled the car into the driveway and walked through the garage. She felt dizzy. Her head pounded. She thought she might throw up. She clutched the walls for support and headed inside to her husband. Being Sonia was becoming tiresome.

CHAPTER 34

Justin and Celia were getting ready to go to Sonia's parents' home for Sunday dinner. Justin thought it was a little odd for his wife to get all dressed up. Usually she wore comfortable clothing when visiting her parents. Justin has been puzzled lately by her actions. He couldn't help but notice that she had changed somewhat. He couldn't quite pinpoint when, but he knew that the minor changes had occurred since they'd gone on their honeymoon.

Lately, Celia had been complaining that she wasn't feeling well. She was tired all the time. Justin had noticed a change, but he didn't want to push it or say anything. Maybe it was the stress of her new store or the fact that she had quit her job. He hoped he had done the right thing by giving her all that money. Maybe the boutique was too much responsibility and it was wearing her down. Yet, at other times, she seemed so happy. He didn't know what to think anymore.

Justin was ready and waiting downstairs. "Sonia, are you ready yet? Let's go. It's getting late."

"I'll be right there, honey." Celia answered. She checked herself one last time in the mirror and straightened out her dress. She smiled. She looked good and was very pleased. She looked a lot better than she felt. Her nerves had gotten the better of her this morning, causing her to throw up again. This acting gig was really upsetting her physically.

As she came down the stairs, Justin said, "Wow, you look beautiful. Your parents won't recognize you."

"Don't I always look beautiful?" Celia said in response. She was worried and hoped Sonia's parents wouldn't notice anything.

"Of course you do sweetheart," Justin said as he leaned over to give her a kiss and then ushered her out the door to the car.

On the way to Sonia's parents' place, Justin stopped in front of a flower shop.

"Why are you stopping?" Celia questioned.

Justin replied with a perplexed expression, "You usually like to bring them something. I thought flowers would be nice."

"Oh, of course honey, I'm sorry. Flowers will be fine. Thank you for thinking about it. I'm just not with it lately."

"I've noticed," Justin said. "What's the matter?"

Celia answered right away, "I don't know honey, I just haven't felt that well lately."

Justin was concerned. "Maybe we should go back home if you're not feeling well. Your parents will understand."

That sounded like music to Celia's ears, but she knew she had to go through with this sooner or later. "No honey, I haven't seen them since we got back and I've missed them. You go ahead and pick out a nice bouquet. I'll wait here."

"All right," Justin said. "You're sure you still want to go?"

"I'm sure, don't worry. If I don't feel well enough, then we'll just leave early."

He quickly kissed her cheek and disappeared into the flower shop. Upon his return, he held a small bouquet of mixed flowers.

"They're beautiful, Justin, thank you." She held the flowers on her lap. They were really lovely, but the smell made her feel nauseous. She leaned forward as if she were about to throw up. "I'm so sorry honey," Celia said as she leaned back again into her seat. "I don't know what's wrong with me."

Justin was beside himself. "That's it," he said, "I'm taking you home."

Celia quickly responded, "Oh no, I'll be fine. I feel much better now," she lied. "I want to see my parents. I really want to see them."

"Of course you do," Justin said as he passed her a bottle of water. Her complexion was pale. "Drink this and see if it makes you feel better." *What was wrong with her?* Justin was concerned. He had noticed lately, that she was feeling sick a lot. And then it hit him like a ton of bricks. "Maybe you're pregnant," he blurted.

With a shocked look on her face Celia said, "Oh no, I can't be pregnant! We took precautions." She looked out the window. She attributed her nausea to her nerves. "I'm fine, honey. Let's just go." Celia gulped the water and motioned for Justin to drive.

After about forty-five minutes, Celia saw a house in the distance that she recognized from the pictures Dameon had shown her. Celia had seen quite a bit of the outside of the house but not much of the inside. It was going to be a challenge to pretend that she was familiar with Sonia's parents' place. All she remembered seeing in the videos was Sonia's bedroom. Why hadn't Dameon taken more footage of this house? It was an important part of Sonia's upbringing.

As Justin drove up the driveway, her stomach tightened. This was going to be the most difficult part of all. She had never even seen these people other than on the video and some pictures. She needed to be totally convincing.

Justin had parked, unbuckled his seatbelt, and stepped out of the car. Celia was still sitting there staring at the house.

Justin opened her door. "Come on honey, what's the matter?"

"My stomach is just a little upset. Give me a minute," she said. Even though her nerves were spiraling out of control, she was thankful for Justin being there. She was really starting to like him and felt guilty deceiving him. He was a nice guy and didn't deserve this, but she was in too deep and had to keep on going with the charade.

"Come on honey," Justin repeated and then continued, "you look so tense."

Celia was feeling ill. She was sure it was just her nerves and that she wasn't pregnant, like Justin had suggested, but it did give her an idea to use that to her advantage.

"Honey, maybe I am pregnant." She saw the look on Justin's face soften. It was working.

He crouched down beside the car and took her hand. "Sweetheart, I love you. It would be wonderful if you were. It makes sense. Maybe that's why you've been a little out of it these days."

Beads of sweat dotted Celia's forehead. "Maybe. But let's not tell my parents anything yet, so we don't get their hopes up if I'm not. We'll figure it out later, and then tell them if I am. Okay?"

"Of course. Let's just say hello and we won't stay long."

"I'm anxious to see my parents," Celia lied. She got out of the car and followed Justin. Her hands were all sweaty. She was worried sick, but she had to pretend that everything was fine.

Celia was about to ring the bell, but thankfully, Justin opened the door. This was her parents' house, and she didn't need to ring the bell. They stepped through the front door. The show was about to begin.

"Hi mom, hi dad, we're here!" Celia called out. She was a nervous wreck. She glanced around quickly and spotted the door that would most likely be the bathroom in case she needed it.

Mary came rushing through the hallway and embraced Celia with a big hug and kiss. It was odd that her daughter had called her "mom," and not "mommy," but she ignored it. She was just happy to see her daughter.

Celia felt awkward. She hoped that Sonia's mother didn't notice anything different. While they embraced, Sonia's father shook Justin's hand. Celia then hugged Sonia's father.

"Well, you guys, good to see you! We've got supper ready," John said.

They proceeded to the dining room with Justin leading the way. They all sat at the table as Mary went to the kitchen to get the soup. Once Mary was seated, the conversation started.

"Tell us about the honeymoon!" Mary began.

Celia felt relieved to tell them about that because she had actually lived that experience. "Oh mom, you have no idea how beautiful it was." She went on and on about the beaches, and especially Maho beach, the uniqueness of it with the planes right there. The beauty of everything. The palm trees. The glittering water. The white sand. Justin talked about the fabulous food, the snorkeling adventures, and the cool night breeze. They also told Sonia's parents about running into Dameon there. They were surprised for sure. As the four of them chatted away the evening, Celia was positive that they didn't notice she was not their daughter.

*****

After Justin and Celia left, something was eating away at Mary. As she lay in her husband's arms she said, "Did you get the feeling that Sonia wasn't herself tonight?"

"No, what do you mean?" John asked.

"I don't know," Mary continued. "It was like she was in another world."

"I didn't notice," John said as he shrugged his shoulders. "I was talking to Justin a lot. It seems they had a really good time on their honeymoon."

"I know," Mary said, "but something is different. I can't put my finger on it. It was almost like she picked up a bit of an accent from the Caribbean."

John replied, "Well, they were there for a whole month."

"And did you notice how she called me 'mom?'"

"So?" John asked.

"She never calls me 'mom.' She always calls me 'mommy.' You know that."

John shifted in the bed and slid down on the pillow. "Honey, I think you're reading too much into things. I don't think you want to admit it, but our little baby is all grown up and married now. Maybe that's why you think she's different, but she's the same girl."

"Just do me a favor, the next time we see them, pay close attention to Sonia," Mary pleaded.

John chuckled. "All right. Now go to sleep please, everything is okay."

As they snuggled up Mary had a hard time falling in sleep. She furrowed her brow. She was happy for Sonia and she couldn't ask for a better son-in-law. But something didn't seem right. It was her eyes. They looked different, empty, scared. Something behind those eyes told Mary a different story.

CHAPTER 35

About a week and a half later, Justin and Celia went to visit Sonia's parents again. Mary was convinced that there was something not quite right with Sonia. She still had a bit of an accent, and she just wasn't as responsive as she normally was. Besides the fact that she called Mary "mom," she also refused to play the piano. Normally, she would jump at the opportunity to play, but claimed she didn't feel like it. Something was definitely wrong.

Not only that, her daughter looked different. Sure, it was the same girl, but her eyes seemed tired and lacked their usual spark. Maybe she was just tired from their honeymoon. The old saying went that you always needed a vacation after a vacation.

After Justin and Sonia had left, Mary expressed her concerns to John.

"She's married now," John said. "She's just changing a little. Kids do that. They have their own life."

Mary wined. "Well I miss the way she used to be." Without realizing it, there was sadness in her voice.

"I know you do, darling," John said. He grabbed her hand.

Mary couldn't stop thinking about it since Justin and Sonia's last visit. What was it about Sonia that was so different? Sure, people change, especially when they got married. It was as if the adult part of the brain kicked in. But something else was wrong and Mary was determined to find out.

"I think you're suffering from the empty nest syndrome," John teased. "It's not like we have any other children to fill the house."

That did it. Flashes of the bus accident raced through her mind. She remembered the reports and how the camera scanned the face of that little girl. And she'd looked so much like Sonia—big blue eyes, heart-shaped face, and blonde hair. Mary felt her heart pounding. For some reason, after all these years, she hadn't forgotten the face of that young girl.

"It couldn't be," Mary mumbled.

"What?" John said.

"Nothing," Mary said.

And that was when she decided to talk to Justin as soon as possible.

*****

At 9 o'clock the next morning, Mary rushed to Justin's office. She decided not to talk to John about it anymore until she was sure. She would feel very silly if her hunch wasn't right; it was a crazy idea after all, but she was worried.

As she walked through the doors of Haines International, she was in awe of how spectacular the building was. A petite girl sat behind the desk, stood up, and walked over to Mary.

"I'm Gwen," she said. "How may I help you?"

"Please tell Justin that his mother in-law is here to see him," Mary said.

"Sure thing," Gwen said and then pointed to a chair. "Please have a seat and I'll get him for you."

"Thank you," Mary said as she sat down.

A few minutes later Justin walked out from his office with a puzzled look on his face. "Hi Mom," he said as he greeted her with a smile and a kiss. "What are you doing here? Is something wrong?"

"Oh no, I just wanted to talk to you about Sonia," Mary answered a little embarrassed. What if her suspicion was totally wrong? Could she really make such a mistake about her own daughter? She had to be careful how she approached Justin.

"Come in my office," Justin said. He placed his hand gently on her back to guide her.

Justin closed the door and offered Mary a seat. He could see that his mother-in-law was concerned about something. "So what's on your mind, Mom?" Justin asked as he settled himself into his chair.

"Is it that obvious?" Mary asked with a shy smile. Was she doing the right thing by involving Justin? "I hope you don't mind," she spoke up, "but I just wanted to ask you about Sonia. I was wondering how she's doing because she seems to have changed a little after you came back from your honeymoon. She just doesn't seem to be herself. The last two times the two of you visited us, she was not quite her happy self. Have you noticed anything strange about Sonia?"

Justin was relieved to hear that he was not the only one who thought that Sonia had changed. "Well, she's not like she used to be when we went out together. I noticed it first on our honeymoon. She seems to have changed a little, but it's okay. She's just so busy with the store."

"Yes, that for instance," Mary interrupted. "We just found out a week ago, and she had already started it. That's not like her at all. She would have mentioned this idea to me a long time ago. Normally, she comes to me when she's excited about something and talks to me about it. She would have asked me to help her, but she never told me anything."

"Yes, I don't know either," Justin said. "I had my concerns initially. She wants to do this all herself. Maybe she wanted to talk to me about it first because it's costing a lot of money to get it started."

"So, you're giving her money?" Mary asked. She knew the answer to her question, but she had to ask anyway.

"Of course I am. I want to help her. But she's insisted that it's a loan. She wants to give it all back with interest. I told her that because we're married, my money is her money and she doesn't need to pay it back. But she insists on paying it back because she wants to prove that she can do it all on her own."

Mary sat back in her chair. She was surprised and didn't know what to think.

Justin had figured that if Sonia was pregnant, like he suspected, her hormones could be playing with her emotions, and maybe that was the reason for her change. She'd promised that she would take a pregnancy test, and made Justin promise that he wouldn't mention it to her parents. But, sitting across from Mary and seeing a concerned mother, he couldn't help himself.

"Please don't say anything," he said with a little hesitation, "but we think she might be pregnant. She hasn't been feeling well lately," he finished.

Mary was dumfounded. Pregnant? Of course this should be happy news, but why wouldn't Sonia want them to know? She suddenly felt so distant from her daughter. She choked back her tears and asked, "How long has she been feeling this way?"

"I can't really recall," Justin answered. "It could be a couple of weeks. I first noticed it when we went to visit you after you got home from your cruise."

Mary sat there trying to take it all in. She was trying to forget what she actually came to see Justin for, and to reset her mind into happy thoughts about Sonia being pregnant. "That would be so fantastic, having a grandchild," she said. But then she got worried again. What if her suspicion was right? She knew that Sonia loved children and if she were pregnant, Sonia would have known by now. Sonia would have told her long ago, even if she weren't sure herself. She would have been too excited to keep it a secret.

Mary crossed her legs and placed her hands in her lap. She thought about what she and John went through, how she couldn't get pregnant. Pain stabbed at her heart. She tried to show some excitement for Justin. "I'm happy for you, if that's what the two of you want."

"Well, we weren't really ready for a baby yet," Justin sighed. "But if she's pregnant, I'm sure we'll be very happy. But we haven't tried. We're actually trying to prevent it for now. We figure that we're still young and can wait before we start a family. Especially now because of the store, we don't really have time for a baby. And I know

Sonia doesn't want a nanny for the baby because she wants to raise it herself. We've been using protection." Normally he wouldn't tell Mary such intimate details, but it seemed fitting for the moment.

"Well, protection isn't always a hundred percent," Mary said, "but it's still strange that she hasn't talked to me about it." And because of that, Mary realized again that something wasn't right. She had conflicting feelings. She decided to tell Justin why she really came to visit him.

Mary continued, "I've noticed other things, but maybe it's because she hasn't been feeling well. For instance, I haven't heard Sonia play the piano at all since you came back from your honeymoon. You know how she loves to play for us. But when you were at our place for dinner, I asked her to play and she said she wasn't in the mood. I've never heard her say that before. She's always in the mood to play the piano. So, I don't know Justin, I'm a little worried. Will you do me a favor?"

"Yeah, sure," Justin answered.

Mary paused. She felt nervous and funny bringing this up, but she couldn't stop now. "I don't know how to ask you this, and you might find it a little odd, but I'd like you to do this for me. Can you have a look under Sonia's feet and tell me what you see please?"

Justin was puzzled by her strange request. "Why would you want me to do that?"

"Well, that doesn't matter," Mary said. "I know this sounds crazy, but will you please look under her feet. Offer to massage her feet or something."

"Okay," Justin said with a shrug of his shoulders not understanding why Mary would want him to do that. "What's this about?"

"Just a feeling I have," Mary explained. "Please do me that favour and I'll explain later."

Although, Justin found it a little odd, he trusted Mary and didn't want to upset her more, so he agreed.

"But don't let Sonia know," Mary warned.

"Why?" Justin asked.

"Please don't let her know; it's really very important," Mary pleaded. "Justin, we've known each other for years and we both want what's best for my daughter and your wife. I promise that I'll explain everything later."

"Okay, I'll be very discreet about it," Justin said.

Mary felt relieved. All she needed was a confirmation that the birthmark was on Sonia's foot and she could stop driving herself crazy. But fear lurched in her stomach. She hadn't even thought about what to do if Justin said the birthmark wasn't there.

CHAPTER 36

After a full day of shopping, Celia was tired. She plopped on the white leather chair and reclined. Her feet were throbbing.

"Want to go for a walk?" Justin asked. He had just gotten home from work. Mary had visited him that morning and he felt some guilt in not being able to tell Sonia about it. But, he had promised Mary he wouldn't say anything.

"Oh, honey," Celia moaned. Usually, she would jump up and welcome him home, but she didn't feel like it. Her feet hurt. "My feet are very sore from walking all day. I've been shopping for the store and I'm exhausted. Can we do it another night?"

"Okay," Justin said in a disappointed tone but realized here was the opportunity that Mary had suggested. He glanced at the bottom of her bare feet. He had no idea why Mary wanted him to check her feet. It seemed crazy, but he had to admit, Mary had him intrigued. "Your feet hurt, huh?" Justin said as he crouched on the floor.

"Yes, they do. I've been out shopping too long," Celia said with pain in her voice.

"Would you like me to give you a foot massage?" Justin asked with a smile.

Celia smiled back. "Oh honey, that would be great."

She stretched out her legs. While Justin massaged her feet he subtly looked for any marks, but there weren't any.

After a short time massaging his wife's feet, he felt himself getting aroused by her moaning. When he couldn't hold back any longer, he stood and leaned over her. His arms reached under her, and before she knew it, Justin had cradled her to his chest and was carrying her up the stairs. The thought of what Mary had asked him to do was no longer on his mind.

*****

A couple days later, Mary went to Justin's office again. Justin was glad to see her, and knew why she had come.

"Hi mom. Nice to see you again." He gave her a friendly hug. "Come into my office. Can I offer you some coffee?" he asked.

"That would be nice," Mary said, "but I'm really here to find out if you had a chance to look at Sonia's feet."

"I did." Justin said, "There's nothing under her feet. I hope that's what you wanted to hear. I don't understand why you wanted me to look in the first place. But no, there's nothing wrong with Sonia's feet.

Mary felt instantly paralyzed. It was true. Her suspicions were right. Her palms grew sweaty. She felt her vision narrowing. Suddenly, she fainted.

Justin quickly knelt beside her and felt her pulse. He sat her up and leaned her against the wall. "What's the matter Mom? Are you okay?" he said in a frantic voice.

Mary's voice was weak. "Justin, call John. Please call John." It was all she could muster before she fainted again.

Justin picked Mary up off the floor and sat her in a chair next to his desk. She was pale and sweating. He raced across the room and grabbed a glass of water. When Mary regained consciousness, he made her drink the water, and then called his father-in-law.

It took a few rings before John picked up the phone. "Hi Dad, Mom came to visit me at my office, and I don't know what's wrong with her, but she fainted, and right now she appears to be in shock. You better come over right away."

While Justin waited for John to arrive, he asked Gwen to fetch some orange juice and a damp towel. Mary seemed to be waking up a bit. Color was coming back to her face and lips.

"I feel so weak," she mumbled.

"Just sit here and relax. John is on his way."

Twenty minutes later, John burst through the door to Justin's office.

"I don't know what's wrong with her," Justin said. "She's just sitting there staring out the window. I can't get a word out of her. She appears to be in shock."

John rushed to Mary's side and held her tightly. After the embrace, John took Mary's face into his hands and made her look at him. She was as white as a ghost. "Mary, what's the matter?" he said. "Sweetheart, come on, tell me. What is it?"

Mary didn't say anything. She just sat there as tears continued rolling down her cheeks. "Sonia, Sonia, where are you?" she called.

"Sonia's at home," Justin said.

"No, Sonia's not at home," Mary said as she shook her head. Her body trembled with fear. "Where's Sonia?" she repeated over and over.

"Please, calm down, sweetheart," John said in a soft voice while he held her lovingly in his arms. "What's the matter Mary? Please calm down and tell me what's wrong."

Justin handed Mary a box of tissues. She blew her nose and gathered her strength. After a few moments, she stared directly into her husband's eyes. "John, you have to believe me. It's not Sonia. It's Celia, her twin sister."

Justin stared at Mary in shock. "What are you saying Mom? What are you talking about?"

"Yeah Mary, what are you talking about?" John echoed Justin's words.

Mary managed to stop crying. "I knew there was something wrong. I knew there was something odd about Sonia. She just wasn't herself. I couldn't figure out, but I knew something was not right, so I asked Justin to look under her feet." She looked at Justin, and then at John and continued. "Remember the 'S' on the bottom of Sonia's foot?"

"Yes, the birthmark." John said with growing alarm.

"It's not there," Mary sobbed.

"Of course it's there," John said in despair. "A birthmark doesn't just disappear."

"It's not there, John," Mary shouted as tears filled her eyes and rolled down her cheeks.

Justin stammered, "It's true Dad. I looked under her feet. There's no birthmark." He stood back. His mind was racing. He didn't really know what was happening, but he knew something wasn't right.

John rubbed his head with his hands not knowing what to think. "I hope you're wrong, Mary. I noticed a slight change in Sonia, but I just thought that once women get married, they change. It's a natural process. But, sweetheart, do you really think...?" John continued as he looked into Mary's eyes.

"Yes," Mary explained as she tried to calm down. "John, remember? A long time ago, when Sonia was around five years old. That bus accident. There were only three survivors and one of them was a little five-year-old girl who was traveling alone with her mother, she looked so much like Sonia. I've never been able to forget her. Her mother had died in the accident. It may be a little far-fetched, but I vividly remember seeing that little girl. She reminded me so much of our Sonia." Mary sat up with a crazed look in her eyes. "What if that five-year-old little girl was Celia, and if it was, who knows what happened to her? She might have found out that she had a twin sister and when she had an opportunity, switched places with her. But when and how could she have done that? Why..." Mary's started to get even more panicky, her eyes wide as saucers. "Where's Sonia? Where's my little girl?" she screamed.

Justin was still in a state of horrific awe.

John tried to pull himself together. His body was shaking. "We'll find Sonia, okay? We have to go to the police. We can't let Celia know that we know she's impersonating Sonia."

Justin ran his fingers through his hair and shouted, "Can someone please tell me what you are talking about? Who's Celia?"

"Celia was the name of the other baby," John said.

"What other baby?" Justin asked. "What are you talking about?"

John sighed. "Sonia is a twin and we adopted her. You know that we adopted her, right?"

"Yes, I know you adopted her," Justin said, "but I didn't know she was a twin. You never told me that."

John continued explaining, "Sonia was one of twins. Celia stayed with her mother. The adoption agent, Sylvia, made arrangements for us to meet the baby's mother, Anna-Marie, before they were born. We knew she was going to have twins. Anna-Marie named her girls Sonia and Celia. She chose to keep Celia and we were blessed to get Sonia. The girls were identical, the only difference being the birthmark. We never told Sonia that she was a twin."

Justin couldn't believe what he was hearing. He felt his stomach lurch. He was with Celia all this time on a honeymoon and he didn't know. He was appalled that someone could possibly do this, and angry with himself for not noticing that she wasn't his wife. He felt sick to his stomach at the thought of going home.

"I can't go home now," he said, "knowing what I know. I don't know what to do."

"You have to go home and pretend that you don't know anything," John said, "Otherwise, you'll give it away. If this girl suspects anything, we may never see Sonia again." He swallowed a lump in his throat and held back his tears. "I'll go to the police. We have to be very careful about this because we can't have Celia suspecting that we know something. For now, we have to pretend that Celia is Sonia until we know what the police want us to do."

John could see that Mary and Justin were losing their senses. He had to remain calm. "I'm going to go to the police right now. Justin, can you drive Mary home and stay with her until I get there?"

"Sure," Justin said while trying to gather his thoughts. He thought of Celia at home, in his house, in his bed. He thought he would throw up. Sonia's face flashed before his eyes. Her beautiful smile, her lips, her kind eyes. He would find her no matter what.

CHAPTER 37

After about 10 minutes into the drive to the police station, John's emotions began to creep up and he started to shake. Normally, he was very calm, cool, and collected. He could usually keep his emotions at bay when he needed to, but he couldn't control his shaking now. Tears were very close to the surface. He told himself not to fall apart, especially while he was driving. He had to be strong even though he was worried and very upset. He arrived at the police station and went inside.

There was a woman behind the reception desk. "Can I help you sir?" she asked.

"Yes, I need to speak with whoever is in charge of missing persons," John said in a shaky voice.

"Certainly" the receptionist said. "How long has this person been missing?"

"I think two months, but we're not sure. We don't really know when she came into our lives, but we just noticed after their honeymoon that she had changed." He was speaking so quickly it probably didn't make much sense.

The receptionist gave him a puzzled look. "Sorry sir, now you're getting me confused. First you're telling me that someone is missing, and then you're telling me that she's back, but she's changed?"

John started to cry. He couldn't hold it in any longer. "We just found out," he said through his tears.

"Calm down, sir. I'll get you something to drink," the receptionist said. She handed him a glass of water and a box of tissues. "Please have a seat."

John sat down. He had held it together in Justin's office, but now, in the presence of these strangers, he let himself go. The receptionist excused herself.

A couple of minutes later, a tall man approached John. "Hello, I'm Sergeant Jeff Wright." He extended his hand. "Please step into my office."

John followed him into a small, brightly lit, tidy room and took a seat.

"I'm in charge of the missing persons division," Jeff said. "Can you fill me in on what's happening?"

John struggled to calm himself down, but he was able to explain in full detail as much information as he could. He started from the beginning—the adoption of Sonia, one of twins, and the birthmark being the only difference between the two. He explained where they adopted her and who the mother was.

Jeff wrote down all the information. "Do you have a picture of Sonia?"

John always carried a picture of his daughter with him. He carefully pulled a smiling photo of Sonia from his wallet and handed it to Jeff.

While staring at her picture, Jeff mumbled quietly, "I've seen this girl before. Where have I seen her?"

"You've probably seen her in the paper when her wedding was announced a couple months ago. She's married to Justin Haines, the son of Simon Haines, our mayor. There was a big thing about it in the paper."

"That's it, of course," Jeff said. He looked at John with kind eyes. "We'll find her, sir. I'll make sure of that. You should go home now, and don't speak to anyone about this until we've done our investigation, especially not around Celia. You need to make sure that you carry-on normally so she doesn't know anything is up. We definitely don't want the papers to get a hold of this because that will hurt our investigation. So please, act as if nothing has changed. All you can do right now is go home and be with your wife. Wait there and I'll contact you as soon as we have more information." He reassured John again. "We will find her."

"Thank you officer," John said, still drying his face with a tissue. "I'm such a mess right now, I'm so embarrassed."

"Don't worry, Mr. Wells. I would be too if my daughter was missing," Jeff said. "Go splash some cold water on your face and try to clear your mind. You can sit in the waiting room until you feel able to drive home, okay?"

"Thank you," John said. He nodded, went to the bathroom and after calming himself down, left the station.

Thoughts of Mary flooded in his mind on the drive home. By the time he arrived home, he had composed himself for Mary's sake. He found Mary and Justin in the kitchen. Justin was trying to make Mary drink some tea, but Mary was too upset to take a sip.

John stared at Justin. "They'll find Sonia. For now the police officer said we have to act normal. You have to go home and act as if nothing has happened. Do you understand, Justin? It's very important that Celia doesn't know that you know who she really is."

Justin felt his face flush. "I don't know how I can do this," he said in a panicky voice.

"You have to!" John insisted. "For Sonia's sake."

*****

That night, when Justin came home, Celia was right there to sweetly greet him. Justin tried to respond in his usual way, but he didn't feel believable. Celia, however, didn't notice. She was too involved with her own schemes.

Once they sat down for dinner, she noticed that Justin wasn't eating. "What's the matter honey, aren't you hungry?" she asked.

Justin stared at her. She looked so much like Sonia. He felt anger swirl through him. How could he be so oblivious? "I'm not very hungry, I'm just very tired. Something went very wrong today at work. I'll have to work a lot the next few days. I have to go back in tonight, I may even have to stay there all night." he lied. He wanted to be anywhere but near Celia.

Celia protested, "But honey, you said that you were tired."

"Yes, and I am," Justin sighed. He couldn't look her in the eye. But, he had to pretend that he loved Celia. He mustered all his love for Sonia and continued. "I'm so sorry, sweetheart, but it can't be helped."

Celia thought it strange that Justin would be staying at the office. He had never done that before, but she was actually happy with the prospect of having an evening or maybe even a whole night to herself. She was getting restless with this whole situation—acting like Sonia—and just wanted to spend more time by herself and with Dameon, not Justin. "It's okay, I understand," Celia said. She turned on the charm with flirting eyes. "But you don't have to leave right now, do you?"

Justin felt like he would throw up. The thought of being intimate with someone other than his wife made his heart hurt. "I'm afraid so," he mustered. He looked at his watch. "I didn't realize it was this late already. I'm sorry, but I have to go now to prepare for this conference call." He quickly got up and kissed her on the cheek. He stormed out of the house without looking back.

As he drove to the office, all he could think about was Sonia. He thought about going to Sonia's parents instead of the office, but what if Celia phoned the office and he wasn't there? He drove on, the road becoming a blur.

He needed to be by himself right now. So many things flooded through his mind. He now understood why Celia wanted a bank account right away, and why she wanted to handle the store all by herself. She didn't want him to know her business. What were her plans with the store and the money he had given her? How could he have been so stupid?

By the time he got to the office, the rain was beating down on his car, and like the rain he was sobbing like a child. He didn't care; no one was there to see him. "Oh Sonia," he cried. "Where are you? I love you. We'll find you sweetheart. I won't stop until I have you back."

He pounded his hands on the steering wheel in anger. He felt so guilty and angry for not noticing that this girl wasn't his wife. He had sex with her. The thought of it made his stomach churn. He swung the car door open just in time, as the rain poured down on his head.

Rain slapped the asphalt. Justin didn't care; he got out of the car and just stood in the rain and allowed the wetness to overtake him. The water splashed his face. He lifted his head up to the sky and opened his mouth. He needed to be cleansed.

*****

Jeff Wright sat at the dining room table, pondering the story that Mr. Wells had told him earlier. It had been a long day. His dinner sat in front of him getting cold. Suddenly it hit him.

"I've got it," he said. "I've got it." He excitedly stood up from his chair. "I think I know where I've seen her!"

Melissa, Jeff's wife, looked up at him, "Got what?"

Jeff stood up and started pacing around the room. After Mr. Wells had left his office, he had gotten everything into motion, but nothing came up. He hadn't been able to get anywhere with the case, so he had decided to go home, have some dinner, and see if he could clear his mind. He could still see the anxiety in Mr. Wells' eyes when he told him about his missing daughter. Jeff couldn't even begin to imagine how he would feel if it had been his own daughter. Of course, Jeff had to deal with missing people all the time, but he couldn't describe it—there was something different with this one. Maybe it was the fact that a fellow father had shown him such raw emotion and fear, or maybe it was the thought of his own wife being impersonated by someone else and how horrible that would be. He didn't know which, but he knew that he felt compelled to find the mayor's missing daughter-in-law.

The picture of Sonia burned a hole in his pocket. Where had he seen this girl? And then, out of nowhere, it had hit him. He had seen her face in a mug shot. A while ago, his coworker, Officer Quinn, had shown him a picture from a case he was working on.

"What is it Jeff?" Melissa asked still confused by her husband's strange behaviour.

"You know that missing girl I told you about when I got home? I think I know where she is. I have to be careful, though. Quinn mentioned something about one of the inmates resembling the Mayor's to-be daughter-in-law. I hadn't thought much of it then, but now it makes sense. I need to make sure I'm absolutely right before I get this thing rolling."

He took a deep breath. "I think Sonia's in jail."

CHAPTER 38

Sonia was sitting in the prison's kitchen peeling potatoes with a peeler since she wasn't allowed to handle knives. That, and working in the laundry room folding towels, seemed to be the only two things that Sonia was allowed to do. Her instincts told her how to do things, but her mind wasn't with it anymore. The poor girl was so mixed up and drugged.

The guards and her cellmates noticed that Celia had changed. She walked around in a catatonic state, and she didn't mention the name "Sonia" anymore. She seemed to believe that she was really Celia. It was as if she accepted her fate.

But, Sonia still cried herself to sleep every night. She was scared and couldn't understand why people said that she had stabbed and killed her boyfriend. She wouldn't kill Justin. She loved Justin. She didn't understand why she would have killed him, but people kept telling her that. She didn't know what was real anymore.

Strangely enough, her dreams were real. Justin appeared to her every night. She felt his hand brush her cheek and rub her back. She heard his voice. She fell asleep feeling his arms around her, but when she awoke, he was gone.

She dreamt of her parents. Her mother sitting by the poolside, laughing and sipping wine. Her father hammering a nail into the wall. And the piano. She would mimic playing, her fingers dancing in mid-air, grazing over the white, ivory keys.

Where did everyone go? How did she end up here? Were these dreams just a figment of her imagination? Was it possible that this alternate life never really existed?

But it was all so real!

Ann made sure to keep Sonia in a medicated state at all times. It was the only way Sonia would cooperate. So, Sonia just sat there, peeling potatoes. She didn't say much anymore, and the nurses started to feel sorry for her. Ann felt torn. No matter what she did, it didn't take away the guilt.

A guard approached Sonia and told her to come with her. She placed the peeler down on the table and stood. Sonia didn't know what was going on. She just did what she was told. She followed the guard to the warden's office.

The guard opened the door, and Sonia saw two men. One man sat behind a desk wearing a uniform. He looked very uptight. The other man stood in front of the desk, closer to the door, and he looked friendly and relaxed.

The friendlier one walked up to her and reached out his hand as she entered. "I'm Jeff Wright. I'm here to talk to you."

From behind the desk, Dameon said, "Take a seat Celia." He turned to the guard and said, "You can go now. I'll call for you when I need you to take her back."

After the guard left, Sonia sat down and looked around the room. She didn't recognize anything in this room except for the uptight man behind the desk. He looked very familiar to her, but she couldn't figure out why. Everything was so mixed up in her head. She sat there like a zombie, wondering what they wanted with her.

Jeff could see that something was very wrong with Sonia. Her eyes were vacant. He assumed she was medicated. He knew he had to be careful not to upset her. He had come to see the bottom of her feet. Jeff turned to Dameon and asked, "Can you have her take off her socks and shoes please?"

"That's an odd request," Dameon responded nervously.

"Yes, I know, but I need to see her feet," Jeff confirmed. After researching it with Officer Quinn earlier that morning, they had discovered that the mug shot he had remembered last night, was Celia Winters, which he now knew to be Sonia's twin sister. He had started the necessary paperwork, and with the help of John and Mary Wells, he found everything that he needed. As soon as he had all of it in order, he made the appointment with the warden at the jail. And now, here stood Sonia in front of him.

Dameon shifted in his chair. He had been nervous ever since Jeff had phoned to make an unexpected appointment to see Celia. *Why did the detective want to see her?* He couldn't deny him meeting Celia. It would look too suspicious. But he had his guard up.

Normally, visitors would see prisoners in the visiting room, but Jeff had made a special request to meet Sonia in a private area. Jeff didn't want to take the chance of anyone seeing him look at Sonia's feet. He preferred that even the warden wasn't present, but knew that was impossible to arrange.

"Celia, please take off your shoes and socks," Dameon said. His voice cracked.

Sonia did as she was told. She slowly took each shoe and sock off and neatly placed them beside her feet. Jeff walked over and lifted up Sonia's feet, one at a time.

And there it was. The S-shaped birthmark. It was really Sonia, just as her parents had told him. He was excited that the case was on its way to being solved, but somehow, someone had switched them. Who was it? Right now, he couldn't react on his feelings. He had to stay straight-faced and pretend that he didn't find what he was looking for. For all he knew, someone working in the prison could have arranged the switch.

"You may put your socks and shoes back on," Jeff said. He turned to Dameon. "I can't find what I'm looking for. You can send Celia back to her cell."

Dameon nodded. Sweat beaded his forehead. He called for a guard, and within minutes, Sonia had left the room.

"I would have a doctor look at her if I was you. She doesn't seem well mentally. Perhaps she should be in a mental hospital instead of here."

"I know," Dameon replied. "She's always been like that, but she's fine. She killed her boyfriend, you know. Apparently, they had been drinking a lot that night and one thing led to another. She stabbed him. No wonder she's like that. I would probably go insane, too. But, she's fine. She does her job and goes back to her cell when she's told to. She's very quiet and doesn't give us any trouble."

Jeff noticed that the warden spoke with some tension in his voice. It was as if he was nervous about something.

"Sorry you couldn't find what you were looking for, but if I can do anything to help, please let me know," Dameon said.

"I'll do that," Jeff promised. He leaned over and shook Dameon's hand. "You've helped me enough already. Thank you."

As Jeff left the prison he couldn't stop thinking about the warden and how he couldn't make eye contact. A sure sign of something to hide. But first, he needed to focus on how to get Sonia out of jail.

*****

After Jeff had left the office, Dameon sat there. His heart pounded. He was sweating through his shirt. That was a close call. What was he looking for under her feet? Did Sonia have something on her feet that Celia didn't? Did somebody find out that Celia was an imposter and went to the police? Someone might have found out that there was a girl in jail that looked just like Sonia.

Uncontrollable thoughts flew through Dameon's head. He knew that something was up and he'd have to do something. They would find out sooner or later. He wasn't ready yet. He had planned to quit his job and take off with the money, but not before he was ready.

Now, he needed a new plan. He couldn't quit his job; he needed to be here. Should he warn Ann? Maybe it was better not to warn her. She might get to nervous and say something. He wasn't sure what he was going to do.

He threw his pen across the room and slammed his desk with his fists. Maybe he should contact Celia and let her know. But, if Celia knew, she might not be able to act like Sonia. Or maybe she might flee with all the money. He was glad that he had asked Celia for the bank account number and password because he knew this was going to happen. It was just a matter of time.

And that was what Dameon needed. More time. He pretended to be sick and left the office in search of a new plan.

CHAPTER 39

The guard brought Sonia back to the kitchen where she was told to continue peeling potatoes. Sonia thought about her visit to the warden's office; she couldn't get that man's face, the one behind the desk, out of her mind. She thought she'd seen him before somewhere, but then again, it was probably just her imagination.

"Ouch," she said as the potato peeler slipped and gashed her finger. She placed her finger in her mouth and tasted blood. Why did that man want to see her feet? Blood gushed out of her finger, down her hand, and onto her clothing. She didn't seem to notice.

"You're bleeding," the guard said. "Let's go to the infirmary."

Sonia looked at her hand and it was covered in blood but she didn't feel any pain. She was led to the infirmary.

Ann happened to be there when Sonia walked in. "What happened?" she asked.

"She cut her finger." The guard explained. "She hasn't been paying much attention the last hour since they talked to her in the Warden's office."

Ann looked surprised, and then started to tremble, hoping the guard wouldn't notice. *What happened in the warden's office?* She wanted to contact Dameon to find out but it would be too suspicious with the guard there. She had to wait until later and play it cool. She'd deal with Sonia first. "Well, let's take care of that finger," Ann said with a forced smile.

Ann put on some rubber gloves, then examined Sonia's finger. She disinfected the wound then dressed it in gauze. "So what did the Warden want?" Ann asked Sonia pretending to be congenial with her patient.

But Sonia didn't hear her at first. She was staring off into space. Then feeling Ann work on her finger, she came back to the present and recalled Ann's question as she looked around the room. With a quizzical tone to her voice she answered, "There was an officer there who asked me to take off my shoes and socks."

"He did?" Ann exclaimed. Then recovering from her surprise, she glanced at the guard and continued with, "So why did he ask you to do that?"

"I...I...I don't know. He asked me to take off my shoes and socks, and then he looked at my feet." Sonia seemed just as puzzled as Ann felt.

Ann blinked quickly. *What was the officer looking for?* "Would you like me to take a look for you. See if there is anything wrong that I can maybe help you with? Do you want to take off your shoes and socks for me?" she asked in a sweet voice pretending to be concerned for her patient.

Without a word, Sonia started taking off her shoes, but it was difficult for her with a bandaged finger so Ann helped her. *Was there something on Sonia's feet that was different from Celia's?*

Once the shoes and socks were off, Ann had a good look. Nothing unusual, but then, just as she was about to help Sonia put her sock back on one of her feet, she noticed a small S-shaped birthmark slightly hidden under her big toe. Thoughts flooded her mind and her heart pounded loudly. *That must be what the officer had been looking for.*

"Well there's nothing wrong with your feet dear. You're okay, so I wouldn't worry about it." Ann pretended to reassure Sonia as she quickly helped her put her socks and shoes back on, and then told the guard, "Celia's okay now, her finger will be fine and there's nothing wrong with her feet. I don't know what they were looking for. You may take her away now." To Sonia she added, "If your finger bothers you, just ask the guard to let me know."

Ann couldn't wait for them to leave.

Celia was done peeling potatoes for the day; she was escorted to the laundry room instead. With her finger bandaged up, she fumbled as she folded towel after towel until it was time for dinner. After the evening meal, she went straight to her cell. She wanted to be alone. She had too many things on her mind and her finger still hurt. Sonia sat on her bed, trying to understand why everyone was so interested in her feet. What were they looking for?

She was very puzzled about the Warden. He had a familiar face. She was sure she had seen him before, but where?

Whether she knew the man or not, the day haunted her. She looked on the bottom of her feet and rubbed her soles with her hands. What was so special about them?

*****

Ann was a nervous wreck. *Had someone found out that Celia was impersonating Sonia? Were they trying to find her?* She felt sick. She was angry for letting Dameon talk her into this. *How could I have been so stupid? If I didn't have to worry about Mike, then I would never have agreed to this.* She felt antsy and couldn't wait any longer. She decided to go over to Dameon's office.

Tom was in Dameon's office. "Where is Warden Smith?" she asked. "I need to speak with him."

"I'm sorry," Tom answered, "but Warden Smith went home. You just missed him. He left about a half an hour ago. He wasn't feeling very well. Can I be of any assistance?"

Ann replied as calm as she could. "No, thank you. I really need to speak with the Warden, but it can wait until tomorrow." She excused herself and left the office, feeling even worse. She was pretty sure why Dameon had gone home sick. She felt like going home herself. She was feeling sicker by the minute. But she couldn't do that. It would look too suspicious.

As she ambled down the hallway, she couldn't help but wonder if Sonia had recognized Dameon as the photographer at her wedding. She shook the thought from her head. If Sonia had recognized him, she would have said something. The drugs were obviously still working.

When Ann got back to her office, she buried herself into her work to keep her mind occupied. She only had three hours left. She could make it.

After her shift was over, Ann drove straight to Dameon's house. She stormed up his front lawn and pounded on the door.

"Ann, what are you doing here?" Dameon asked as he opened the door. He saw the worried look on her face. "I'm glad to see you, though. I was just going to give you a call. I knew you'd be almost home now."

"You went home sick," Ann replied. "I was worried about you."

Dameon faked a calm and relaxed smile. "Well, no need. I feel better now. That was nice of you to worry about me sweetie pie."

Ann was on the verge of a breakdown. "You don't have to act as if you invented the word calm because I can see that you're very worried. You went home after you saw the officer who came to see Sonia's feet. You better tell me what you know and how we can get out of this." She started to cry and angrily pointed at him. "I should have never let you talk me into this. We're in big shit now aren't we?"

"No, Ann, calm down," Dameon said. He led her into the living room and shut the front door. "I have everything under control. I was going to give you a call. I have good news for you."

The first thing Dameon did when he got home was take care of the money in Celia's bank account. He'd transferred all of it on to an offshore account, which he had under an alias name. He had received quite a few checks from Celia, which he had put on his Store Works business account. He had already taken a lot of that out in cash and been storing it at his house just in case. He'd known an emergency like this could happen, and he had wanted to be prepared.

"What's your good news?" Ann said stifling her tears. Within seconds she noticed Dameon's suitcase on the floor. She gritted her teeth. "So, you're about to take off on me again, aren't you? Is that the good news?"

Dameon tried to calm her down. He handed her a fat manila envelope. Her trembling fingers reached out and took the envelope. When she opened it, she saw bundles of money bound with elastic bands. She couldn't believe her eyes. While still in shock, she asked, "How much is this?"

"Fifty thousand," Dameon smiled.

Ann felt slightly relieved. Maybe this would all work out. This would be enough to get Mike started in the rehab centre. "I'm sorry, but I was just so upset and worried. I guess I wasn't thinking straight." Then she continued, shaking like a leaf, "But what are you doing with that suitcase?"

Dameon wrapped his arm around Ann's shoulders and led her to a chair. "Calm down sweetie pie. Have a seat. I have a plan."

Ann could feel what was coming. He was about to take off again, and it could be for a couple of months or maybe years. He'd done it before. Right before Mike was born. She'd never told Dameon that he was the father. He wouldn't have believed her anyway. His suitcase stood ready in the hall and she knew he was about to take off again. What could she do?

Ann started to cry again and through her tears she said, "I'll go home and pack my suitcase and go with you." *But what about Mike? He's only just 16 now, I can't leave him!* She could hardly think straight.

"No, Ann," Dameon said, "You have to stay calm. You're right, there was an officer there today, an investigator who wanted to look at Sonia's feet. I'm not sure why he was so interested in her, or why he wanted to see her feet, but I want to be prepared in case he's figured out that Sonia and Celia were switched. I have to warn Celia, and I'm going to take her away somewhere. I'll have to hide her for a little while. When the coast is clear, I'll let you know where I am. By that time, I'll have a lot more money for you, but for now, I need you to go back to work like nothing happened. You need to stay here for Mike. You can't just leave him. You need to act like nothing has changed. Can you do that for me? Just don't say anything, and no one will ever know that you were even a part of it all."

Ann sat there, shaking and crying. "I can't go back to work! They're going to find out that I was involved, I just know it."

"No, Ann, nobody will suspect that you had anything to do with this. But they most likely will suspect me because I was Justin and Sonia's photographer." His eyes scanned the floor. *I should have used an alias and a disguise. I'm usually more careful than that. How could I have been so stupid?*

Ann sobbed uncontrollably.

He looked Ann straight in the eyes. "This is not your problem, Ann. You have nothing to worry about. Just go back to work like nothing's happened. You'll be fine."

Ann started to calm down a little, but then realized that Celia knew who she was. "Celia knows who I am!" Ann screamed.

"That's why I'm taking her away," Dameon said. "Don't worry about Celia. I'll take care of it."

Ann could do nothing but pray and hope that she trusted Dameon enough to get her out of this situation. She unwillingly left and headed back to work the next day.

It was only a matter of time before everything was exposed.

CHAPTER 40

When Jeff returned to his office, the first thing he did was phone Mr. and Mrs. Wells. He told them he had found Sonia. He wanted the two of them to come to his office tomorrow.

"Why not today?" Mary cried with emotion. "I want my baby back today."

"I know, and I'm very sorry," Jeff said, "but I need to take things easy. She's safe, but we have to be very careful. We don't want the people who made the switch to know that we're on to them. We want to make sure that we find those people before they get wind of our investigation and flee. So for now, we can't risk moving too fast. I have to make sure all the pieces are put together right or we may just lose the people responsible for this. Don't fret! I'll be working all through the night to make this right. Sonia is fine, you don't need to worry, I saw her myself, and she'll be all right until tomorrow. Please meet me in my office at 10 o'clock tomorrow morning."

Mary and John couldn't understand why it would take that long and they were anxious to see their daughter.

Jeff didn't tell Mr. and Mrs. Wells that he found Sonia in a prison because that would worry them even more. He would have to get the proper release papers, which would take some doing. He also wanted to make sure that Sonia had a good night's sleep before he took her out of her environment. Because of her mental state, he needed to be gentle with her. He also wanted to talk to Mr. and Mrs. Wells in his office and prepare them for Sonia's mental state.

Like the past few days, since Mary had realized that Celia had been impersonating Sonia, Mary couldn't sleep that night, all she could do was cry. She was so worried! But unlike the past few days now her crying was filled with hope not fear. Jeff had found their daughter. Still, she didn't understand why they couldn't get Sonia back right away. *I want to hold my baby.*

Millions of questions flashed through her mind. Where was Sonia? John wrapped Mary into his arms in their bed and lay there also unable to sleep. All they could do was wait.

CHAPTER 41

It was nine o'clock in the morning when the doorbell rang. Martha, the maid, opened the door.

"Good morning ma'am," Jeff greeted. "I'm Jeff Wright and I'm here to see Mrs. Haines. Is she home?"

"Oh, I'm sorry, but Mrs. Haines left last night, and as far as I know, she hasn't returned yet. But, I'll double check. Give me a moment please. You may wait here."

"Is Mr. Haines home then?" Jeff stopped her before she went off to see if she could find Mrs. Haines.

"He's not home. He's at his office. He told us he wasn't coming home for a couple days. Apparently, they're very busy at Haines International and he was going to sleep there whenever he could get a few hours."

Jeff suspected that Justin was intentionally staying away because of Celia. He also suspected that Celia had taken off because someone must have warned her about the investigation. That could only have been someone who worked at the jail.

Martha interrupted Jeff's thoughts. "I'll go now and have a look to see if I can find Mrs. Haines for you." But as soon as she had said that, they both heard a noise coming from the garage.

Since

"Oh," Martha said, "That might be Mrs. Haines."

But instead, they saw Justin walked into the foyer from the garage. Neither of them had heard Justin's car coming up the laneway.

Justin wondered whom the man was standing in his front hall so early in the morning. He had noticed a very nice car in his driveway, so he knew that someone was visiting. "Who might you be?" Justin asked extending his hand.

"I'm Jeff Wright, sir," Jeff answered. "I'm the investigator. Your father in-law came to see me two days ago," he said quietly. He still wasn't sure if Celia was there to overhear them.

"Oh," Justin said with slow realization. He didn't know what to say. Jeff could see that Justin seemed troubled. "Is there a private place for us to talk?"

"Yes, of course," Justin said. Before leading Jeff to his office, he quickly turned to Martha and asked, "Where is Mrs. Haines?"

"I'm sorry, I haven't seen her this morning sir," Martha answered. "I was just going to have a look and see if she's in her room, and then you walked in. I know she left last night, and as far as I know, she hasn't returned yet, but I'm not sure."

"Well," Justin said, "I'm pretty sure she's not home. Her car isn't in the garage anyway. She left last night, huh? Maybe she came home late last night and left again early this morning." Justin tried as hard as he could to maintain his calm. "She's very busy with the store, and I had to stay at the office again last night. That was the second night in a row, but it couldn't be helped. We're just so busy with work that I didn't even have a chance to phone her. Why don't you have a look and see if our bed has been slept in."

Martha nodded and went upstairs.

"I'm sorry, sir," she said when she returned, "it doesn't look like anyone has slept in your bed last night."

Jeff took the initiative because Justin was staring into space. "It's okay, we'll find her." Then he asked Martha, "Could you make us some coffee?"

Concern for her missing employer started to show on Martha's face. "Yes, of course I'll do that," she said.

Jeff wanted any excuse to be alone with Justin so he could tell him that he'd found Sonia. He wasn't happy with the idea that Celia had possibly fled. But since she most likely had, he would first get Sonia out of prison. Jeff knew he couldn't ask her family to wait any longer. He would send out an APB about Celia in the meantime. After he got Sonia out of jail, he would look for Celia himself and whoever her accomplices were. He knew that Celia couldn't have done this on her own. Getting out of jail and switching with Sonia—there must have been more people involved and he would find them all.

As soon as Martha left, Jeff said, "Mr. Haines, we've found your wife and she's safe and well."

Justin's eyes widened. He couldn't believe what he just heard. He was so overcome with the good news that he hugged Jeff, his tears building up and falling down his face. "You found her? Oh my God, you found her!" He wiped his face with his hands and tried to catch his breath. "Where is she, and when can I see her?"

"You'll see her soon," Jeff answered, "but I want you to come to my office first. I'm meeting your in-laws there at ten o'clock. I need to talk to all of you before I go and get her."

"Why?" Justin asked surprised. "Why can't we get Sonia now? And why did you come here if you want me to come to your office?"

"Because I was hoping that Celia would have been here so I could arrest her. But obviously, somehow she found out that we were looking for her. She must have gotten wind of it because she's gone. I'll send out an alert to the police to start looking for her as soon as I get back to my car. I'll do my own investigation after we get Sonia. My priority is Sonia and you guys, right now."

Martha stepped into the room with a tray of coffee. Jeff was grateful for the caffeine; it had been a long and stressful couple of days.

Justin was too excited and nervous to drink anything. When Martha left, he said, "Where is Sonia? Can you at least tell me where she is? Please, Mr. Wright, I need to know."

Jeff had been in these situations before—seeing desperate family members of those who were missing. But this case was nothing like any other case he had worked on, and he saw the desperation in Justin's eyes. He took a sip of coffee and said as compassionately as he could, "She's in jail."

"Oh my God!" he cried as the tears ran down his face. "My poor Sonia, in jail? I can't believe it. Why? What happened? I don't understand!" His voice choked. He thought of his beautiful Sonia alone in a jail cell. He tried desperately to push that thought from his mind.

"I was up late last night getting everything ready for today. I haven't stopped working on this case since I found out where Sonia was. I had to impose on a few people in their private homes last night to get them to sign the proper release papers and that wasn't easy! But when I explained what it was all about and that it involved the mayor's daughter-in-law, people felt sorry for Sonia and were more than willing to help. Now I've got everything, and as soon as I talk to Sonia's parents, then I'll be on my way to get her out." Jeff explained.

"Oh, I'm sure you've done everything you could," Justin said with a shaky voice, "I'm just so upset knowing that Sonia is in such an awful place. She must be so scared."

"Its okay, Mr. Haines," Jeff said. "I realize that this is not easy for you. Let's see if your in-laws left to go to my office. If they're still at home, we can meet them at their house."

Justin agreed and phoned John and Mary. They were still at home and happy to hear from Justin because they hadn't been able to get in touch with him to let him know that Jeff had found Sonia.

"They found Sonia," John said immediately.

"Yes, I know." Justin answered. He tried to sound upbeat, but he couldn't, knowing that she was in that awful place. "Sergeant Jeff Wright is here with me. He said he was going to meet you at his office, but since you haven't left yet, we can meet at your house. Just stay put and we'll be there as soon as we can."

"Okay Justin," John said nervously. "We'll see you soon." He turned to Mary and smiled reassuringly as he hung up the phone.

"Before we go," Jeff said to Justin, "we need some clothes for Sonia. We want her to wear something that Celia hasn't worn yet. Would you be able to grab something quick before we go?"

"Yes, I think so," Justin said. "I'm sure I can find something from before we got married. Just hold on a minute."

Justin rushed upstairs and picked out one of Sonia's favorite sundresses. He wanted Sonia to feel good in clothing that she was familiar with. He came downstairs holding a small bag.

Jeff asked Justin to call the maid back; he wanted her to know they were leaving. Although he couldn't let on what was going on, he needed to know if Celia showed up while they were at the Wells' house.

Martha entered the room still worried about Mrs. Haines.

"I need you to do me a favor," he said to Martha, "if Mrs. Haines comes back, I need you to call me immediately. I'll be with Justin so you can just call his cell. Can you do that?"

Martha nodded in agreement while visualizing Mrs. Haines in a car accident or worse. What was going on? Tears were beginning to form in her eyes.

"Everything's okay. We just need to know when Mrs. Haines returns," Jeff said seeing that Martha was worried about her employer.

Justin gave Martha a reassuring smile. "Please make sure you make a nice dinner for us tonight." He thought, in a couple of hours, his real wife would be in his arms again.

"Just let us know as soon as possible if she comes back before we do," Jeff reiterated.

*****

John and Mary were waiting nervously in the living room when they heard the front door open.

Justin closed the door behind him, but before he could say anything, John and Mary were standing in the hallway. Mary gave Justin a comforting hug. "Oh Justin, I was right," she cried. "She wasn't Sonia, and I knew it." Mary couldn't stop crying, but they were now tears of happiness. She turned to Jeff. "You must be Mr. Wright?"

Jeff reached out to shake Mary's hand. "Yes, and you must be Mrs. Wells. It's nice to meet you."

"I'm so grateful that you found my little girl." Mary couldn't help the tears flowing down her face. She was so overcome with emotion.

John took Mary in his arms. "We're so lucky that you found Sonia. When are we going to see her?" he asked.

"Can we sit? I want to talk to the three of you first," Jeff said.

"Is something wrong?" Mary asked. They sat down on the couch.

"Nothing that won't be fixed over time," Jeff said, "but I have to warn you that Sonia's mental state has been scarred by this ordeal." Jeff tried to be as gentle as he could, but they had to know why Sonia was in her current mental state. So, after taking a deep breath, he blurted, "Sonia's in jail."

Mary let out a wail and caved into John's arms. John couldn't move.

Jeff continued with, "You have to be gentle with Sonia when she gets back home. She's confused right now. It will be difficult for her at first. She might not understand that this is her real life."

Then Jeff turned to Justin, whose face was pale, "It appears that she's been given a lot of sedatives. And, I think, she actually believes that she's Celia. The people in the prison have convinced her of that. That's why we have to be very careful. She may need some help readjusting. I thought it might be better if she's with her parents first because she's confused about you. They made her think she killed you, and that's why she's in jail. I think it might be a good idea if you were not here when I bring Sonia home, or maybe you can just make sure that she doesn't see you right away."

Justin understood, but he didn't like it. He wanted to bring his sweetheart home. "Do the people at the jail know that you're picking her up this morning?"

"Yes," Jeff answered, "they do. They're expecting me in about an hour."

"I had hoped that I could come along to pick her up. But I guess that's out of the question now?"

"Yes," Jeff answered firmly. "I don't think it would be a good idea. I really think she shouldn't see you right away. I should go by myself. That way, I can talk to her in the car and prepare her to meet you all. It's probably a good idea for you to stay here with Mr. and Mrs. Wells. Just make sure you're in another room. She might recognize all of you right away and want to go home or she may need some time to adjust and want to stay with her parents first."

Justin felt his heart drop but he loved Sonia so much he would do anything for her, no matter how hard it would be for him. He sighed. "I'll stay out of the way as long as I need to." As he watched Jeff leave to pick up Sonia he couldn't help but feel overwhelmed. He was going to get Sonia back, and all he could do was hope that she remembered him.

CHAPTER 42

It was six o'clock in the morning. The bell rang and a guard walked through the hallway to wake everyone up. It was the same routine every morning: six o'clock wake-up, shower, get dressed and have breakfast. However, this morning was different for Sonia.

As the guard passed her cell, she spoke through the bars. "Celia, you can sleep longer." The guard went on her way.

Sonia was surprised. She sat up in bed. Why would she be allowed to stay in bed longer? She lay down again, rolled over and curled herself into a ball. It didn't take long for her to fall asleep and dream about that big house again. She didn't understand where the images came from. Her dream seemed so real, and she was happy, but when she finally woke up again, she was still behind bars. Why did she keep seeing these visions? The more she thought about it, the more mixed-up she felt.

Around 7:30, the guard told her to get up. This guard usually had a grim look on her face and was never friendly. But, this morning, the guard was actually smiling.

"Come on," the guard said. "You can take a shower by yourself, and when you're finished, we'll have breakfast ready for you."

Sonia was sure she was still dreaming. She pinched her arm. *Ouch!* She was definitely awake! So why was the guard being so nice to her? She did as she was told. She had a long shower all by herself without the guards watching her, which was very unusual. After she got dressed and had breakfast, the guard brought her to the recreation room and told her to watch TV. *What's going on? Why am I getting special attention? Did I do something? I don't understand.*

The guard turned on the T.V. and left the room. Sonia didn't pay attention to the movie, but questioned the bizarre morning. *Why was I allowed to sleep late? Why did I get to have a long shower alone? Why the special breakfast? Why am I allowed to watch television? Is this a special day or something? Do I have to go to court maybe?* So engulfed in her own thoughts, she didn't even realize it when the guard came in and turned the television off. Sonia had no idea that she'd actually been staring at it for over an hour. She hadn't even noticed the guard come in.

The guard startled her. "Celia, come with me."

Coming back to the present moment, Sonia stood up and followed her.

The guard brought Sonia back to her cell, handed her some strange clothes, and told her to change into them. Sonia had never seen these clothes before. They weren't very pretty. They were actually quite old and well used but it was nice to not wear the jail jumpsuit for a change. She slipped on the jeans and t-shirt. She found it odd that they fit her so perfectly. She still didn't have a clue what was happening.

"What's going on? Why are you being so nice to me? Why am I wearing these clothes?"

"Those are the clothes you came in with," the guard said. She wasn't surprised that Celia didn't recognize her own clothes. After all, Celia had been in jail for over five years. "You really don't recognize those clothes?" the guard asked. "They're yours!"

Sonia crinkled her brow and tried to remember. "Well, they might be, I don't remember."

"That's okay," the guard said. "You stay here. In a little while someone will come for you."

Sonia didn't hear what the guard was saying anymore. She just stared at the clothes now on her body with a blank look, trying to remember something of her previous life, but nothing came.

CHAPTER 43

Jeff was led into a holding area by a security guard. After he was screened and identified as the investigator for the case of Sonia Haines and Celia Winters, he was escorted to the administration area where he handed in his release papers. It would not be long before Sonia would be back with her family. Tom, who was covering for Dameon because he was still home, sick, had a stack of paperwork to sign. Once everything was completed, Jeff handed Tom a bag with some of Sonia's clothes in it.

"What's this?" Tom asked.

"Some fresh, clean clothes for Sonia to change into before I take her home. They are her own clothes. I think they'll make her feel better."

Tom handed the guard the bag and ordered her to get Sonia changed.

Jeff had asked Tom to keep everything as quiet as possible since the investigation was not over yet.

Jeff waited impatiently for Sonia in the warden's office. He still had to find Celia and the people involved in the switch. But for now, he just wanted to take Sonia home and reunite her with her family.

"How long has Dameon Smith been the warden?" Jeff asked.

Tom replied, "For quite some time."

"How long has he been out sick?"

"Just a couple of days," Tom said.

Jeff realized that Dameon had been sick ever since his visit. This seemed very peculiar and Jeff knew that he would start his investigation with Dameon Smith.

*****

Sonia was sitting on her bed staring at the walls when the door of her cell opened.

"Change into these," the guard said as she handed Sonia the bag of clothes.

"What? Why?" Sonia was confused by yet another set of clothes for her to change into. "Why do I have to change again?" She was baffled.

"The Warden told me to give these to you to change into. I'm not sure why. But these are nicer, don't you think?"

"Yes, they are." Sonia replied still in a daze and confused.

The clothing seemed so familiar to her. "I think I've seen these clothes before. Are they my clothes?" she asked.

"I don't know. Don't worry about that right now," the guard said. "Just change into them. They'll look nice on you."

Sonia did as she was told and changed. She looked at herself, and for a moment, she knew that she was Sonia, but then she started to doubt herself again.

The guard noticed her confused look. "Don't you like these clothes?"

Sonia didn't hear the guard at first and didn't respond right away. She didn't know for sure who she was, but something about these clothes made her feel good. She felt happy but she wasn't sure why.

Then slowly and still a little distracted she reacted with, "Yes, I like them."

"Well, then," the guard said, "you look nice. Come on, Celia, let's go, the Warden's waiting."

They left her cell and made their way to the warden's office.

Jeff and Tom were still talking when the guard knocked on the door.

"Hi Sonia," Jeff greeted her with a friendly smile.

Sonia was surprised to hear someone calling her "Sonia."

"Who are you?" she asked.

"I'm Jeff Wright," he said as he extended his hand out to her.

Sonia shook Jeff's hand. She recognized his face, but she couldn't remember where she'd seen him before. But then it came to her: this was the man who had come to look at her feet. Or was that one of her dreams again? It was hard to keep reality and the dreams separate.

Jeff noticed Sonia's confusion and she seemed drugged, but not as much as she was the first time he saw her.

"Who are you?" Sonia asked again.

"I'm Jeff, and I'm here to get you out of prison and bring you home to your family."

"What do you mean?" Sonia asked. She felt suspicious, surprised, happy, and scared all at the same time.

Jeff knew it was hard for Sonia to understand. She appeared to be in a trance. *Poor child. She probably had an awful time in jail and didn't deserve it.* "Sonia, do you recognize the clothes that you're wearing?" he asked.

Sonia paused, then said, "Yeah, I think I've seen them before. They feel good, they make me happy, like I've worn them before."

"Yes," Jeff said, "exactly, you're right, you've worn them before. You may not remember me. I'm the one who came to look at your feet the other day. You probably don't recall that, they had you on a lot of drugs. I'll explain it all later."

"No I remember you," Sonia said still feeling confused.

"I'm going to take you home Sonia. I'm going to bring you to Justin. Do you remember Justin?"

Sonia's face dropped. "Justin is dead," she said and started to cry.

Jeff's heart ached. He spoke in a calm, reassuring voice, "No, no Sonia, Justin isn't dead."

Sonia looked surprised. She choked on her words. "The people here told me that I killed him." She paused. "Justin isn't dead?" She felt her mind whirling with all the confusion.

"Yes, I'm sure, Sonia. It's okay. You didn't kill Justin; he's alive and worried about you. He's waiting for you at your parents' house."

Sonia wiped the tears from her eyes. For the first time since she could remember she felt truly happy.

Jeff took Sonia's hands and said with a caring voice, "Come sit down for a minute." He helped her into a chair while Tom handed her a box of tissues. Jeff looked into Sonia's eyes and continued, "You'll be okay. I'm going to bring you to your parents."

"My parents?" Sonia asked, as she blew her nose into a tissue.

"Yes. Mr. and Mrs. Wells, remember?" Jeff said and then reinforced it again, "Mary and John Wells."

"Yes, I remember those names, Mary and John Wells. Are they really my parents? I thought I dreamt it." Sonia was totally shaken up.

Jeff could see that Sonia was trying to compute everything in her mind. She was still very drugged up. She needed to see a doctor. "We should go," he said. "I think once you see your parents, things will start to come back to you again. You'll remember who you are and what your life is supposed to be. You'll be with the people you love, they love you and want you to come home."

"Why did they put me in here?" Sonia asked. "Did I do something wrong?"

"No, Sonia," Jeff said, "it's very complicated and it was a very big mistake, but I'll explain more on the way to your parents' house." He didn't want to explain everything all at once; she'd been through enough and may not be able to digest it all in one go. He didn't want to confuse her. She was not in the right frame of mind. Also, he didn't want to say too much in front of Tom. He still needed to find out who had been involved in the switch and didn't want to jeopardize his investigation. He didn't know if he could trust Tom or not, or if Tom was also involved in some way.

Jeff reached out to help Sonia stand up. "As soon as you see your parents, reality will start to come back to you. Seeing their faces and hearing their voices might clear things up for you," he said as he guided her out of the office.

As confused as Sonia was, she trusted this man for some reason. As she stepped outside into the sunlight, she knew that everything was going to be okay.

CHAPTER 44

A string of emotions shuffled through Sonia's head as she sat in the backseat of Jeff's car. A man she didn't recognize sat in the driver's seat and drove. It had felt like forever since Sonia had driven in a car.

Sonia stared out the window. She watched the buildings pass by her in a blur and squinted her eyes in the sunlight.

The trip would take about an hour, which would be enough time for Jeff to fill in Sonia on the details. He had to tell her some things about her family and about herself, who and what she was before she ended up in jail. As far as Jeff knew, Celia Winters was guilty. But, he still didn't know how Celia managed to switch with Sonia. Obviously, someone had helped her. He couldn't think about that now though. So he turned his attention back to Sonia. "Do you know anything about a twin sister?"

Sonia looked puzzled, "A twin?" *What was he talking about?* "What do you mean?" she was so confused.

"I guess your parents never told you. Do you know that you were adopted? Can you remember that? Your parents told me that you were adopted and that you were one of a set of twins."

Sonia started to cry. "Yes, I thought I was adopted, but they told me I was just dreaming. Is it real?"

"Yes it's real. You are Sonia, not Celia. You are adopted and you do have a twin but you never knew that part I guess." Jeff looked straight into Sonia's eyes as he spoke. "Someone was trying to make you think you were Celia. I don't know who yet, but I think that the guards didn't know any better. I believe they thought you were Celia."

Sonia was staring in Jeff's direction but only hearing half of what he was saying. "I always felt so drowsy and so numb, like everything was a dream and not real. But now I'm starting to feel shaky and I'm getting a headache. I feel very mixed-up, like this isn't real either."

"Don't worry," Jeff comforted. "I think you'll feel better soon. Whoever put you in there probably kept you drugged on purpose so no one would get suspicious. I bet once those drugs wear off your thinking will become clearer and you'll start feeling better in a couple of days. I don't think they have given you drugs long enough for you to have serious withdrawal symptoms, but I'll make sure that you get checked out by a doctor."

Sonia stiffened.

Jeff gently placed his hand on top of hers. "Soon you'll be yourself again. I'm going to tell you the whole story so just relax and listen. It's not going to be easy to hear, but you need to know what happened before you see your parents, at least as much as I know of it anyway."

Jeff shifted in his seat and rolled open the window. "You have an identical twin sister. The only difference between the two of you is that you have a birthmark on the bottom of your foot."

"Yes, I know I have a birthmark," Sonia echoed. She was trying to listen and understand what Jeff was saying. "Is... is that why you wanted to look at my feet?"

"Yes, that's why. And when I saw the birthmark, I knew you were Sonia, and Celia, your biological sister, your twin, had somehow switched places with you."

Sonia looked shocked and confused, but Jeff continued. "I don't know exactly how she did it, but we'll find that out when we find Celia. She vanished, but we'll find her. And we'll find whoever else was involved. She had to have had some help; she couldn't have done it alone."

Jeff noticed the pale look on Sonia's face and could see that he was starting to make a connection. She was obviously getting a bit clearer minded now, so he continued, "I just knew you were Sonia when I saw that birthmark. Your mother told us about the birthmark under your foot."

Sonia sat there and didn't know what to say. "You mean, what I thought was a dream was not a dream at all? It was real? I'm really Sonia Wells?" She was so unsure of herself she repeated the same sentence over again.

Jeff looked at her with kind eyes. "I want you to understand what has happened to you. Your birth mother, after giving you up for adoption, kept Celia and raised her on her own. Celia had a very different life than you and ended up in prison for killing her boyfriend.

Somehow she managed to steal your identity, put you in jail in place of herself, and has been living with Justin pretending to be you. It's been a while now since the switch happened, but we're not exactly sure when."

So it was all true. I really am Sonia! And Justin is alive! Sonia looked like she was about to cry again.

Jeff quickly said, "I'm taking you to your parents place right now. They're so excited to see you. When you're feeling better and your mind is more clear you can tell us what you remember."

Millions of thoughts raced through Sonia's head. She cried out, "I'm so happy you got me out of there." It was all she could muster.

"I know it wasn't a very nice place," Jeff said, "and it was a terrible thing to happen to you. But we found you, and now you are going back home where you belong." He smiled at her.

"Yes, home. Justin..." Sonia remembered. "I love Justin so much. I'm so glad he's alive." Her emotions swelled as she tried very hard to recall everything. "I'm starting to remember... I know I'm Sonia. I'm sure of it."

Jeff smiled again. He was relieved to hear her say that. "I'm so glad you're coming out of that mixed-up mental state you were in."

Sonia was starting to remember more and more. "I know I'm Sonia Wells...Haines...and I'm married to Justin. I remember the beautiful wedding we had and I'm so excited to see my parents again. Jeff!" she squealed. "I'm going to see my parents and Justin!"

"Yes, you will," Jeff said with a chuckle. This was what he loved about his job. He was going to reunite a family. She seemed to come around quicker than he thought she would, which would make the transition a lot easier.

Jeff hesitated but then seeing how well Sonia was doing he finally asked, "Does the name Dameon Smith mean anything to you?"

"Yes, I remember Dameon," Sonia said. "He was our photographer. His photos were amazing! It's all coming back to me. I remember Dameon was nice enough to work for us for a whole year. He made a great movie from our engagement party and our wedding, and he also made lots of movies and photos from the new house we were building. It's a beautiful house, I remember it all now!" Sonia clapped her hands together in excitement.

It was all starting to make sense to Jeff. The pieces of the puzzle were coming together. Now, he had to find Dameon Smith, and he was sure that wherever Dameon was, Celia would be close by.

CHAPTER 45

As the car pulled up the driveway, Sonia couldn't wait to get out. Everything now was much clearer in her mind. She was so happy to be home. She barely waited for the car to come to a full stop as she tried to open her door. Once she was out she ran up the lawn, with Jeff rushing behind her to catch up, and busted through the front door. "Mommy, Daddy, I'm home!" she shouted in excitement.

Mary couldn't believe her ears, and when she saw Sonia, she couldn't believe her eyes. Tears of joy clouded her vision as she took Sonia into her arms, never wanting to let her go again. Sonia held on tight like a little girl.

"Oh honey, you're back!" was all that Mary could muster, and both mother and daughter couldn't stop crying.

"Oh, Mommy," Sonia said through her tears. "You must have been so awfully worried."

"I certainly was," Mary cried. "We were all so terribly worried. I'm so glad you're back." Mary let go of Sonia with difficulty so that John could take his daughter into his arms. John held her tight as tears ran freely down his cheeks. He couldn't let go. He didn't want to let her go. He didn't want anything bad to happen to her ever again.

As they embraced, Jeff motioned for Mary to get Justin. As soon as Sonia saw him, she let go of her father and flew into Justin's arms. They were all crying. Even Jeff had a hard time keeping his eyes dry.

Justin was so happy to have Sonia in his arms again, and tears flowed from his eyes in pure gratitude. But, he also felt so guilty about mistaking Celia for Sonia. He felt tormented, like it was his fault that Sonia was in jail for so long and like he had cheated on her. *If I'd noticed sooner, Sonia would have been home a long time ago. I should have noticed it as soon as the switch happened. I can't forgive myself for not knowing the difference. How could I not know it!* He held onto Sonia with all of his heart. *I don't even know when the switch occurred!*

None of them knew.

Jeff cleared his throat and asked, "Can we sit down somewhere?"

"Of course we can," John said. "Let's sit in the living room." He turned toward his daughter. He couldn't believe his eyes. She really was back home safe and well.

They walked into the living room and sat down. "We've missed you so much and we're so happy you're back, we were so worried." Mary said as she held Sonia's hand. They all sat there smiling at each other through their tears.

Jeff decided to break the silence. "Would it be terribly impolite if I asked for some coffee?"

They all laughed, and after gently squeezing Sonia's hand, Mary stood and said, "Of course, I already made a pot. We're all ready for some, I'm sure."

Jeff felt that Sonia was well enough to ask some more questions. As they sipped their coffees, he asked if she remembered when or where the switch had occurred.

Sonia stopped smiling and tried to remember. "It must have been at the airport because I remember going there. We were going on our honeymoon and then after that everything went blank. I don't remember anything else from the airport. Except," she stared down at her coffee, "Coffee...I remember coffee. Yes, Dameon spilled his coffee on me. But after that I just remember waking up in a cold room with bars." She paused for a moment and choked back her tears. "I've missed all of you. I was so scared, and I was really starting to believe that I was Celia. I didn't know who I was anymore. And then I thought I'd dreamt all of this. That this life wasn't real but just a dream. But it is a dream, a dream come true!"

Justin gently rubbed Sonia's back.

Feeling Justin's loving touch, she remembered the horror and buried her face in her hands. "I thought I had killed you because that's what everyone told me. Oh Justin, I'm so happy you're alive!" She sat up and hugged him and continued, "I'm so happy to be home. THIS dream is real! I know it is." She pinched herself just to make sure she was right.

"Yes, sweetheart, this dream is real, you're not in that nightmare anymore," Mary said. "You're our daughter, you're home and you're safe. Oh, I'm just so happy your back home!" *Thank GOD I followed up on my gut feelings!*

When Jeff finished his coffee he excused himself. He wanted to leave the Wells family alone with their newfound happiness. He had learned a lot from Sonia's story. He knew that he had to start looking for Dameon Smith. He was pretty sure that Dameon was not at home, sick, like they had told him at the prison, but probably somewhere with Celia Winters. He wanted to get back to the office as soon as possible and he also knew that Sonia needed to be alone with her family. She would have questions for them about never having been told about her twin. But that was for John and Mary to deal with, not him. He had to catch the offenders.

"Thank you so much for the coffee," Jeff said, "I must be going."

Mary, John and Justin thanked him over and over again for bringing Sonia back home to them.

As Jeff was about to leave, Sonia ran up to him and wrapped her arms around him. "I cannot thank you enough," she whispered.

With tears now in his eyes, he turned and left.

As soon as Jeff was gone, Sonia went back to her parents; she had some questions for them.

"Mommy, Daddy," Sonia said approaching the group again, "I need to know. Jeff told me I am a twin. Why didn't you ever tell me?" but she was too happy to be back home again to feel any hurt.

"We wanted to sweetheart, but we just didn't know how, and the right time never came up to tell you. We didn't mean to keep it from you. I'm not sure why we didn't tell you sooner. Maybe we were scared that you'd want to find her and maybe leave us. I don't know. I'm sorry. We're sorry."

"I don't care. I'm just so happy to be home again! I love you so much. YOU are my family, that's all that matters. I have you and I have Justin. Oh Justin…" Sonia held onto her husband. She was starting to feel overcome by it all. Exhausted. Oh what it would be like to sleep in a real bed again! She wanted to lie down. "I'm feeling so tired."

"Of course," Mary said. "Why don't you take a nap in your bedroom? It's all ready for you."

She kissed her mother and father on the cheek and grabbed Justin's hand. "Please come with me? I don't want to be far from you."

At that moment, Justin thought he would cry. He squeezed her hand and followed her upstairs.

Once they lay down, Sonia snuggled into Justin's arms. "I've missed you so much," she cried.

Justin smiled and kissed her forehead. His wife was back in his arms, but he couldn't shake the guilt he was feeling. Less than a week ago, he was lying with Celia in his arms. He wanted to punch a hole through the wall. *How could I have been so stupid?*

"I love you so much, sweetheart," Justin said. He choked back his tears. Celia's face flashed before his eyes. The morning sickness. The throwing up. The mood swings. Bile rose in Justin's throat but he stifled it. Somewhere, Celia was out there and possibly pregnant with his child. His body tensed.

"Are you okay, honey?" Sonia mumbled. She could hardly keep her eyes open.

"Yes. I love you," Justin said.

"I love you, too," Sonia whispered. She inched closer to Justin and allowed him to engulf her in his arms. This was where she was supposed to be. She quietly drifted off to sleep.

Like this book and want to share it?

Simply send your friends to:

www.StolenIdentityBook.com

Where they can review the first 5 chapters for FREE!

About Lucia Van Der Gulik

Lucia came to Canada in 1970, together with her husband of just 3 weeks. Without any knowledge of the English language, it was hard for her to communicate.

However she was determined and learned the language, little bits at a time while she worked as a babysitter and housecleaner. With little education and no English background at all, she didn't have much of a chance of getting anything better than that.

She and her husband lived in British Columbia for the first year and then moved to Ontario, where she has been ever since.

As the years went by she learned more and more of the language, and started working in restaurants and did sales jobs. She read a lot of English books and joined the local barbershop chorus to help her master the English language.

Lucia has raised two daughters, who have blessed her with three beautiful granddaughters and one handsome grandson. With the encouragement of her family, the dictionary and spell-check close by, she has written her first novel.

Visit Lucia Van Der Gulik's Blog...

Learn how Lucia came up with the concept for Stolen Identity and how she was able to overcome her lack of knowledge for the English language to write this incredible tale.

www.LuciaVanDerGulik.com

Made in the USA
Charleston, SC
07 July 2016